OUIJA & HAINTS in the SILENT CITY

A Cardboard Cottage Mystery

JANE ELZEY

Scorpius Carta Press
Arkansas

For all the women

"Well-behaved women rarely make history."
—— *ELEANOR ROOSEVELT*

CHAPTER ONE

Amy studied her ghostlike reflection in the kitchen window above The Cardboard Cottage, her anchor to everything she loved. The historic limestone building with four shops and an infamous closet was the center of her universe. That and the people connected to it.

Victor jumped onto her lap and circled twice before settling into position, balanced on her thighs like a sphinx looking eastward. The sun pushed a soft amber glow through the trees on the ridge. As its rays reached the kitchen, her reflection disappeared.

The creek below the building was no longer rushing through the rocks, but the current was brisk enough to float the flotsam and jetsam washed down from the hillsides. The summer rains had filled the creeks and plumped the hillsides into an expanse of green. The leaves had turned now that cooler temps were here. The oaks were orange. The maples wore spotted green, scarlet, and yellow as if they couldn't make up their mind which color to show off. The dogwoods were the color of flaming red roses, and the sassafras wore crimson tie-dye. Even if you didn't know a single tree by its name or heritage, you could be enraptured by the Arkansas Ozarks showing off its Autumn.

Victor's purr-engine rose to full roar as she stroked his tiger stripes. His tail twitched as they watched the birds flirt with the morning, flittering among the branches and twittering to each other with their tremulous calls. The scent of cinnamon drifted up from Crumpets and Cones below, filling the corner of Bluff and Main Street with the aroma of freshly baked sweets. The streets were still empty, the tourists still lazy in their beds, shopkeepers cherishing a few more hours of uninterrupted quiet.

Fall in Bluff Springs was a busy season with tourists drawn to the changing leaves and then shoppers filled the sidewalks right up until Christmas. Adding to the bustle, Amy and best friends Zelda, Rian, and Genna were playing roles in a fundraiser. The event was set in the Silent City, also known as the graveyard. Actually, it was the cemetery, because the church once attached to the graveyard had long since fallen to the elements of time, weather, and unruly tree roots.

Called *Tales from the Silent City*, the event was a series of vignettes highlighting characters from Bluff Springs history. The actors, or rather the volunteers, would share the stories of the residents of the Silent City—residents meaning the buried—and their historic contributions. This year they were celebrating the women who made history in Bluff Springs.

The event wasn't spooky, and that put the kibosh on the story about the man hung for the first murder in town. Had he been a woman, they would have found a way to include the tale of the hanging and the haunted tree above the grave that howled like a haint in purgatory when a cold wind blew from the north.

She shivered involuntarily at the thought. That wasn't one of the stories in this year's program, thank goodness. But that gnarled tree was only a few rows over from where she would be waiting in the dark with a lantern to light the scene.

Victor jumped to the floor as she stood up. "Sorry, buddy," she said as he chirped his disapproval at being dumped from his warm perch. "It's time to get to work. Are you coming today?"

As if he understood her question, Victor trotted ahead, his plumed tail straight in the air. Amy followed, counting the steps as she always did—twenty-nine in all—down the azure painted stairway and onto the sidewalk, past Crumpets and Cones bakery, under the shop sign with colorful daisies and curlicue letters, past the hopscotch grid on the sidewalk, and then right to the front door of The Cardboard Cottage. Twenty-nine steps. Not a bad commute to work.

The front door was ajar.

Tentatively, she pushed the door with her fingertips and Victor scooted in between her legs.

"Hello?" she called into the dark hallway. "Is someone in here?"

A clip clop sounded on the wooden floors. "Hello?" she called again, the skin tingling on the back of her hands. "Who's there?" Victor shot down the hallway before she could scoop him up.

"Shoo, you!" Zelda called and then poked her head out of the door of her shop. "I'm here early today, Sparks. I have big plans for these boxes that arrived yesterday. But it doesn't include you, Victor, so shoo," she huffed.

"And good morning to you, too," Amy said, watching Zelda disappear inside the shop without another word. Zelda Carlisle's shop was a cubby-hole pantry at the back of the building, crammed floor to ceiling with shabby chic doodads for the home. Zsa Zsa Galore Décor looked much like the farmhouse in the Green Acres sitcom from the 1960s. Eva Gabor was the star of that show, not her sister, but Zelda had decided that Zsa Zsa Galore Décor had a much better ring to it than Eva Galore Décor. No one would know the difference, Zelda claimed, and Amy remembered Zelda's declaration, hands on curvaceous hips as she stood her ground. "It's Zsa Zsa, and that's all there is to that." She knew what she was doing. Zelda's shop was popular.

The shop door across the hall was closed. The Pot Shed was all things bird, bee, and gardening. And for those who knew Rian O'Deis, the name made you smile. Her plants and herbs thrived in the bright, humid space which used to be a Victorian-era kitchen that now smelled like a greenhouse. The Pot Shed was but one of Rian's businesses. An on-demand vintage car dealership was another. A newly acquired vineyard was yet a third. The OG was Rian's cannabis farm that had nearly gone under when Zelda's former husband stuck his nose in not-his-business. For those who knew Rian O'Deis, The Pot Shed was one hundred percent Rian's humor. Just like her *dealer* car tag. Rian had laughed when the vehicle registration clerk said she had to have a *dealer* tag to deliver the vintage cars.

Amy smiled as she glanced at the infamous closet door nearly hidden under the stairwell where a shiny brass plaque read, G. Gregory, Rock Star. The sign was a gag gift from the three of them. Genna didn't need nor maintain an office in the building, but they often joked that the closet under the stair was Genna's place at the Cardboard Cottage, her stake in the investment. Genna was a public relations guru who helped promote their businesses, although her passion was politics. They teased that the closet was where Genna kept her broom. A broom for a witch with a "b" for someone with a very demanding nature. Genna took that in good humor.

Amy keyed the lock to Tiddlywinks and let herself in. Victor followed with his tail in the air.

Tiddlywinks Player Club anchored the old two-story building as vintage game shop and parlor. The shelves were full of games that fit the everything-old-is-new-again trend as a new generation of game players returned to retro roots.

Morning at Tiddlywinks was a brief and pleasant set of chores. Amy turned on the lights, dealt with the cash register, set out a puzzle for the day on the big library table and then straightened the chairs. She also dusted the shelves even though they didn't need it. The cardboard spines of the game boxes as they were stacked on the shelves inspired the name of her collaborative business. She had faith a shop with cardboard was stronger than a house of cards. So far, so good.

Amy glanced up when the bell over the door jangled. She forgot to shut and lock the door. The shop wasn't officially open yet, but she caught herself before she said so out loud.

"What have you got there?" Amy asked instead, eyeing the young woman who entered.

"A bunch of old games," the woman said with a friendly smile. She placed a cardboard box on the table, then after dusting her hands on her pants, straightened a collection of necklaces strung around her neck. "I was hoping you would buy them." She pulled the games from the box.

Amy eyed the stack of Ouija boards and then glanced at the young woman. She stood with her fingers laced in front of her, her long fingernails painted the color of marmalade. She wore a fuzzy fleece jacket and baby tee with Buckle Up Buttercup printed across her chest. Amy recognized the character. She had a whole shelf of Powerpuff Girls games left over from Y2K. Amy noticed the woman's slim physique, guessing it belonged to a late twenty-something who had understanding yet what damage hormones, gravity, and fast food take out could do to a body. But she would. Eventually, she would.

Amy tugged at her purple tee and smoothed the wrinkle at her waist. It was hard not to compare. She had a middle-aged spread at her midriff. Her hair was copper colored and so curly it could spring wild. This other woman's was straight and sleek and oddly silver-white. She was tall and Amy was not. She was young and Amy was not. She was pretty and Amy certainly wouldn't describe herself that way. The freckles on her cheeks being her most despised feature. That and a small scar at her hairline she knew would never go away.

She reached out and touched the top box. "Where did you get these?"

The young woman looked at Amy and frowned. "I didn't steal them or anything. If that's what you're asking. They belong to me."

Amy eyed her curiously, wondering. How did she come by a dozen vintage Ouija boards she wanted to sell? "I wasn't suggesting that," Amy said. "I like to know the history and backstory on the games I buy. A vintage game with a story behind it has a lot more value in my shop."

"Oh," the woman said simply. "I don't have a story or anything, but I heard you buy vintage games. I inherited a house here in Bluff Springs and these were in the attic. Buried at the bottom of a trunk of old clothes."

She could tell the woman was itching to pull her phone from her matching marmalade-colored bag and multi-task her way through their conversation. Somehow she fought the urge.

Amy ran a finger over the edge of the box. "Are all they all intact?"

"I don't know. There's not much to them. A board and that thingy. I don't know what it's called."

"A planchette," Amy offered.

"Ok, sure. Then it's all there. They have to be worth something. Right? They're really old."

Amy lifted the lid and breathed in old cardboard and dust. The board was burnished dark with age, the surface scratched where the planchette had made many a trip over the letters. Instead of *Goodbye* at the bottom, it said, *Au Revoir.* Amy's heart quickened. That was French for *goodbye till we meet again.* The board must be from the early 1900s. Maybe even older. She leaned in and brushed at the grime with a fingertip. The manufacture's mark was barely there, but it was there. Made by J.M. Simmons & Co, Chicago, 1920.

"This is very cool," Amy breathed and then straightened, trying to control her excitement. The more she looked at the boxes in front of her, the more excited she felt. She was itching to pull her own phone from her pocket and run an eBay scan to check the selling prices on vintage Ouija boards. "I don't think I've ever seen one like this. Can I look at the others?"

The woman clicked her fingernails together. "Are you going to buy them, then? Like maybe today?"

"Probably," Amy said, still trying to hide her excitement. "I won't know what they are worth to me until I do a little research and, to be honest, there's not a big call for Ouija boards. They spook people, you know."

"I get it," the other woman said flatly. "I got spooked when I found them. I was alone in the attic." She widened her eyes and grimaced for effect.

Amy laughed and then shifted her attention to the next box in the pile. "Where is this place you inherited?"

"Over on Piney Top. That little house that sits back from the road. The front yard is so overgrown, the house is almost hidden.

It's on the other side of the graveyard. The one with all those cool old tombstones."

"That old homestead has been empty and abandoned for a long time," Amy offered. "If I'm thinking of the right one."

"Abandoned, maybe," the woman said. "But not empty. It's full of stuff. Some of it's pretty cool and all of it is old."

"The house has been in your family awhile, huh?"

The woman nodded. "The house belonged to my great aunt Mable Rose. Well, great, great, great aunt or something like that. I didn't know her. I came down here once, but I don't remember much. I was more into Barbies. I do remember it was a long car ride."

She smiled warmly. "And now I am the rightful heir and owner. That's what it says in the documents, anyway. The Piney Top house and acreage in Bluff Springs, Arkansas, has trickled all the way down the line. Lucky me."

Amy wasn't sure if her tone was sarcasm, but she nodded in reply and lifted the lid on another box, noticing that they all seemed to be from the 1920s. It was a time in American history when Ouija Boards were a popular parlor game for young girls flirting with their future and widows seeking solace from the beyond. Millions of boards were made.

"If you want to leave these with me, I can do some research and give you a fair price." She put the last lid in place. "You can stop by tomorrow or leave me your number."

The woman frowned and reached for her bag, digging in the pocket for her phone. "Actually, I could use the cash today, if you're interested. I maxed out my credit cards getting here. Airfare and a rental car, you know. The lawyer had the utilities turned on so I could stay in the house instead of a hotel, but the estate used all the assets to get this far. I think that's how he put it. There isn't money left for anything else."

"Are you going to live there or are you going to sell it?"

"I don't know," she said and shrugged, tapping the top of the Ouija box with her fingernails. "The house wasn't what I was expecting, but I don't really know what I was expecting. It was pretty dumb to think it would be one of those big old mansions you see in the movies."

Amy raised a brow. "Big old mansions can be money pits. Trust me. I bought one." Amy motioned to the building with her hand. "I love this place, though. Every penny I put in it makes it more valuable. Thank goodness it has good bones and was taken care of through the years."

"Well, that's not the case with this place," the woman said, punctuating her comment with a quick huff of a laugh. "The house is a dump, but I guess it's better than nothing." She tugged at her sling bag strap. "I let my old apartment go. I couldn't afford it anyway because my roommate moved in with her boyfriend. That's never fun." The corner of her mouth jerked into something akin to disapproval. "I'm into a new scene, though. And so far I like Bluff Springs. It's pretty hip."

Amy smiled. "Hip?" She hadn't heard that expression in a long while. Everything old was new again, including the slang. "I guess you could say we're hip."

"Well, you know, you got old hippies and new hippies, and Pride flags, and musicians in the park. I can literally hear them from my porch. What do you call that?"

"Music?" Amy said with a chuckle.

She let out another quick huff. "I mean, when they play for money."

"Busking. That's what it's called."

The woman nodded. "You think they make any money?"

"Enough to survive, I guess."

"Busking. That's cool. The music is a little twangy, but I like it, okay." She stuck her phone in the pocket of her cargo pants and shuffled in her Doc Martens. "So, about this stuff. I'd rather we make a deal now if you're chill with that. I need groceries. Peanut butter in that health food store was ten bucks a jar."

Amy laughed again. If she were set on organic fair trade peanut butter, it would cost ten bucks a jar and then another ten for a loaf of good bread. Or maybe she was a spoon right out of the jar kinda gal.

"I'll give you a hundred bucks for each one," Amy said impulsively.

The woman inhaled in surprise. "A hundred bucks! Each? That's twelve hundred dollars!"

"Yep," Amy said and moved toward the counter. She didn't have that much in the register, but she could write a check. She'd call ahead to the bank and let them know the check was real and for them to honor it.

"Twelve hundred bucks!" she exclaimed again as she followed Amy to the counter. "I didn't know they would be worth that much!"

"They may not be," Amy said as she pulled the checkbook from the drawer. "But I will at least get my money back over time and you can consider this a welcome to the neighborhood gesture. I think what you're up against is big. Life altering, maybe." Her own journey to Bluff Springs in a broken-down VW and a heart full of hurt sprang to mind.

"There's a reason you landed in this town. There's a reason you landed on my doorstep. This is not a charity check, mind you. It's an investment."

Tears welled in the young woman's eyes. She turned slightly and focused on the dust on the toe of her boots.

"I need your name," Amy said, as she opened the check book, pen in hand. "And I should draw up a bill of sale, too, but I can get that to you later." She waited expectantly.

"Camellia," the woman said, looking at the pen in Amy's hand. "My name is Camellia deRossier."

"Well, Camellia deRossier," Amy said as she filled in the blank and pulled the check from the page. "Nice to meet you. I'm Amy Sparks, proprietor and owner of Tiddlywinks Players Club and The Cardboard Cottage. And this is Victor," she added as the cat jumped to the counter and nuzzled Camellia's hand. "He's not shy about asking for attention."

Camellia petted his head, and Amy could tell she knew cats. Cat people petted cats one way. Dog people pet cats like dogs.

"Victor," Camellia echoed, and let him bump her hand for more. "That's a good name for a fuzzy little gentleman." Victor looked up and chirped. "You steal hearts, don't you?"

Amy grinned. He did indeed. "So, don't be a stranger," she said, handing over the check. "There aren't any strangers in Bluff Springs if you don't want there to be."

Their eyes met and Amy could see her younger self in the flash of those dark eyes. Young, lost, broke, maybe even broken. Looking for a new life. A new way to be. She remembered being in that place herself and how the town had healed her. Or more to the point, Bluff Springs and three best friends healed her.

Camellia deRossier stuck her hand out abruptly and gripped Amy's with a handshake. Amy could tell she'd rather have a hug. Maybe next time.

The bell jangled and Zelda swept in just as Camellia was folding the check into her bag.

"*Yoo hoo!*" Zelda called. "I'm going after tea and scones." She looked at Amy and then at Camellia with a bright smile, and Amy watched as Zelda looked her over head-to-toe. Camellia was maybe close to thirty and average height. Her hair was cut shoulder length and silver-blonde, but Amy noticed a fine line at her roots was beginning to grow in darker. The hoops in her ears and her lips and her fingernails and her sling bag were the same bright shade. Zelda nodded and wagged a finger at the collection of necklaces at her chest.

"That's a really good look," Zelda said, her green eyes sparkling with warmth. "Very stylish. Quite vogue."

"Hip," Amy said and grinned. "Zelda Carlisle, meet Camellia deRossier. She's new to town," Amy added.

"Welcome," Zelda answered, reaching out a hand. She was considerably shorter than Camellia, and a whole lot curvier. Definitely on point on the fashion scale. "It's good to see that you're already shopping at The Cardboard Cottage. Most interesting shops in town."

Camellia nodded and grinned. "For real!"

"Zelda is one of my business partners. She runs the shop down the hall."

"She's also your best friend," Zelda added with a huff. "You forgot that part."

"And she's my best friend," Amy repeated.

"Are you in for a cup of tea?" Zelda asked Camellia.

"Who, me? Are you asking me?" She looked surprised by the invitation. "Well, thanks, but I guess I need to fly."

"Another time then," Zelda said as she turned toward the door. "I know we will see you again, Camellia deRossier," she said over her shoulder. "No one can hide from us. And there is no reason why they would. We're the most fun in this entire town. Ask anybody. And don't believe them when they say we're trouble."

CHAPTER TWO

"Dress rehearsal at my house at six," Zelda called as she passed Tiddlywinks and headed toward the front door. "I'll spring for pizza. I've already called Genna and Rian."

Amy looked up from the counter where she was batching out the receipts for the day. She waved and hollered back, "See you at six, then. Should I bring anything?"

Zelda paused in reflection. "If you have more of those date bar things you made last game night. They were great."

Amy nodded. "Got it." She had made a double batch and froze one.

"Oh, and you could bring a flashlight. I think we should try rehearsing in the dark. You may need to light up your script because Genna will howl if you get it wrong."

"I know my script already," Amy said. "Don't you?"

"Of course I do," Zelda countered. "Well, almost."

"You only have two more days, Zelda," Amy scolded. "And you've had a month to get it memorized. What's the problem?"

"The problem is that Genna is wordy and long winded," Zelda said and put her hands on her hips. "It's like the entire encyclopedia in a ten-minute chat. Nobody can pay attention that long. Nobody standing in the dark in the graveyard, anyway. I plan on improvising a little. I'll hit all the high points. Dazzle them with my charm."

Amy rolled her eyes. This could be really fun. Or it could be a disaster. It was going to swing one way or the other.

"Genna worked really hard on those scripts," Amy said finally. "You can at least appease her by learning the script she wrote for you. If you improvise at the event, she won't know, but for tonight…"

"I know, I know," Zelda interrupted. She folded her hands in front of her and recited. "*I am Catherine Duncan, the first female mayor of Bluff Springs, sworn into office on January 4, 1925. I am responsible for the first Petticoat government of my town, population nine thousand three hundred and ten. Not all the citizens voted for me, I assure you. More about that, later. But I did have the vote of the women in town, and I couldn't have achieved my mayoral success without them or my best friend, Maude. She was highly influential at the Bluff Springs Weekly Times because her husband owned the newspaper, and Maude had full command of the front page. You'll meet her next at her residence a few plots over. She's waiting patiently for you to arrive, although I cannot say that was one of her qualities in life. She had many, mind you, but patience wasn't her virtue. Now, let me tell you more about myself and the advances I was able to bring forward in Bluff Springs…*" Zelda paused, and Amy applauded.

"I'm a bit iffy after that," Zelda said. "The script seems to go on forever."

"Close enough for a start," Amy said. "You'll get the rest of it memorized. I know you will." Genna had layered the stories with history, personality, and a bit of gossip to keep it interesting. Petticoat government was the term used to describe an all-female governing body. Given that women were constitutionally afforded the vote only a few years earlier, this was quite a conquest.

"I promise to practice. I will," Zelda said. "Toodles," she added and waved a manicured hand. "See you at six. Sharp."

Amy returned to her task, thinking how history seemed so far in the past but also not far at all. The theme for the *Tales from the Silent City* was the women of Bluff Springs now residing in the

Silent City. The program was a nod to the one-hundred-year anniversary of enfranchisement as amended in the U.S. Constitution. The 19th Amendment essentially prohibited the nation and its states from denying the right to vote on the basis of sex. That felt like a rather awkward way to recognize women's right to vote, a sort of back into it kind of approach. The right to vote was a hard won victory for women, and it had only been a hundred years. It seemed more like ancient history.

While the anniversary year wasn't calendar exact, it did acknowledge that not all women were given the right to vote at the same time. Native American women didn't receive the right until 1924 because, prior to that, Native Americans were not considered citizens. That was a hornet's nest Genna had ranted about over dominoes when she unearthed that fact. Women of color wouldn't receive the right to vote for another four decades. Amy thought Genna would blow a fuse over that. Genna was passionate about the things Genna was passionate about. Like powerful women and politics.

Amy sighed at how much time had passed. Decades were elusive if you wanted them to be and history was easy to forget in the day-to-day grind.

She was almost fifty and much had changed in her lifetime. The advancement of technology was an easy given, but things like civil rights, equal housing, and equality in the workplace were relatively modern-day advances. She didn't know that many young adults, but she knew they had no idea how much had been gained on their behalf in the last one hundred years.

She thought of Camellia deRossier. Of her quirky style and mix of fashion eras. Of her right to inherit property, to pack up and jet across the country, to make decisions on her own. A lot had changed since Camellia's aunt lived on Piney Top.

The thought made her feel good about being generous with the check for the Ouija boards. High tide floats all boats. Sisters supporting sisters. Sisters doing it for themselves, just like Aretha Franklin and Annie Lennox sang.

Besides, with a quick search, she learned that one of the Ouija boards she bought could be worth as much as five or six hundred bucks. It might sit on the shelf awhile before it found a buyer, but it would find a buyer, eventually. She knew that as sure as she knew rain followed thunder and synchronicity was ever-present if you used your eyes to see.

CHAPTER THREE

Zelda pointed to the Ouija board sticking out of Amy's bag. "I can't believe you brought that thing." Zelda patted her hair and straightened the trim of her jacket, which Amy thought might be an authentic 1920s silk kimono. That wouldn't be out of the question. The pattern was full of greens and golds that suited her completion.

"I brought it to show you all what I bought today. From the woman you saw in my shop. Camellia deRossier. They were in the house she inherited. A dozen of them."

Zelda shook her hair, and her earrings dangled. "Ouija boards. That's so up your alley, Sparks. But you're not going to talk me into touching that thing. I know better."

"Why would anyone have a dozen Ouija boards?" Genna asked, eying the board with disdain. "One will do the trick."

Amy agreed. She thought the same thing.

Rian raised a brow above her espresso brown eyes. "I don't believe in that nonsense," she said, shaking her head, brown curls bouncing, as she rolled the sleeve of her flannel shirt. Zelda once claimed Rian invented the lumberjack look, which was what this next generation of adults were claiming as their own. Rian had plaids much older than they were, but now her old-style look was trendy.

"Well, I can't say that I do believe in it or don't believe in it," Amy said defiantly, noticing that Rian's t-shirt read: I love dirt. "But I do know there are some things we can't explain."

"That's an understatement, given your history." Genna tossed her silver braid over her shoulder. Amy noticed Genna was wearing jeans, which was not usually Genna's style. But then, at six-foot, it was hard to find jeans that covered her ankles. Amy glanced at Genna's feet. Ballet flats. The usual. Her sweater was well-loved robin's egg blue cashmere; the beads around her neck were the same color. They matched her eyes.

"I mean really, Amy, you're four for four on your crime-time antenna," Genna continued. "What kind of snippet will you conjure up if you start messing with that mystic-board-hoodoo-business? Heaven only knows how many spirits have used that thing like a telephone from the other side. I can't imagine you want to add talking to spirits to your list of spidey-sense dreams."

"And I don't want it in my house," Zelda said. "I get the heebie jeebies just thinking about ghostly spirits rapping on tables and scratching on doors. What if we bring back one of the dead husbands?"

"That's not how it works, Zelda!" Amy realized her tone was defensive. She hadn't brought the board to use it; she only brought it for show and tell. Zelda's reaction seemed overly dramatic if not out of character.

"You wouldn't think twice about the Ouija board if not for that movie," Rian offered. "People weren't afraid of sharks until *Jaws*. No one looked twice at birds until Hitchcock went all psycho on Tippi Hedren. And it wasn't until they found the Ouija board in the attic that—"

Zelda threw up her hands to interrupt. "Nope! Don't even say it."

Rian grinned. "Touchy subject."

Zelda narrowed her eyes.

"It sounds like you had an unfriendly experience with the Ouija board. You should share it with us," Genna urged. "Maybe you have a teenage memory you want to get off your chest. Do enlighten us."

"No." Zelda crossed her arms across her chest. "I will not."

"People have been talking to the dead for a long time in more ways than one," Genna said. "Haven't they Amy?"

"How would I know?" She shot back. "I don't talk to spirits. I don't see ghosts. I don't know anything about that."

"We know," Genna said and smiled. It seemed genuine even if a bit gloating. "You aren't psychic, and you can't read minds. You aren't clairvoyant. You can't channel wisdom or move anything with your mind. We know all that. But you do dream things that aren't there and that is what? *Telepathetic.* Isn't that what you call it?"

"I call it a pain in the rear," Amy blurted. But she didn't really mean that. She was beginning to see her dreams as a gift. Something passed down through the generations the same as red hair and hazel eyes. It was a gift, of sorts, but not one you raced to open on Christmas Day. She thought of her snippet dreams more like an obligation to set things right, to return the equilibrium of cause and effect. She couldn't stop bad things from happening to people, but she could be part of righting the wrong. The trick was figuring out the dreamtime clues that seemed too warped and whacky to make sense. Plus, she never knew when the snippet would come. Or who it would be about.

"It would be okay with me if we skate right through this graveyard gig without any weirdo things happening," Zelda complained. "I'm on edge enough being out there in the dark, let alone trying to dig up somebody else's dirty deeds."

"Boo!" Rian poked Zelda in the ribs. Zelda threw up her hands and the dregs of her wine splashed over the top of her head.

"Now look what you did!"

Rian laughed but Zelda was not amused.

"This is not a scary gig, Zelda," Genna scolded. "It's a history lesson. It just happens to take place in the graveyard."

"In the dark," Rian said.

"On the eve of Halloween," Amy added. She could feel Zelda tense beside her.

"Stop it!" Zelda slammed her hand on the table. "If you want me to play Catherine Duncan in the graveyard, you're going to have to back off the scare tactic. I mean back way off." She wagged a finger at each of them in turn.

Amy smiled. Zelda grinned. Rian and Genna broke into laughter and Genna had to spit her pizza bite into her napkin to keep from swallowing it down the wrong pipe.

"At least you get to wear a really nice costume," Amy offered. "That's a plus."

Zelda nodded. "And I'm going to keep it, too, since I had the outfit made special for my curves. The pattern is right out of a 1924 fashion magazine with buttons and a little inset plaid flair. Kind of like an ascot but not at the neck. And a cute little cap hat covered in roses on one side. You'll see. That's why I called this little soiree," Zelda added. "Your costumes came today, too. This is our first dress rehearsal."

"But it's not in the cemetery," Rian teased. "Although it is getting dark outside." Rian widened her eyes at Zelda like the ghoulish Igor.

Zelda sighed impatiently and left the room. When she returned, she held a zippered clothes bag, which she draped over one of the chairs.

While Genna was in charge of researching and writing the scripts for the vignettes, Zelda was charged with the costumes. She had taken her role seriously since fashion was her thing, and she culled the vintage shops for weeks. For most of the volunteers, she hobbled together skirts and shirts and shawls that reflected the era and occupations of the characters. For herself, Amy, and Rian, she had sent a vintage fashion book to a local tailor. Together they had spent hours looking over his stock bolts of material for just the right patterns and tweeds. It hadn't been cheap, but then, *she* wasn't cheap, and Zelda loved to play dress up, especially for a cause.

Genna was assigned the role of hearse master. She would welcome guests at the cemetery gates with an oratory about the event they were about to experience in the Silent City. She wasn't driving a 1920s hearse wagon, but it sure looked the part. And so did she. Genna had taken her late husband's tux from the closet and had it altered to fit her slender frame. The top hat had been ordered online. Almost six feet in bare toes, Genna in a top hat made her a fiendishly looking presence.

Rian begrudgingly accepted the hanger holding her costume. Appropriately, Rian was playing the town's druggist, Bella St. Claire, who became one of the state's first certified female pharmacists after her husband passed.

"The movie was actually a story written by Daphne du Maurier," Rian said as she wiggled into the jacket.

"What movie are you talking about now?" Amy asked as Zelda handed her the hanger. She was playing Mayor Duncan's best friend, Maude Calhoun, who ran the newspaper single handedly after her husband's death.

"*The Birds*," Rian answered. "Daphne du Maurier wrote a short story about birds attacking a town unprovoked. Alfred Hitchcock turned it into a scary movie success. Daphne du Maurier liked all that paranormal stuff. She may be known for *Rebecca* and *Jamaica Inn*, but her short stories took her moody writing into the macabre."

"Good to know," Zelda muttered with sarcasm. "Maybe I'll do a little light reading before I go to bed tonight. Now let's rehearse Genna's scripts one more time. They need to be perfect. Or else."

CHAPTER FOUR

The night of the event finally arrived, and the Silent City was even darker than Amy thought it would be. A crescent moon hung in a clear sky, and the ancient pine boughs broke the light with eerie fingers. The scene and setting at the foot of the gravestone was lit by three lanterns that circled at her feet, which were feeling cold in her T-strap shoes—the shoes Zelda insisted she wear because they fit the fashion. Amy would have preferred her sneakers on this cold, uneven ground. No one would look at her shoes and think them out of place. No one but Zelda. Next time—if there was a next time—she'd pack her sneakers and change when Zelda wasn't looking.

She could hear the low hum of the voices at the vignette before hers. It was so quiet in the graveyard the sound carried. The crowd was maybe twenty-five yards away, but they weren't much more than shadowy figures in the lantern light.

Her face was lit by a lantern hung on a hook, and she squinted into the light. Silently, she rehearsed her lines once again, although she had delivered them several times already, and they had less than an hour to go. Judging by the number of groups who already passed through, the event was a successful fundraiser. There had been a steady flow of people moving from one vignette to another, led by a resident of the Silent City, so to speak, swinging a lantern to light the path for the crowd. She turned and peered into the night behind her. It was indeed much darker than she thought it would be. No doubt Zelda had noticed that, too.

The crowd applauded and then she heard the crunch of shoes on the path. It would be her turn to perform next.

Something caught her eye as it fell from the tree beside her. It landed with a loud crashing thump. She stifled a scream and turned toward the sound, but the night veiled her vision. She pulled the flashlight from her pocket and scanned the ground just as a dark form rose from the ground and darted away. She screamed, and every flashlight in the graveyard turned toward her. Light beams flickered over her. Over the ground. Over the tombstones that stood between her and… whatever that was running away.

Still rooted with fear, she trained the light to see into the dark. A limb lay a few feet away, snapped and fallen to the ground. A widow maker, they called those tree limbs. They may not look dangerous on the ground, but a knock in the head would knock you dead.

The volunteer leading the pack trained the light on her face when he reached her. "I hope you're okay."

She blocked the beam from her eyes with her hand. "It was just a big branch," she said, and noticed her voice was trembling. "But it scared me."

"It's a good thing you weren't ten feet that way," he said. "We'd be planting *you* in the Silent City."

She knew he meant to amuse her and ease the tension, but it rankled a little simply because it was true. Had she been standing ten feet in that direction she would be as dead as Maude Calhoun.

One of the docents sprinted up the path. "Tell me everybody's okay," he said breathlessly. "I heard a scream."

"It was me," Amy said quietly. "I'm okay. A branch fell over there, and it spooked me. Some wild animal fell with it and ran off."

He directed his light to the ground and then back to her. "Are you sure you're okay?"

Amy nodded in the light; her eyes squeezed shut. "Let me catch my breath and I'll be ready to continue."

"We'll take the group to the next stop," the man said, with a nod to the volunteer leading the group. "They can loop back through here afterwards. No harm done. Here, sit down for a minute," he said, motioning to one of the chairs placed for the guests. "I'll stay with you if you need me to."

"I'm okay," she said, sitting in the cold metal chair. "Really, I am. It just surprised me. I'll be ready to tell my story when the group comes back through."

"If you're sure."

She watched the white tread of his tennis shoes moving away, a ghostly-looking sight as he left her in the darkness.

Amy trained her flashlight on the limb. It was big enough to hold an animal, and she hoped that what dropped to the ground wasn't a bear. Or a mountain lion—either one having watched and waited from its perch above. Whatever it was it would be as surprised to drop to the ground with a crash as Amy was to hear it. Whatever kind of animal it was it was long gone by now.

Something winked among the pine needles in the flashlight beam, and curious, she rose. Her knees were not as steady as she thought they would be, but she managed the soft, uneven ground between her and the limb and the shiny something. She bent down and peered at the tangle and then pulled it from the pine straw.

Hanging it from her fingers, she played the light over it. It was a necklace. Old and very worn. The chain was broken. It resembled a locket, but rectangular rather than round. The shape was larger by a good half inch than a picture locket, and it didn't open when she pried her thumb to the edge.

She looked up and realized what had just happened moments ago and at her good fortune at not standing closer to the tree. She returned to the cold chair in the light beneath the hanging lantern which was bright enough to see what she held in her hands.

The locket was metal, maybe tin or brass, she couldn't tell which. Not gold or silver. The pattern on the outside was decorative, maybe a bough of Christmas holly. The other side made her think of a musical harp. She ran her finger over the edge and discovered a hinge on the outside. There was something lodged in the hinge, and she worked it with her fingers. It was a tiny pencil, not much bigger than a toothpick. With the pencil removed, the locket opened. Inside was a booklet, the pages old and yellowed with time. The pencil marks drawn on the pages were crude and unreadable. Not crude like someone illiterate, but as if writing from an angle as it hung from the neck.

In the background she heard the applause and then the crunch of shoes on the path. The next group was coming. She slipped the necklace into her pocket and took her position on the makeshift stage. She glanced again at the branch only a few feet away. Whatever had made the branch fall—whether bear, lion, or old age and rot—it wasn't there now.

The group gathered around her, lanterns flickering in the night, and she began to speak.

"My name is Maude Calhoun. My friends call me Maudie, but I prefer Mae. And when I put my name on the newspaper I publish, I call myself M.A. Calhoun. This is my gravestone, next to my husband, Frank, who retired to the Silent City long before I did. This is my story, and if you'll gather near, I will tell you about the woman behind the Bluff Springs news."

CHAPTER FIVE

She walked toward the circle of light, confident this was her destination, although she didn't know why. Everything was in black and white, like an old movie of the film noir age. As she drew closer, she recognized the tombstones of Franklin and Maude Calhoun, side by side in the cemetery. She approached the table where a man sat solemn in a dark suit, eerie light from the lantern casting deep shadows across his face.

She grinned with incredulity when she saw who it was.

"Good evening," Alfred Hitchcock said in a slow intonation. "I knew you would be along shortly."

He motioned to the table. "I would ask you to join me, but as you can see, the seats are all taken." His jowls lifted briefly into a near smile and then settled again.

There were four chairs set around the table. Three of them were empty. Hitchcock sat in the center seat, looking at her intently. She looked at him, amused and confused.

"You can never believe precisely what the deceased will tell you." He motioned solemnly to the Ouija board at the center of the table. "Especially on one of these popular talking board contraptions. They are often inclined to spell out the most harrowing tales of deception. And murder."

She drew in a breath.

"But then, you are the one. The one to tell. If you were bold enough to ask."

Ask who? She glanced again at the empty chairs. She saw now there were objects on the table at each place setting. One looked like an old apothecary jar. Another were four queens from a deck of cards. The last was a silver thimble, like the playing piece on a Monopoly board. A lace handkerchief was tossed carelessly beside it, as if someone had risen abruptly and left it behind. She saw a dark spot in the fold. Dark like old blood.

"I have it on good authority that unfavorable habits lead to sleepless nights. I also have it on good authority there is a most useful remedy for insomnia."

He placed a single bullet on the table.

"Guaranteed to put you to sleep. Forever."

"No!" Amy yelped. "This is just a dream!"

"A dream? Or a nightmare? It is always a pleasure to wake up from both. Some do not." He folded his hands in front of him. "Good night," he added. "Or perhaps, I should say, au revoir."

Au revoir?

CHAPTER SIX

Genna bustled through the Tiddlywinks door like one of the witches of Eastwick. She was dressed in a long, flowing shirt-dress with silver moons and stars on a deep purple background. The dress was cinched at her impossibly narrow waist, and the hem went almost to the ankle of her Oxford lace up pumps in a cauldron goo green. She didn't wear a hat or a broom, but Amy suspected her witch's broom was within reach in the hall closet.

"Honoring your true stripes, I see," Zelda said teasingly and grinned. Zelda had joined Amy earlier to see the trick or treaters on their downtown run.

Rian trailed in behind Genna, and Amy was surprised to see her. Rian had not opened The Pot Shed today, and Amy knew that trick or treating was not her favorite social event. Rian didn't want grubby hands and fake blood anywhere near her precious plants and illegal edibles.

"What brings you here?" Amy ventured.

"Genna, if you must know. I'm getting new tires on the Fiat. She agreed to be my chauffeur. I was hoping she would show up in that hearse and top hat from last night, but no luck."

Rian was in her usual baggy blue jeans, t-shirt, and flannel. Amy and Zelda were in the same costumes from the fundraiser. Today, Amy chose sensible shoes.

"I thought we could all walk down to the pub and have a witchy cocktail," Genna said. "Maybe something like Absinthe and Champagne."

"Like we are going to find that at the pub," Rian mumbled. "You'll be lucky if you can get a warm beer on a day like today."

The streets were absolutely packed with tourists. Some were in costumes already. Some would return after dinner for a block wide Halloween crawl.

"I'm going to stay open for another hour at least," Amy said. "The newspaper said we were trick or treating until seven."

Genna looked at her watch.

"You'll have to go to the pub without me," Amy said.

"And without me, too," Zelda said. "I'm hanging out here."

"Is there anything in your fridge?" Genna asked hopefully.

"There's a box o'wine. Glasses are in the cupboard to the right."

Genna nodded and disappeared. When she returned, she had the box with four glasses laced through her fingers. Amy put the box beneath the counter when the glasses were poured. No sense in advertising the obvious.

"You caused quite a stir in the graveyard," Genna said, as she settled into her seat. "Your scream was loud enough to wake the dead."

"Eww," Zelda said. "You have absolutely no discernment, Genna. What a thing to say."

"I have no discernment?" Genna countered, with a hand gesture toward herself. "Kettle and pot," she added. "You're the one who asked that lady in the Heathrow Airport if she could point you to the ladies loo."

"It was necessary," Zelda said. "I really, really had to go. I was just being colloquial."

"What was necessary was *discerning* the guide dog at her feet and the red tipped cane. She was much more polite to you than I would have been."

"She was very polite," Zelda countered. "She understood my plight. And that's not what it means, anyway. Discernment is knowing the difference between right and almost right. You agree, don't you, Amy?"

"Not barking up that tree," she answered, rising to meet the next round of trick or treaters at the door. She noticed that the streets were finally thinning and put the bucket of candy on the stoop outside and closed the door. "They can help themselves," she said, as she returned to the table and settled into her seat with a glass of wine. She reached into her pocket and then leveled her arm over the table. She opened her hand to let the necklace slither through her fingers. It landed with a tinny plunk.

"What's this?" Rian asked.

"Probably more show and tell," Genna answered.

"I found it last night in the graveyard," Amy answered, looking from face to face. "It was right where the branch fell." She narrowed her eyes at Genna. "Which is why I screamed, if you will remember."

"What is it?" Rian asked again.

Zelda tapped her finger on the table. "It's a necklace, duh."

"I think it's a dance card necklace," Amy said, ignoring the snark. "It could be from the late eighteen nineties."

Rian picked up the chain and brought it closer for inspection. "A dance card what?"

"Open it," Amy said. "See that little pencil in the hinge? Pull that out. You'll see."

Rian fumbled with the pencil and then opened the locket. "It's a notebook," she said. She leafed through the pages gently, careful not to tear the pages that were not much bigger than a large postage stamp.

"You've heard the expression, my dance card is full," Amy offered. "This is where that expression came from. It was the guy's job to secure the dance from the women. She would then write the dance and her dance partner in her notebook. That way everyone was booked, and no one sat like a wallflower in the corner."

"Very Victorian." Rian passed the necklace to Zelda.

"This looks vaguely familiar," Zelda said.

"You weren't around in the eighteen hundreds. Or maybe you were," Genna quipped.

"You've seen this before?" Amy asked.

"Well," Zelda answered slowly, as she turned the locket in her fingers. "I'm not sure that I have, actually. Not that I remember where, anyway."

"Another thing that dates this is the *repoussage*." Amy added.

"The re-poo what?"

"*Repoussage* is the metal working technique used on the surface. It's where they take a malleable metal like brass and create designs by hammering from the reverse side. This one looks like Christmas. I think that's a spray of holly. I know it's old because after the war made metal scarce, they started making dance cards out of paper and ribbon."

Genna accepted the locket from Zelda. She opened it and turned the pages. "I can't read this scribble."

"Some of it is not discernible," Amy agreed. "I guess it was hard to write with that tiny pencil on tiny paper hanging from your neck. At least that's how I picture it."

"What do these numbers mean?"

Amy shook her head. "Beats me."

"And what are the drawings of?"

"Your guess is as good as mine. But there are also a few names in there. Names you might recognize, Genna," Amy added dramatically.

"Oh, so now you're implying I am old enough to be from the eighteen hundreds."

"Just look again. You'll see."

Genna squinted to study the pages. "Evangeline. Elysa. Della. Cat. Coleman." Genna brought the page closer. "No, that says Calhoun." Genna gasped. "Calhoun! As in our own Maude Calhoun."

"Or maybe Frank Calhoun," Amy answered. "Or Frank senior. Who knows how far back this goes."

Genna turned the pages slowly. "Here's a Teddy."

"Look at the page."

"Duncan!"

"Mrs. Teddy Duncan," Amy corrected. "With all those fancy scrolling letters and curlicues. Like she was trying out the monogram for her wedding linens and lace handkerchiefs."

Genna handed the necklace back to Amy. "You said this was on the ground at the cemetery?"

Zelda gasped. "Do you think it was buried in Catherine Duncan's grave and was dug up?" She looked at the necklace with renewed suspicion. "Someone robbed her grave!"

Amy shook her head. "If so, it was dug up recently. It wasn't dirty enough to be on the ground long."

"How old would someone be in nineteen twenty-four if they were dancing socialites in the late eighteen hundreds?" Genna asked.

"Older than dirt," Zelda answered.

"They would be in their twenties," Rian answered. "No, that's not right. They would be in their forties if they were a young adult in the nineties."

"That's the 1890s," Amy said, with a side look at Zelda. "Not 1990s."

Zelda scrunched her nose. "Too much math for me. If you want to talk fashion, however, I might have something to add."

"If Rian's math is right, the necklace is too old to belong to Catherine Duncan. At the time she was a young dancing socialite, paper and ribbon were the style used. They wore them on their wrists. Each card became a souvenir for their scrapbook. This necklace would have been considered very old-fashioned." Amy dangled the chain from her fingers.

"It was probably a family heirloom," Zelda argued. "Passed down from her mother or grandmother who did live in the *eighteen* nineties." She looked at Amy with a self-assured smile.

"Then why didn't it get passed on to Catherine's heirs?"

"She didn't have any," Genna answered. "At least, I never found any children mentioned in the archives."

"That doesn't mean she didn't have children," Zelda said. "It just means they didn't make the news."

Amy knew Zelda was right. And so was Rian. It would not have been stylish for a young woman to dance in the early twentieth century with such a Victorian-looking piece. Especially with bob shorn hair and her hem to her knees. She thought of the brooches that came her way through family lines. They were treasures, for sure, but they were not something you tacked onto your t-shirt and called it good. But then, everything old was new again. Vintage was hip and old school was cool. Maybe a brooch would look good on a blinged up tee.

"What are you going to do with it?" Zelda asked, breaking into her thoughts. "Are you going to wear it? I would wear it if you gave it to me."

"It belongs to someone," Amy replied, ignoring Zelda's not-so-subtle plea. "I think I should try to find who that is."

"And how would you accomplish that?" Zelda asked. "Assuming it belongs to someone now residing in the graveyard. It's not like they are going to answer a Finder's Keepers Want Ad in the newspaper."

Amy didn't answer. Her thoughts had turned to Alfred Hitchcock showing up in her dream like one of his movie cameo appearances. All the seats were taken. Were there ghosts sitting at the table that she couldn't see but he could? He sounded like he was laying out the riddle for her to pick up and solve. Either that or she had bad dreams after too much Ben and Jerry's ice cream and a scare in the graveyard.

If ever there was a time to tell her friends—her best friends—about Alfred and his stranger than strange appearance, now would be the time. Somehow, the words wouldn't come out when she opened her mouth to speak.

They would probably believe her. After all they had been through, her friends now understood the veracity of her snippet dreams. If she could use that strong of a word. But in fact, she was beginning to recognize the difference between a dream and a snippet herself. Not always. But there was a difference. One had all the markings of a fretful mind working overtime on day-to-day problems in the middle of the night. The other had spine-tingling dread attached.

She wasn't sure which one Alfred was. Not just yet.

He had been amusing in his odd sort of way as he talked about murder and deception. But the fact that Rian had been talking about Alfred and his birds only a few days ago made *snippet* questionable. And the fact that he talked about the Ouija board in her dream made it even more suspect. Hadn't she just bought a dozen?

Her mind was definitely trying to sort out something, but was this a foreboding snippet dream? She wasn't sure about that.

"Genna," she said at last, turning to face her friend. "When you were researching for these vignettes, did you run across any murders?"

Genna raised a brow. "Murders?" Genna tapped the table with a fingertip. "Did I forget to mention that Winslow T. Duncan was murdered? He was Catherine Duncan's husband. She was Mrs. Winslow T. Duncan before his demise. He was gunned down after a card game. Left for dead in his Model T."

"Genna!" Amy exclaimed. "How could you leave that out?"

"I didn't think it was germane to this year's vignettes. The story wasn't about him; it was about the mayor. And he was already gone when she was elected."

Amy shook her head. The edges of her snippet dream were beginning to solidify. A murder. A card game. And another dead husband.

"What does the T stands for?" Zelda asked.

"I know that one," Rian piped in. "The Model T was the twentieth model car that Henry Ford made. He started at letter A and T followed twenty car designs later."

"I don't think you know what you're talking about," Zelda stated as a matter of fact. "I've never heard of a Model B or a Model Q."

"I meant the other T," Amy said. "As in Winslow T."

"Theodore," Genna answered. "Winslow Theodore Duncan. Maybe they called him Teddy for short."

"And the plot thickens," Zelda said. "Mrs. Teddy Duncan became mayor of Bluff Springs after her husband died. You left the most interesting part out of your script, Genna. Somebody murdered poker playing Teddy! If that necklace belonged to Catherine, I say she did it!"

Genna frowned. "I was focused on the wives, not their husbands. I was looking at the women who were just getting a few civil rights and liberties. For the first time, women voted, and they worked outside of the home. They cut the hair off their heads and moved their hemlines up to their knees. I was focused on a very exciting time for women beginning to come into power, not their husbands!" Genna sounded defensive. She sipped her wine and feigned a look of indignant satisfaction.

"The trend to put women in power didn't last all that long," she added a moment later. "Although Petticoat governments did find favor in rural towns. Jackson, Wyoming was the first Petticoat government in world history."

"What kind of work did Winslow T. Duncan do?" Rian asked.

"I don't remember. But I do know how to find out. I still have access to the historical archives. I'm sure I can find a story about the incident."

"What if we're holding a clue to a crime," Amy said finally, her hand closing tightly over the dance card locket.

"Did you have one of your dreams?" Genna arched a brow. "Are you talking about a present-day crime? Or something old and already buried in the silent—"

"Here we are talking about ghosts again!" Zelda interrupted. "I don't like it when we talk about ghosts."

"Haints," Amy said quietly.

"Haunts," Zelda echoed.

"No, the word is *haints*. It's an old Creole Gullah word. My grandmother used it."

"Haints and hollers and hoodoo," Rian said.

"What if finding this necklace wasn't an accident? What if someone planted it there so someone else would find it and start asking questions."

"Someone like you?" Rian mused with a smile. "If ever there was someone prepared to ask questions, that would be you, Amy."

Amy tensed. Alfred Hitchcock said something very similar.

Haints and hollers and hoodoo.

And a graveyard full of secrets.

CHAPTER SEVEN

The days following a busy Halloween weekend, replete with the eventful Silent City fundraiser and trick or treaters, left Amy ready for downtime in fuzzy slippers with a fuzzy cat for company. She often took Sunday afternoon off because there wasn't much business since most of the tourists were packing up to head home. There was only so much a person could do while still being polite when a tourist asked, yet again, if the streets were always this crooked and how come the hills were so steep. It was a fun answer when it was fun to answer. It was a labor of love when she was beat. Victor had opted to stay home all weekend by hiding in his favorite spot when it came time to leave. The shriek of the costumed witches and vampires and Marvel heroes in the street below had put his tail in full puff. She was just dozing off for the second time during the movie when her phone rang. Victor opened his eyes with a squint and looked annoyed.

"Hey, Genna," Amy said, recognizing the caller.

"Not… believe… found…" her static stuttered.

"I can't hear you!" The line was silent for a moment.

"Said… found … send… you…"

Amy's phone chirped as the text from Genna arrived. She knew Genna was out of town dealing with a client crisis, and the hills and hollers of Arkansas had dead spots where cell phones couldn't signal out. It was one of the reasons why Genna and Rian had invested in a cell tower scheme. Neither got rich quick, and the hills and hollers were still standing and so was the poor connection.

The call dropped and Amy turned her attention to the text. It was a picture of a newspaper article. She strained to read the block of print.

Genna had scored.

Winslow T. Duncan of Bluff Springs was found dead in the seat of his car, on the morning of January 11, shot in cold blood with what is believed to be his own gun. The gun was not found. Robbery is suspected, since the deceased man's wallet was missing from the vehicle when searched. A fellow gentleman not identified by name said he believed there would be a considerable amount of cash still in his possession, as Duncan, known to friends as Teddy, had won the bounty of a card game held the evening prior at the IOOF meeting hall.

Amy stared at her phone. A poker game. Of course, a poker game was involved. Hadn't Alfred Hitchcock all but spelled that out for her? Four queens from a deck of cards and a warning about deception and murder. Had Duncan's winning hand been four queens?

Amy's phone chirped again.

Known to Bluff Springs, Ark. as a successful businessman with considerable real estate holdings and the first Ford car dealership in the county seat, Winslow T. Duncan was laid to rest in the Bluff Springs Cemetery, Wed., Jan. 16, following his untimely death. The Rev. Cecil Hayes did preside over the internment at 10:50 o'clock and gave a humbling sermon to a sorrowful gathering of many on the fragility of life and the inevitable call home. The widow, Mrs. Winslow Duncan, was present. The widow wore a mourning dress of the simplicity required for the occasion with

just the right touch of chic in a panel of crepe on black taffeta.

Was she reading a fashion magazine or an obituary? Definitely written by a woman who would notice those details. Probably Maude Calhoun.

Amy blinked and refocused.

The local chapter of the IOOF presented a handsome spray of yellow chrysanthemums to adorn the casket. Fellows will take responsibility to erect the Woodsman of the World statuary ordered to adorn his presence once the stone has been received. The pallbearers were J. Earl and Edgar Langford, Franklin Calhoun, Oscar St. Claire, Delano and Alfonso Slater, and the Baker brothers, Charles M. and Stanley.

It didn't say if the widow would take over Duncan's car businesses or his real estate, but Amy suspected it was worth a tidy sum, if he was a successful businessman. She made a mental note to ask Genna if she knew what IOOF stood for and who were the Woodsman of the World. Certainly, Genna had come across that in her research. She would also ask Rian about a Model T dealership in the 1920s. That had to be a pretty big deal.

Mostly, she wondered who had grabbed the gun and the poker cash and disappeared into the cold winter night, leaving Duncan, even colder, behind the wheel.

Her phone chirped one more time and a picture popped up.

Winslow Duncan was a looker. She could tell that even in the newspaper photo. He had a crown of thick, dark hair and piercing black eyes beneath a heavy, brooding brow. His mustache nearly reached his ears, the ends resolutely curled and waxed. He appeared to be smoking a cigarette in the picture, but the most prominent item visible was a signet ring with the initials WTD engraved in the center. The ring looked like something he would use to seal a deal and document in wax. Or leave a hefty bruise in a fight. She thought he looked like a brawler. A card player. A winning card player. Definitely a man used to getting his own way. His expression was menacing and yet slightly amused at the same time. She sensed he was a man who could be really fun until he wasn't, and then he would be cruel and unforgiving.

She knew she was pushing a lot through the filter of the camera lens, but he struck her as someone who knew the fragility of life and didn't care one whit, regardless of what the Rev. Hayes had to say.

Catherine Duncan did well as his widow. Genna's script for the Silent City was full of facts and anecdotes about this courageous woman who took the reins of power in a time when women were neither celebrated nor esteemed. Her leadership and civic involvement made a big impact on the town. Genna highlighted her most memorable achievements. Getting women appointed to the town council was one. Then she created educational opportunities for women and children and supported women-owned businesses at a time when enterprise was dominated by men. She even sold the town's tiny jailhouse, putting the revenue toward her civic projects. Mayor Catherine claimed they didn't need a jail if the crooks could escape easily enough to attend the popular dance locals called the Barefoot Ball. There wasn't enough time to tell the story of that jailbreak in the mayor's vignette, but it was the event that motivated her to sell the jail. Under Catherine's mayorship, minor lawbreakers didn't spend lazy time behind bars. They were given stiff fines and community service work. The plan seem to work. Criminals went to the state prison. Delinquents went to work.

Those were all astonishing feats, but Amy wanted more than the headlines reported. She wanted to know what did *not* make the headlines. The kinds of things people didn't talk about in polite society. The most pressing was whether Zelda was right, and Winslow was shot by his wife, and if she did, why?

Amy settled against the cushions and let Victor reclaim his spot. Was this the crime her snippet dream was guiding her to solve? It was a big leap to make buy why else would Alfred Hitchcock show up in her dream in the graveyard with a bullet and a message about deception. And murder.

She stroked Victor's soft fur and wondered what mad little rabbit trail she was about to follow. What if Catherine Duncan purposefully moved her husband out of the way of her success? What did it matter, now, about something that happened more than a hundred years ago? What would anyone gain from that knowledge now? Genna claimed Catherine Duncan never had children, so, there were no heirs left behind to complicate matters or ruin family history. And yet, there was Sir Alfred Hitchcock, goading her into a visit to the Ouija board for answers. A little Q & A, as Genna liked to call polite interrogation. A "creepy Q &A" is how she would put it. Amy wasn't any keener to use the Ouija than Zelda was, and she had her own reasons to keep her fingers off the talking planchette. She hadn't touched the boards since buying them, other than to stow them in the closet until she could research their history and worth.

She wouldn't begrudge the money she gave Camellia. The gesture might have been a bit more generous than wise, but something had told her to help this young woman through a tough spot. She would make her money back and then some. She knew that. Tiddlywinks Players Club was getting a reputation as the place to score hard to find games. Her email list of collectors was growing. Maybe there was a Ouija collector on the list. But why in the world did Aunt Mable Rose have a dozen Ouija boards? And where was she in the Bluff Springs history books?

"Okay, Sir Alfred," she said out loud. "What am I missing here?" Victor yawned and stretched across her lap.

The necklace fell into her lap, so to speak. Which, in her mind, meant it had to be a clue. A clue to something. Synchronicity and all that. If that clue was to an unsolved murder, then it had to be connected to Winslow Duncan. It was his name in the pages. Not a coincidence. Unless she was missing something subtle. That would be Alfred Hitchcock's style, wouldn't it? Subtle. Until she drew back the curtain and screamed.

Amy pulled the necklace from the box on the coffee table in front of her. She put it there for safe keeping until she decided what to do with it. She pulled the tiny pencil from the hinge and opened the locket, realizing how fragile the pages were. She also noticed, then, that the little notebook was removable. That made sense. One could use up the pages in one notebook and then replace it with another. The necklace was permanent. The booklet was not. Perhaps women keep them after the pages were full, or more likely they tossed them in the fire. Some people kept everything. Some people kept little.

She opened the booklet with gentle fingers and then opened the camera on her phone. She didn't want to ruin the pages thumbing through them too many times. By snapping a picture of each page, she could study the images more closely and share them with her friends.

She recognized some of the names now. Of course, St. Claire and Calhoun were prominent members of society at the time of Duncan's demise. Their wives became prominent later. She didn't see the names of the pallbearers, but she would be on the lookout. But, if this was a dance card for a young socialite, why the names of married men?

"Well, because they weren't married, yet," she said with excitement to Victor, who opened his eyes and blinked. "I love you, too," she said and blinked back. Cat language. She was fluent.

That made perfect sense if the locket had belonged to Catherine Duncan. She may have been considering other marriage options on the dance floor. But why were there women's names in there, too? Evangeline. Elysa. Della. Cat. Maybe they were contemporaries. She turned her attention to the writing on the pages. There were names and numbers and drawings. Maybe the numbers were telephone numbers. It couldn't be a sketch book, especially hanging from a chain at the neck, and the pages were not much bigger than a postage stamp. What were the sketches and what did they mean?

The list of things she didn't know was growing. She didn't know much about life in the 1920s. She knew Prohibition was in full force and mostly ignored. Bathtub gin and moonshine were illicit enterprises. She knew Flappers had more fun than anyone. But she doubted the ideal of Gatsby's Roaring '20s in high society New York would look anything like life in Bluff Springs. Arkansas was a scrappy place with rutted roads and steep hills, and houses clinging to the cliffs. So, what did life look like in the 1920s and who were the people who lived it? Genna had done a good job with her ten-minute history vignettes, but people were much more than that. People were more than their obituaries of school graduations, church memberships, and family left behind.

Her phone chirped again.

"The usual suspects," Genna typed. An image followed, and Amy was once again drawn back in time.

The front-page headline read: **TOWN LEADERS QUESTIONED FOR MURDER**

Authorities have arrived at the unfortunate conclusion that Winslow T. Duncan, deceased, was a victim of homicide.

"Duh," Amy said to Victor, who looked up and blinked.

Town leaders have come forward to say that they were engaged in a friendly game of cards with Duncan the evening of his death. It appears a tangle of tempers was exchanged, according to a statement by Oscar St. Claire, owner of The People's Drug at the corner of Mountain and Main. The argument in question was anchored by a misunderstanding between J. Earl Langford and Duncan. It was reported that Langford had put up a parcel of land as assurance in a bet that was subsequently won by the now deceased. The parcel, according to Langford, is of more value than agreed upon for the debt. The argument ensued when Langford attempted to retrieve the note of promise from Duncan. St. Claire and others who wish to remain unidentified were successful in defusing the argument before it rose out of hand. It is unclear whether the argument continued to the street, where Duncan was found beyond resuscitation in his automobile the following morning. When questioned about his whereabouts at the time of the incident, J. Earl Langford told authorities in charge of the matter that he returned home to his wife and family immediately after the altercation. He claimed he saw a man helping Duncan free his car from the icy slush in the road and then saw him rushing from the scene. He believed him to be the indigent colloquially known as Hobo Joe. Other witnesses said they did not hear the fatal gunshot. "All I can say is the death is ruled a homicide at this point,

and homicide and murder are synonymous. We have a crime here, and we are looking for the suspect," Constable Wallace said.

Wow. The usual suspects, indeed. A poker player who scammed a fellow player out of a nice piece of land. The thought landed suddenly that perhaps this was how Duncan had acquired his real estate holdings. And that meant there could be a whole slew of suspects lined up and waiting to be questioned for murder. If they were still alive. There was a lot of anonymity bandied about, but the names Langford and Hobo Joe took front and center.

The wife was not mentioned as a suspect. Was that conspicuous? Or inconspicuous? Maude Calhoun could be protecting her best friend from that direction of inquiry since Maude held a great deal of influence in the pages of the Bluff Springs Weekly Times. Her husband sat at the helm. It made sense that the person who wanted anonymity was publisher Frank Calhoun himself. He would want his name omitted from the article to give the appearance of journalistic objectivity. She read the story again. The appearance of objectivity. Not that neutrality was all that different then than now.

Amy looked over the article again, noting the names that were now familiar. Brothers J. Earl and Edgar Langford were pallbearers at Duncan's graveside service. J. Earl lost money in the game. She knew there were Langfords still living in the community today. One was the owner of a motel and the other had a campground not far from the cemetery. They wouldn't be the same people mentioned in the article, of course, but they could be descendants. The thought pinged in her head. She could hunt them down and ask a few questions. Maybe they remembered the story.

After dressing quickly, Amy scooted out the door, leaving her cat snoozing in his favorite spot in the windowsill. The air outside was chilly, and she was glad she thought to grab her purple knit cap. The embroidery said, *Cat Mama. Beware.* She pulled it over her ears and walked briskly down the block, watching the leaves rustling in the breeze from sidewalk to street to gutter. The street sweeper would be along soon, and the leaves would be stirred into a frenzy before being vacuumed away.

The coffee shop across from the courthouse was a favorite hang for locals. You could get a plate of bacon and eggs and gravy for $6.99 and coffee refills were free all day. Sunday was the day the husbands went for bacon and eggs and man chat while the women went to church. Or brunch. Or shopping. Or whatever the wives were motivated to do.

She figured the Langfords were regulars. She opened the door and stepped in.

She found a place at the counter and ordered. She held her warm mug in two hands and spun around on the stool. The room was full, and she knew most of them by face if not by name. They were pleasant faces. Men of all ages. A couple of tourist families getting a late start on the road. A woman and her husband. Amy couldn't remember their names. They ran a sports excursion off the highway. ATVs or something. She recognized one of the Langfords sitting at a table near the counter. She couldn't remember which one he was. The motel keep or the RV man.

"I just met your new neighbor," Amy said when their eyes met in greeting.

"What new neighbor?" His voice was deep and resonant, reaching through the din and chatter of the room.

"Over on Piney Top. That old, abandoned house."

His eyes narrowed in confusion. "No one's living in that dump. It's a tear down. You're thinking of my brother, though," he added. "He's the one that wants it. His campground is on the back side of that acreage."

"You mean he wants to buy it?"

"Well, sure he wants to buy it. It's sitting in the way of his spread. That property has been deadlocked in probate forever. He's just waiting for it to go up for sale on the courthouse steps for back taxes. Going to add another fifty RV pads in the pines." He grinned. "Not a bad name if you ask me. Pads in the Pines. I'll have to suggest that. My place is the Palace in the Pines. I got thirty rooms, all facing the edge of the ridge. Got an outdoor jacuzzi, too. And a wedding gazebo big enough for twelve. Twenty if they don't sit down. And two honeymoon suites."

Amy nodded and drank her tea, letting the steam warm her face. Two brothers with property in the pines. She was trying to figure out how to turn the topic to the past and ask if he recalled a story about some distant relative that lost a game of poker. Somehow no opening seemed to fit.

"Well, he may have to wait a little longer," she said finally. "I don't think she's decided whether to sell or renovate. Time will tell. I'll be sure to give her your name in case she decides to sell. I think renovation will be a pretty costly project to take on."

He nodded curtly. "She?"

"Her name is Camellia deRossier. She's a relative of Mable Rose deRossier."

Amy detected the slightest nudge of a frown. "Any idea what she might want for it before she gets too far in the swamp on repairs? I know my brother's sitting with cash in hand."

Amy shook her head. "No, but I can ask. You want to give me your phone number?"

He pulled his wallet from his back pocket and produced a card. Grant Langford. Palace in the Pines. Weddings, Honeymoons, Reunions. We top all your expectations.

"I'll pass this along. Say," she said and waived the card. "Are you related to Edgar or J. Earl who lived here in the 1920s? Your family has been here a long time, haven't they?"

It was barely visible, but his face lost a fraction of a shade. He studied her face, and Amy knew she'd hit a sore spot. "Edgar was my great grandaddy," he said finally. "Good man. Honorable man. Pillar of the community."

"And J. Earl? What about him?"

"Why are you asking?"

"Oh, just because," Amy said and smiled innocently. "We were part of the fundraiser for the museum. You know, the *Tales from the Silent City*. We got bit by the history bug while learning our parts. Langford was mentioned in the history books."

"Really?" A wry grin took over his bristled face. "In the history books. J. Earl? Well, I guess he did make history. I guess he did indeed."

Amy pounced. "What did he do? What happened?"

"I thought you just said he was mentioned in the history books."

"Yeah, but…" Amy swallowed her tea and sputtered. "I don't remember what happened."

The wry grin was back. "Well, you just go back and look him up in your history book. I bet you can read all about the jailbird from Arkansas. No one ever figured out how he escaped. And you can be sure they tried."

He rose before Amy could drag him back into the conversation, tipped his ball cap, and was out the door.

CHAPTER EIGHT

Dominoes was a weekly occurrence among the four friends. The day of the game changed now and again, but the place they played rarely did. They loved to hang on Genna Gregory's deck in the woods, with its overgrown gardens and ancient trees. There was a pergola on the deck with a twisted wisteria vine that was probably planted when the house was built. In late fall, it was nothing special, just a dark tangle of vines Genna never bothered to prune. In the spring, though, the pergola would absolutely glow with purple blossoms that hung from the vines like bunches of grapes. The scent of wisteria in full bloom was remarkable.

Now that fall was well entrenched in the Ozarks, the leaves in the trees were what glowed. She never tired of looking out at the expanse of color laced over the mountain tops. Or the way the sun sunk behind the trees and sparkled like a golden goblet full of magic and promise to rise again tomorrow.

"I'm going to have my tailor make an entire wardrobe of 1920s fashion," Zelda was saying, as Amy brought her attention back to her friend. "I have received more compliments on that outfit I designed for the fundraiser than I have all year. I could single-handedly bring back the fashion of that era," she added. "I could be responsible for bringing back the roaring twenties and all that jazz."

Rian chuckled under her breath. "Bring back opiates in your cocktails while you're at it."

Zelda raised a brow.

"Back then you could put swamp water in a bottle and call in a miracle cure," Rian explained. "It's not like the FDA was around to prove your claims. Pharmacies were allowed to sell alcohol even during Prohibition. You could get an alcohol prescription for your nerves and anxieties and the pharmacist could fill it every week."

"Sounds like you did your own research," Genna declared.

Rian nodded. "Oscar St. Claire had his own little prescription. There was more than one inference that he had an addiction—to what, no one said—but there were two instances where he dispersed the wrong remedy for the wrong illness. It was covered up quickly, but there were two deaths attributed to his snafu. People felt much better when Bella took over the pharmacy."

"The thing about marriage was," Genna pitched in, "if you had a husband you didn't like then you were stuck. Divorce was out of the question. Society wasn't designed for women's independence. Staying married to a cad wasn't about the moral compass, it was about survival."

"What do you mean society wasn't designed for independence?" Zelda asked.

"A business could refuse to hire you just because you were a woman. There were laws that regulated how, when, and where a woman could work. Silly things, too, like you couldn't drive a taxi, work in a pool hall or a bowling alley. Those jobs were considered a negative influence on women's behavior. A vexation to her honor and servility. Even if you had a job and made a living, a realtor could refuse to sell or rent to you, especially if you had children. You couldn't get credit, and you couldn't get a passport unless it was in your husband's name."

"But you could vote, and that was a big step in the right direction," Zelda claimed.

"Sure, but from what I've read, women were encouraged to vote the way their husband wanted them to vote," Genna said. "The balloting process wasn't all that private. There was a guy with a box, and you handed him your ballot. Who's to say he didn't look and then tattle to your man later. It was societally acceptable for women to be told what to do, how to think, and how to behave.

"You may think the 1920s was all flapper fashion, silk stockings and long beads, but there were laws about how much skin a woman could show or how high your heels could be."

Zelda looked inquisitively with a raised brow.

"Two inches," Genna answered automatically. "Women seemed to think that it wasn't really the safety issue as they claimed. It was really because anything more than two inches could make a woman as tall as her mate. Heaven forbid if she towered over a man. That was a social taboo. Oh, woe to the tall girl." Genna grimaced and then took a sip of her wine. Defending the rights of women was thirsty work.

Amy could tell Genna was revved up and back on her soapbox. They were used to Genna's soapbox. She was passionate about everything political, and since she and Merriweather Hopkins had reconnected after a skirmish in the wine country of Arkansas, Genna was high on her soapbox about advancing the welfare of Arkansas women.

"The suffrage movement was having a tremendous impact of society, and much of the old ideology was changing," Genna continued. "The 1920s was the decade when radio entertainment and washing machines came into existence between war time and the depression. When you look back on it, it happened fast. Time-warp fast. Fashion and lifestyles were turned on their heels. Hemlines rose to the knee. Corsets got thrown in the trash. Women went to school so they could earn an income. Even married women went to work. Women learned to be teachers and dressmakers and typists and salesclerks and telephone operators who were affectionately called the 'hello girls.'

"The twenties were a fascinating decade of social, political, and cultural changes. There were tremendous advancements in technology and convenience. There was widespread economic growth, and cultural phenomena like jazz, sexy literature, and art were everywhere. People in the twenties were having fun. And then it came to a screeching halt."

"The Great Depression," Amy said.

Genna nodded. "The stock market crash ushered in a totally different era. Totally different vibe. That decade was about anguish and suffering. Unemployment and lack. Nobody was having fun. Not even the rich guys."

"Thank goodness that horrible time ended when it did," Zelda said. "But still, I do love the fashion of the twenties. And I'm glad we're in this century. I appreciate my freedoms and independence."

Amy agreed. Her generation had seen women gain incredible ground against societal misogyny. In her lifetime, women not only voted, but they won stature, high honor, and significant leadership roles. In her generation, women had autonomy over their bodies, their environment, their bank credit, and their lifestyles. There were many things that women—and some men—still didn't have agency over, but the world was evolving. Technology—warp-speed like Genna said—was ushering in an understanding that the world was diverse, and yet, akin.

"You know what else was happening in that era," Amy said, when the lull in conversation had gone on long enough. "Spiritualism was all the rage."

"Like Harry Houdini," Zelda said.

Rian laughed. "Harry Houdini hated them. He knew they were fakes, and he spent his life outing mediums and their fraud. He was not a believer. He was all about engineering the distraction."

"Engineering the sleight of hand," Amy added.

Rian nodded. "He was a master of illusion."

"I ran across an article about Houdini in the Bluff Springs Weekly Times," Genna said. "Houdini was in Kansas City giving a magic performance and a speech about Spiritualism. There was a rumor he would detour to Bluff Springs for an impromptu performance."

"Did he?" Rian asked.

Genna shrugged. "There's only so much you can dig up in the newspaper morgue and museum archives but that would have been pretty big news if he did. I uncovered a regular sermon on the mount, though. Reverend Cecil Hayes published a column every week about the sins of the flesh, the suffering of the wicked, and the evils of drink. I got the impression he published his sermon after the fact for the benefit of those who didn't attend his service."

Rian turned to Amy. "What's your interest in spiritualism?"

"Just that it was popular at the time. And I did just buy a bunch of Ouija boards."

"Oh, not that again," Zelda complained. "You know how I feel about that."

"The same way I do, I think," Amy answered. "But the Ouija board was really popular in the twenties. They had Ouija parties where people gathered to communicate with the dead. It wasn't seen as evil or macabre. It was a way to connect with people you loved and missed. It was a game to some, like checkers and mahjong, but it was important for people who were into secrets and the hidden unknown.

"It's not real," Amy continued, as if trying to convince herself. "But people loved it, and it wasn't until the pious saw their power slipping that it got such a bad rap. And well, we know where it went from there."

"Right to the big screen," Rian said with a wicked grin, wiggling her eyebrows at Zelda.

"Not funny," Zelda said.

"What is funny is that we haven't played a single tile all evening," Genna said, and spun the domino tiles in the center of the table. "We're slipping. We used to be able to talk and eat and drink and play at the same time. We may be getting old."

"Speak for yourself," Zelda said, pulling a single tile from the pile. "Double six," she said, plopping it down for all to see. "This is going to be my game to win, Sparks. You and Genna and Rian can hash out your role as losers however you see fit."

Amy laughed. She loved winning. She didn't mind losing. Mostly, she was grateful she had three best friends who would go to the ends of the earth with her if she asked them. She was going to have a great big ask in the not-too-distant future because they were going to have to go to the ends of the Ouija board to ask what Alfred had put into motion. If she really was out to solve a cold case, the Ouija was part of it. That was clear. And she sure as anything wasn't going to do it alone.

"Get thee to the boneyard," Genna said gleefully as Amy studied the pips in her hand with a sorrowful eye. "I know you don't have any fives."

The dominoes in play had scored Zelda a big fat twenty points, which she had added to the scorecard with an exaggerated flair. Zelda was always the scorekeeper, which was a novelty for someone who despised math. Her method to tally the points was to mark a single \ for every five points won. Another / made for ten. By looking at the Xs—each worth ten points—it was easy to keep score without a single number or equation required. Zelda wasn't always paying attention when points were scored, but she was honest, and they could count on her to do the right thing. Genna, however, was always suspect in the game. One of her favorite things was to cheat and not get caught. It wasn't easy to cheat at dominoes, but Genna had invented a number of ingenious moves. The most stellar, to date, was when she hung a bagua mirror, positioned so she could see everybody's hand. She was found out and scolded—in good humor, of course—and they hadn't caught her at any big cheats since then. Genna's hard edges, it seemed, were softening. Amy thought it had to do with Merriweather Hopkins, an old friend turned enemy who was once again an old friend. They never saw the two together unless it was in a photo op, but Amy knew the two of them were doing great things for women in Arkansas in their non-profit organization they called Project X. A fun play on the chromosome.

It was no accident that Genna was the one who suggested the women of history as the focus for the *Tales from the Silent City*. Nor was it an accident Genna assigned herself as the writer for the scripts. Amy knew Genna's research was going to come in handy in this cold case murder. If Genna didn't already have the information memorized, she'd know where to find it.

"And you don't have any blanks, either," Genna quipped now as Amy absently pulled tile after tile from the boneyard, her pile in front of her growing. And growing. And growing, still.

"I don't think there are any blanks or fives left," Amy yelped.

Rian wiggled her brows.

Amy finally pulled a blank sided tile from the boneyard and played. "No points," she declared.

"Obviously," Zelda said with a gloat.

"What do you think about those articles I sent you," Genna said, as the play moved to Zelda once again, who took her time examining her tiles and counting the pips.

"The usual suspects," Amy answered. "Langford sounds a likely suspect if you ask me, but I'm still wondering if Catherine did the deed."

"What are you talking about?" Zelda asked, playing a tile with no points, even after all that scrutiny.

Amy shared the gist of the articles Genna had sent by phone, and the story about what had happened to Duncan, catching Rian and Zelda up to date. She pulled up the text on her phone and handed it to Rian to read.

"It's the whole lot of them," Amy added. "The usual suspects at a poker game. Players who lose and lose badly."

"St. Claire was one of them," Rian said, looking up from the phone.

"He's the one who squeaked to the paper," Genna answered. "The other guy didn't give his name."

"That was probably Frank Calhoun," Amy responded. "He wouldn't dilute the credibility of the report in his own newspaper."

Genna chuckled. "But he didn't mind throwing Langford under the bus."

"Right," Amy agreed. "Making Langford a top suspect. The only person who could give Langford an alibi was his wife.

"I think the story sounds like it was written by a woman," Amy continued. "Probably Maude Calhoun. There were unusual details in the story, like the flowers and the dress the widow wore. I can't imagine a dude noticing that."

"That verbiage was the norm back then," Genna said. "But I bet you're right. I'm thinking Maude wrote the article to keep Frank's name out of it."

"She kept Catherine Duncan's name out of it, too," Rian said. "This line about how Duncan *was living in harmony with his newlywed wife'* is a bit veiled and suggestive." Rian scrolled to the next frame.

"Is this Winslow?"

Amy nodded.

"Let me see," Zelda called out. "Don't bogart the phone, Rian. Oh my!" Zelda exclaimed, as she looked at the photo. "He's a handsome one. And dark. He's got the kind of look so many women fall for even when they know they shouldn't."

Amy nodded. Zelda was probably talking about herself. About how she seemed to fall for dark and handsome. The kind of man women fell for, even when they knew better. Men like that were dangerous. Capital D.

"You haven't heard the best of it, yet," Genna said loudly, obviously eager to spill the tea. "Once I started looking for unexplained deaths—unexplained deaths of men," she added, "I found two that might surprise you." Genna paused and drank from her glass, her eyes glistening over the top. She loved the drama of anticipation.

"Frank Calhoun died six months after Winslow Duncan was gunned down in the street."

"Shot in his car," Amy corrected. "He wasn't gunned down in the street like some gangster."

"Spoilsport," Genna muttered. "Gunned down in the street is so much more headline worthy. I don't understand why the newspaper didn't use it."

"Do we know the cause of Calhoun's death?" Amy asked.

"Died in his sleep. Natural causes, they said. A heart attack most likely. He was forty-five, quite a bit older than Maude, and he had been feeling ill. Oscar St. Claire was treating him with a remedy guaranteed to cure what ailed him."

"Castor oil and cocaine, no doubt," Rian added. "Those seem to be the pick-me-up vices of the era."

"It wasn't insomnia was it?" Amy asked, remembering Sir Alfred's permanent remedy.

Genna shrugged. "I don't know that it said what was wrong with him. He went to bed. He didn't wake up. But hear this," Genna added, her eyes twinkling. "Less than a year later, Oscar St. Claire was dead."

"What?" Rian said. "That does sound suspicious."

"We could be looking at another black widow society," Zelda squealed. "They seem so popular back then. Remember that opera about the barber who women paid to off their naughty husbands so they could be free? He wasn't just a barber, he was a surgeon, a botanist, and a killer of bad husbands in Seville. Which, by the way," Zelda added with a raised finger, "is in southern Spain and on my bucket list."

"That's not at all what that opera was about," Genna said sharply. "You're thinking of Sweeny Todd and that doesn't fit this at all."

"Well, excuse me for having a senior moment," Zelda huffed back. "They were both barbers."

"Who's talking about barbers?" Rian asked. "I missed something."

"There are no barbers in the line up," Genna said, sternly. "Not a single one."

"I think the victims were witnesses to the crime," Amy said quietly, hoping to still the rancor at the table. "The men were at the poker game, if we can assume the unidentified person was Frank Calhoun. This Langford guy is getting more suspicious. Did he die, too?"

Genna laughed. "It was a hundred years ago. So, yeah, he died, too."

"You know what I mean," Amy said. "Was his an unexplained death?"

"Not that I read," Genna admitted. "But I agree, there is a pattern here. Maybe not one as overly dramatic as Zelda colors it, but there is something here. The biggest pattern I see is that each of these women rose to an unlikely level of success after the husband's death."

"All after a poker game and Winslow bit the dust," Zelda insisted. "And Catherine Duncan became Mayor of Bluff Springs!"

Amy nodded. "Maude Calhoun became the publisher of the Bluff Springs Weekly Times."

"And Bella St. Claire took over the People's Drug," Rian added.

"See. There it is," Genna urged. "They all flourished once their husbands were out of the way."

"I still think the barber did it," Zelda declared and grinned.

"Maybe it's just a coincidence," Rian suggested.

Amy shook her head. "Maybe it's no coincidence at all."

CHAPTER NINE

Amy hung the "Be back in an hour" sign on the door of Tiddlywinks and locked it behind her. With a bag lunch from Crumpets and Cones, she set out for her destination. Choosing a back route that took her down a hidden set of stairs, she turned on to a paved road that only locals knew. It followed a quiet, narrow holler with a brook on either side. The pavement was impossibly narrow, the asphalt eroding away into the creek from age and rushing spring rains. Today the woods were full of color, and she let the melody of the water set the tempo for her gait.

It was a fair walk, not too far but far enough for much needed exercise and time enough to think things through. She wanted to return to the scene in daylight. The necklace hadn't just fallen out of the sky. It had lain tangled in the pine needles waiting for someone to find it. Was it really intended for her as her snippet suggested? Or did it connect to her at all? Hitchcock didn't mention the necklace, and it wasn't among the objects on the table. So, was there a connection? Or was she grabbing at air?

As she walked, she wondered about these three women in Bluff Springs that Genna had highlighted in her vignettes. They weren't the only successful women in the town's history, but they stood out to Genna. Would they have accomplished the amazing things they did if not for this turn of events? The events being the fact that their husbands died? How would anyone know? Anyone but destiny, that is. The Moirai. The three sisters of ancient Greek mythology who ensured that every being lived out their destiny. One thread for each mortal, intertwined and tangled, knotted to the threads of hundreds of other mortals along the way. One of the sisters spun the thread. One decided the length of the life. The last sister cut the thread. She wasn't sure whether she believed in fated destiny, but she wasn't ready to discount it either.

Don't mess with the Fates.

When she reached the pasture where the white horses lived, she knew she was almost to the back gate of the graveyard. She stopped, delighted when the horses ambled over to the fence, tails swishing with hope. She didn't have anything to give them, except adoring praise, and they seemed to tire quickly of that and moved on.

She had only been through the back gate of the graveyard once. Rian showed her the hidden entrance when they were hiking. It was used by the maintenance crews mostly, and there was a small building next to the gate for tools. In the summer, no one would dare cross the weedy path for fear of chiggers and ticks. Now that fall was here, the weeds had died down and, she hoped, so had the pests. She pushed the gate open, surprised when it squeaked ominously, and then entered the quiet.

That was the thing about graveyards. They were quiet. There was a calm about them if you didn't let the spooky get to you. Today, she didn't feel spooked at all. She was on a mission. The information she needed to solve the mystery of the murder of Winslow T. Duncan was within her grasp. At least she felt that way. The big question was why did it matter? Everybody involved was long gone. There was no one left to blame. No one left to punish. No one left to care.

She felt certain the necklace had something to do with it. And so did Sir Alfred Hitchcock. Eventually, she would have to pull out one of the Ouija boards and ask the question. But which question? The dream-time advice said she would need to be bold enough to ask. Was she bold? Not bold enough to do the Ouija alone. Zelda wasn't going to budge. Maybe she could talk Genna and Rian into playing the Ouija with her. There had to be someone else she could ask. Someone she could trust. Someone brave and adventurous.

She realized that she would have to share her snippet if she wanted Genna and Rian's help. She would have to find the courage to speak the words out loud. That was never easy. Sometimes it proved disastrous.

She made her way to the plot block where she performed her role as the newspaper publisher, M.A. Calhoun, noticing that the branch had been removed, along with all the signs of the fundraising event.

No one was sitting at a table in the daylight. There was no table.

The thing about snippets was that they came when they came. She had no control over her premonitions. Half the time she didn't know if she was just dreaming or having one of those kinds of dreams. She was beginning to recognize the difference, but it wasn't something she was ready to trust completely. She remembered her first snippet dream when she was a teen, and how unsettling it had been. Grandmother Ollie had been patient and kind, although sterner than Amy had ever known her to be, as she explained what was nearly impossible to explain to a child. Although she didn't think of herself as a child at sixteen, she knew better now.

If Grandmother Ollie was here, she would ask how long these dreams would come. She would ask if they faded over time. She would ask if they stayed to the end. She would ask all of that and more. If Grandmother Ollie was here, she would embrace Amy in a warm hug and pat her hand with her dark-spotted, wrinkled one and tell her how much she was loved.

Amy touched the peridot necklace she always wore. It was Celtic knot inlaid with a peridot stone and a tiny diamond. The charm brought her a sense of peace when she touched the stone that always seemed warm to the touch. As long as she wore the necklace, she would be connected by an invisible thread and the knowledge that she and Grandmother Ollie shared something few others shared.

She spotted a bench and made her way there for lunch, unpacking and nibbling her ham and cheese. She heard the twang of the banjo before she saw him. He was a good ways away, but she could see him sitting on a bench, much like the one on which she was sitting. She could definitely hear his banjo. He was facing a grave, as if serenading a loved one.

How sweet.

She listened to the words and the melody, recognizing neither. And then, she rose and made her way toward the music, as if drawn by yet another invisible thread.

He looked up as she approached and paused at a polite distance. He stopped strumming and waved.

"Sorry," she said. "I didn't mean to interrupt you."

"It's okay," he said. "Everybody's probably ready for me to quit, anyway. My wife always said the banjo was loud enough to wake the dead."

Amy frowned. She sure hoped not.

"I guess you have loved ones in here."

Amy shook her head.

"Just taking a walk, then."

"I needed to clear my head."

"This place will do it," he said and smiled again. "No one to argue with you here but yourself."

Amy laughed. "No, I guess not."

"Bad jokes are my specialty," he added. "A good laugh is a good way to make friends. They call me Banjo Man. Name's Charles. Never felt that name fit me much. I've been Banjo Man for more years than you've been on Earth."

"Probably not," she debated with a smile, as she moved closer and accepted his outstretched hand. "My name is Amy Sparks."

"Well, Amy Sparks, at least we're both younger than everybody in here. If that's any consolation. You live around here? Or are you visiting?"

"I own a shop downtown. The Cardboard Cottage and Tiddlywinks Players Club. You know it?"

He shook his head. "I don't make it downtown much. Arthritis."

"I live downtown, too. My apartment is above my shop," she offered, and then instantly wondered why she volunteered that information to a stranger.

"You know much about this cemetery?" he asked. "It's historical, you know. Been here since 1867. That's what the monument says."

"What's the deal with these headstones that look like concrete logs. There's a lot of them."

"Oh, yeah," he said. "Woodsman of the World. There was an insurance company that came through town after the war. Nineteen twenty—twenty-two, I think. Every man in town who had any cash on hand bought a life insurance policy. It came with a headstone for when you needed it. Not all the same size, mind you. If you notice, some are tall and some are small. I guess it had to do with how much insurance you bought. If you look, you'll see they also have secret symbols engraved on them when they mark the grave of a fellow of the IOOF."

"I've heard that term," Amy said, "but I don't know what it means."

"Independent Order of Odd Fellows," he recited. "It was a benevolent social society. They were all about promoting the ethic of reciprocity. But, only if you were white and male. I'm sure things have changed a lot, but back then, that's the way it was."

Amy nodded. Reciprocity. The practice of exchanging with others for mutual benefit. Especially the privileges granted by one group of men to another. That might not have been how *they* looked at it, but it was probably close to the truth. No doubt they did good deeds. Most fraternal orders did. But now she wondered if reciprocity included covering for a crime—a homicide as the constable put it.

On first pass of the article Genna had sent to her phone, it read like a group of men had gotten into a scuffle at a poker game and one of them had lost. Permanently. She could picture Langford following Duncan in the aftermath of his anger. Did he shoot him? Did he steal back his deed and money and then go home to his family?

The other poker players could know what happened. Perhaps they told the truth but not the whole truth. One of the best ways to hide the truth was to stay as close to the truth without telling the whole truth and nothing but the truth, so help you God. Rian was good at that. She could skirt around details you'd never know she left out. She just didn't volunteer what she didn't want you to know.

Not like herself. She was always spilling more than she intended.

"That salesman must have made himself a small fortune," Banjo Man said, breaking into her thoughts. "There are ten WOW gravestones in the first block alone."

Amy gasped when the thought struck her. Maybe the strange symbols in the dance card notebook were symbols from the fraternity.

"Are you okay?" he asked with kindness. He put his banjo in the case at his feet and slid over on the bench.

She hesitated for a brief moment and then sat beside him. "Do you know what the symbols mean?"

"The one you see most is a chain with three links," he answered. "It stands for friendship, love, and truth. I don't know much more than that, but I do know hobo signs."

"Hobo signs?"

He grinned. "I can talk all day about hobo signs. It's my hobby."

"Hobos are your hobby? Is that word even politically correct?"

He laughed loud and long, and Amy could see that Banjo Man would make friends easily and probably keep them until they were gone from this earthly realm. He had to be in his late seventies, but his face was carved with age, not worry.

"It's a real part of American history," he said, as he drew a handkerchief from his back pocket and wiped the laughter spilling from his eyes. "Trains, hobo culture, ballads about life on the road. I love listening to those stories. I used to go to the hobo conventions and sit in the jungle to listen to the old timers talk. The jungle. That's what they call the place hobos gather near the railroad tracks. Most of the storytellers were railroad workers who had firsthand hobo knowledge. Some of them were kind to the men who rode the rails. Some not so much."

"Did you retire from the railroad?" Amy asked.

"No, I was a meter reader. Spent twenty years reading water meters until I got arthritis in my knees. Had to retire early." He patted the top of his knee with a thin hand. "I sure am glad it didn't reach my fingers."

She noticed, then, that his cane was resting on the bench beside him.

"Tell me more about these symbols," Amy urged.

Smiling, Banjo Man obliged. "The thing you need to know about the hobo culture is that they were willing to work. And some of them had special skills. Like whittling or sharpening knives, or even carpentry. That's how they made money. They could split firewood or hoe a garden or rake leaves for a handout and a meal. They were homeless by choice, and they worked to travel and traveled to work. They mostly traveled by rail.

"Tramps, on the other hand, travel but aren't willing to work. And bums, well, bums do neither."

Amy grinned. She appreciated the vernacular.

"Some were illiterate, but most were not," he continued. "Some had disadvantages, like maybe they were disfigured from the war, or maybe not quite comfortable melding with polite society."

"You mean they were mentally ill."

"Well, they didn't have that term back then. But mostly it was about having a free life. The ability to roam, to see the country, to depend on themselves and the kindness of strangers to get by."

Amy nodded. She understood that.

"I don't guess anybody knows for sure how the signs got started, but the secret hobo language allowed them to communicate without saying a word in whatever language they spoke."

He reached for his cane and drew a symbol in the soft dirt at his feet. It was a circle with an X in the middle. An X just like the ones Zelda used to mark their domino scores.

"That means 'good place for a handout'," he said, and then drew another. This time it was a circle and square side by side, with a single dot in the middle of each. "That meant 'a bad-tempered man lived there' and you should approach at your own peril.

"The hobos marked sidewalks and carved gates and fenceposts and trees, and bridges and all kinds of places to offer guidance to travelers coming behind them about what they might find ahead. The signs were everywhere, but you wouldn't notice them unless you knew where to look."

She could imagine an entire manifesto of images marking the nature of the town.

"Bluff Springs was a big railroad town and so it saw its fair share of hobos. At least until the railroad travel became obsolete for the masses. Cars, you know. Everything changed then."

Amy found herself looking off into the woods beyond them. Something was tickling her memory.

"Well," he said, as if noticing her attention had drifted. "That's enough of my yammering. The day's getting on and I need to get on, too." He rose as if it pained him, and he leaned heavily on the cane. "Hope to see you again," he said with a smile. "Always nice to have two-way conversation in this place."

Amy smiled warmly. Somehow, she knew that's all he really needed. She watched as he ambled toward his car parked nearby and put the banjo case in the front seat. He probably wished his wife was sitting there instead, ready to buckle up and go for a ride in the countryside. Maybe stop for ice cream.

Amy pulled out her phone and opened the photos of the images she had taken of the notebook. Her hour was up, but this seemed more important than racing back to open Tiddlywinks on time. She hadn't said what time she would be back, only that it would be within the hour. That gave her some leeway.

She headed for the block nearby that had several WOW tombstones. Maybe she would find the symbols she was looking for.

She was comparing photos to the gravestone when a rustle above her grabbed her attention. She glanced up into a gnarled old redbud tree and saw a pair of Doc Martens dangling from a limb.

"Camellia!" Amy called. No one answered. "Camellia deRossier is that you up there? What are you doing up a tree in the graveyard?"

A heavy thud sounded as she dropped from the tree to the ground. Camellia deRossier now stood in front of her, a sheepish grin on her marmalade lips. "Hello, Amy," she said.

"What are you doing?" Amy demanded without pleasantries. "Aren't you too old to be climbing trees?"

Camellia shrugged. She was still wearing the same Buttercup tee and cargo pants, but the collection of necklaces was gone from her chest and so was her sling bag. Camellia didn't answer and Amy wasn't sure what to think.

"You know the house I inherited is just on the other side of those trees," Camellia said finally. "I saw you go in at the gate. I didn't know anybody else knew the gate was there but me and that mower man."

"Are you following me?" Amy asked, surprise taking over her features. "Are you stalking me?"

"Why would I do that?" Camellia demanded, and for the first time Amy felt uncomfortable.

"Then tell me what you are doing in the tree."

"I'm not doing anything," Camellia said, defensively. "I'm minding my own business. You're the one lurking around all these headstones. It's obvious you're looking for something."

Amy narrowed her eyes.

"If you lost something, I could help you look," Camellia said, her tone less edgy. "I've got nothing better to do today but whack at cobwebs and sort through old magazines. There must be five years' worth of fashion magazines in that attic."

"Why did your Aunt Mable Rose have a dozen Ouija boards?" Amy blurted. "Was she a Spiritualist or something?"

Camellia startled. "A what?"

"A Spiritualist," Amy repeated. "They believed they could reach people on the other side and bring back messages to their loved ones. Messages of faith and hope and maybe where the money tin was hidden."

"Cool," Camellia said. "I wonder if there is a money tin hidden somewhere in my attic. That would be fantastic."

Amy pondered for a brief moment, gauging whether Camellia was really someone she could trust or if that was her hope meter pegging the red. "I found something in the graveyard the other night," Amy started, wondering if she should hold back Rian-style or tell it all. "It's a notebook. Sort of. And there are a bunch of symbols written inside."

Camellia's interest seemed piqued. "What kind of symbols?"

"That's what I'm trying to find out," Amy answered. "That man I was just talking to said the WOW gravestones have secret symbols engraved on them. They're the headstones with the log looking bases." Amy turned the phone toward Camellia. "I'm looking for something like this." The picture looked like a hashtag with one extra vertical line.

Camellia's eyes widened.

Amy flipped the screen to another picture. "And this one," she added. "Have you seen any of these on the headstones?"

Camellia didn't answer at first and Amy wondered if she was thinking about the question or ignoring her altogether.

"Camellia?"

"What's so special about these symbols?" she asked finally. "Do they mean something?"

"I don't know," Amy admitted, "but I think it's a clue to a crime. Something that happened a long time ago. For some reason, it's fallen into my lap to solve."

"What kind of crime?"

Amy let the question hang for a moment. Was Camellia someone she could trust, and better still, would she be willing to join her at the Ouija table? If so, the four of them might summon the courage to ask the question: Who murdered Winslow Duncan?

Camellia shuffled her feet with impatience. "What kind of crime?" she asked again.

"A murder," Amy said. "A cold case murder."

CHAPTER TEN

If the telephone directory for 1923 was a fair assessment of the times, most of the townsfolk of Bluff Springs had a telephone in their home and a connection to every business and household. Those who lived on the outskirts still had to rely on gossip and the mail.

Amy rifled through the pages and sighed. Genna sat across from her in the stuffy room that held artifacts, the microfiche, and a cabinet full of old photos.

Genna had dragged Amy with her for another foray into the belly of history as she looked for details on what happened to Winslow Duncan. Amy could tell Genna's interest was beginning to pale now that her obligation for the fundraiser was complete. Eventually, Genna would pass the research baton altogether, Amy was sure of it, moving on to something with intrigue. Like a politician who needed handling.

"If they hung anybody for shooting Duncan, I sure can't find it," Genna grumbled. "Contrary to his obit notice, he wasn't all that beloved. Here's a legal notice naming him as a defendant. Are you having any luck on your angle?"

"It looks like the suspect pool is bigger than we thought," Amy answered. "Look at this." She spun the phone directory that was all of thirty pages counting the cover and tapped the page.

"This page is a listing of the Odd Fellows and their occupations. In addition to our poker playing guys, there was a lawyer, a banker, a doctor, a livery stable owner, an undertaker, a minister, a jeweler and locksmith—that's an interesting combo, but I guess those two trade skills would go hand in hand. There are several listed as gainfully employed. Not sure what that means. Oh, and here's a barber. That will make Zelda happy."

Genna closed the newspaper morgue book with a snap. "If they all belonged to this reciprocity organization, they were probably all in cahoots. Maybe they were in cahoots to get rid of Duncan. Maybe the card game was the set up. Maybe they were on to poor old Frank and Oscar, too. I can see Winslow playing one too many high-stake games. What goes up must come down. The widow angle may not be as strong as we think it is."

Amy studied the list in front of her. Four queens. It had to mean something. No queens on this page. No queens in this all-male organization.

"I'm getting bored with the hunt," Genna said and exhaled. "The only interesting thing I've found all morning was this little announcement." She reached for her notes and read, "A gathering of like minds to console the bereaved with deep understanding and spiritual affirmation available to all those who seek answers. Ask and ye shall receive." Genna looked up from her notes. "Sounds like someone was calling a coven of witches."

"Not witches," Amy said. "A Spiritualist meeting. Maybe a séance around the Ouija board. Does it say when and where to meet? There had to be some way they announced where they were meeting without anyone knowing. Anyone opposed, that is. It would be a pretty daring thing to put a meeting out in the open for anyone and everyone to show up."

Genna reached for the morgue book and thumbed the pages quickly, careful not to tear the fragile newspaper. "Genius," she said finally, tapping the page. "There are two small ads on the same page with that announcement. One is for a Model T and the other is for a dressmaker."

Amy inhaled sharply. "Either Winslow Duncan was a Spiritualist or the dressmaker was. And my money's on the latter. What's in the ad?"

Genna read, "**First Class Dressmaker. For Style, Economy, and Good Fit, come to Miss Mable Rose, skilled dressmaker, discreetly located at 7 Piney Top. Appointment required.**"

"Bingo!" Amy yelped. "That's why a dressmaker has a dozen Ouija boards! The same dressmaker that had stacks of fashion magazines!"

"Because she—"

"Because she did more than fit women for the latest fashions," Amy interrupted. "Because she ran the town Ouija parlor under the guise of style, economy, and good fit!" Amy could barely contain her enthusiasm.

"Get ahold of yourself. This doesn't have anything to do with Winslow Duncan or the other husbands."

Amy's face fell. "Well, no. But it does solve the mystery of why Mable Rose had so many Ouija boards and that was a conundrum that's been puzzling me for days."

"You're so easily engaged," Genna quipped.

"I can just imagine how the widows in town went to Mable Rose to find answers about their husbands' deaths. They would be looking for answers from the beyond. They might be looking for deep understanding and spiritual affirmation like the ad said. They would be seeking answers Mable Rose promised to deliver. I wonder what else Camellia deRossier will find in that old house." Her mind was already drifting. Maybe there really was a money tin hidden in the eaves.

They put away the papers and ephemera and left the stuffy room. The hallway was empty and the other doors on the second floor were closed. "What's in these other rooms?" Amy touched one of the doors as they passed toward the stairs.

Genna halted mid-step. "Only one way to find out," she answered and turned the knob. They peeked inside. "Furniture." Genna breathed as the dust now disturbed danced in the morning sunlight. "Very old furniture. They must get a ton of donations when people clear out an estate." Genna moved to another door and swung it open. "Hmmm," she said, eyeing the gray interior. "Suitcases and steamer trunks. Worth a fortune on the vintage market. I wonder if they are still full of clothing and stuff. Zelda could have started her costume haul right here."

"It must take them forever to go through it all," Amy said, eyeing the small mountain of luggage. "They wouldn't want to toss anything in case it has some historical value for a future exhibit, and it wouldn't work to cram it all in the exhibits downstairs. I wonder if there is any one person who knows what's in these suitcases."

"Of course there is," Genna said simply. "Now whether they still have all their faculties about them is another matter. I'm not sure how information gets passed down at a small museum. I suspect there are lists and lists and files of lists."

They heard steps at the bottom of the stairs and Genna hurriedly closed the door.

"False alarm," Amy whispered with a guilty grimace, as the footsteps seemed to move in another direction. They descended the stairs. As they turned the corner at the landing, Amy stopped abruptly. Standing at the bottom of the stair looking up at them was a woman who made Amy think of her fifth-grade history teacher. Her expression was just as dour.

"I assume you put everything back where it belongs," she said, her voice as thin as the skin on the back on her hands. Amy noticed they trembled slightly as she gripped the knob of the newel.

"Yes, ma'am," Amy said. "And thank you for letting us look."

The woman's nod was barely perceptible, but the look of disapproval eased. "You found what you were looking for, then?"

"I think so," Amy said. "But then, I'm not all that sure what I was looking for."

"If you don't know what you want, you'll never find it," the woman scolded. "That's the rule of logical reasoning." Amy couldn't disagree more, but she wouldn't say so. She hoped Genna wouldn't either. Looking with eyes open only to the goal ahead left out a lot of things to be seen. The woman stepped to the side to allow them to pass.

"I know you were part of the fundraiser," the woman added and nodded to Genna, who towered over her by a good two feet. "I was under the impression your research was concluded. If research ever ends," she added quietly, like a tender afterthought. "I started that event, you know. Twenty years ago. It wasn't held in the cemetery back then; I assure you that."

The disapproval was back. She glanced up at the stairs. "Too steep for me these days. And no one seems to want to bother with all that—" she gestured with her hand, "all that wonderful history to sort in the rooms upstairs. There are never enough docents young enough to be useful. Young people don't care about history."

She waited for a retort from Genna, but Genna was suspiciously quiet, and Amy realized she was eyeing an exhibit on the museum floor.

"I never noticed this exhibit," Genna said. "Is it a new?"

"Nothing in here is new," the woman said curtly. "We're a museum. We collect and preserve *old* things."

Amy stood ready to stomp on Genna's foot if she made a snark about that, but Genna's attention was elsewhere. Amy followed her to the exhibit cordoned off with red velvet ropes.

"Oh, yes," the woman said, following slowly behind. "This is Mayor Catherine Duncan. We decided to change things up for the fundraiser."

Better late than never. Amy looked at what was certainly not the real thing. A female mannequin was posed studiously behind a desk as if writing some great tome, a fountain pen in one hand and a lace handkerchief in the other. A gray cloche hat hid the fact that the mannequin was bald, and a fur collar was draped around her neck over a strand of pearls. A beaded clutch bag and pair of gloves sat on the desk at her elbow. Her feet, dressed in black t-strap shoes, like the ones Zelda made her wear in the graveyard, were crossed at the ankles under the desk. No small feat for a mannequin. On the wall behind her was a picture of four women sitting on a park bench, laughing. She recognized one of the popular springs in the city.

"The Petticoats," the woman said with fondness. "Bluff Springs' first female government. A powerful statement for that time. Those who knew Catherine always knew she could accomplish great things. Even under the circumstances."

Amy's ear pricked up. "Circumstances?"

"Her father forced her to marry Winslow Duncan, who was beneath her in every way. She was better educated and certainly came from a better economic class." The bitterness seemed personal.

"Why the arranged marriage?"

The woman looked at Amy as if she had flunked the pop quiz. "We've only speculation," she answered after a bit of silence.

"Oh," Amy said, knowing not to provoke it further. "Who are the women in the picture?"

"Catherine is the one in the middle," the woman said, pointing with a thin finger. "The woman to her left is Bella St. Claire. To her right is Maude Calhoun."

"And the woman on the end?"

"We believe that is Mable Rose deRossier," the woman said. "Although there is still some conflict of opinion on the matter. She was not a member of this progressive government, but it was said she was one of Catherine's most trusted allies. She was the dressmaker in town. I've always presumed that was the sum of their relationship but there is evidence they were good friends."

Evidence. That was what she was looking for in the stuffy old room upstairs. The photo was black and white, but she could see clearly the women on the bench. Catherine was taller than the others, and she was wearing the same fur collar as the mannequin. They were dressed in the style of the day; straight, blousy dresses with adornment and layers. Both Bella St. Claire and Maude Calhoun had short bobs. Catherine's hair was lighter. Mable Rose was the smallest of the four, her short hair curled under in tight, smooth rolls. Her face looked older than the others but not by much. It was the serious expression on her face that made her look older. They were laughing at something outside of the picture frame. Everyone except Mable Rose. Her gaze was somewhere else.

"We think this photo was taken a few months before she was married," the woman said. "It came from her scrapbook. That was one of the items donated to the museum after her passing. A very insightful piece of history."

"Can I see it? Does she mention Winslow's murder?" Amy felt excited by the prospect.

One brow shot above her glasses. "It's not part of the exhibit," the woman declared. "It's packed away for safekeeping and requires special permission." She glared at Amy. "Special permission and good cause. I question if you have either."

"I'm confused," Genna admitted as they turned away from the exhibit and out of ear shot. "You would think a murder in a town of this size would be big headline news, plastered across the pages every week until it was solved. Especially as it centered around the future mayor.

"But it wasn't," Genna continued. "Big headlines, I mean. Maybe that's because Frank Calhoun knew something the rest of them didn't. Or maybe Maude Calhoun censored the news so her friend Catherine wouldn't go to the gallows. Or there could be something else we're missing because the whole thing was just swept behind the scenes. Of course, she wasn't mayor yet, so maybe I'm ahead myself. Except I still think it would be big news."

"Four queens," Amy said absently. She was thinking about the women on the bench.

"What about four queens? Are you talking about us?"

Uh oh. Now she was stuck. Amy looked at Genna and made up her mind in an instant. "You said before that there were four husbands who died around the same time," Amy said. "The last one was the preacher. What was his name?"

"Hayes," Genna answered. "The Reverand Cecil Hayes."

"And they all had wives. Four queens."

Genna twisted her lips and gazed at Amy with a dubious look. "You're reaching. Duncan was killed by gunshot. Obviously murdered over money. He was a cad and card shark. Frank had a heart attack in his sleep. Oscar died of an accidental overdose. The only thing that connects them is that they were at the poker game. And the good reverend wasn't there. At least we don't think he was. There's no confirmation he was there."

"How did Rev. Hayes pass?"

Genna rubbed her eyes. "Reading those newspapers make my eyes feel like sandpaper. Another heart attack, I think, but I'll look again another time. The pattern doesn't fit, anyway. His wife never made big news after his demise. I don't remember reading anything about the Mrs. Rev. Hayes."

"It could be that she was the only one that felt guilty after the fact," Amy offered. "Like if they made a pact she couldn't live up to. Maybe Mrs. Rev. Hayes was so overcome with guilt that she never got over it."

Genna sighed. "Your imagination is working over-time. There is nothing in the books to suggest a pact of any kind. Except for maybe Mable Rose taking money for talking to the dead."

"Haints," Amy said quietly as they exited the museum. She held the door for Genna. "Haints are the restless ones that can't move on. My grandmother said the only way you can get rid of haints is to paint your ceilings blue."

Genna laughed but Amy knew that it was not funny business. Haints were never something to laugh at. Never.

CHAPTER ELEVEN

Genna dropped Amy off at the door of The Cardboard Cottage. She and Genna were at the museum for more than two hours and it was now just after ten. That only made her a few minutes late to open. The front door was unlocked, and she noticed both Zsa Zsa Galore Décor and The Pot Shed were open. Their doors were pushed to the hall as they always were when the shops were open for business. Zelda's shop had its familiar wheelbarrow full of pillows greeting the shoppers with bright colors and designs. Across the hall, The Pot Shed door was propped open with a potted palm, and the sign on the door said, 'We're Blooming Open.'

Life back to normal. She opened the door to Tiddlywinks.

She was busying herself with her morning shop chores when she noticed a car pull up to the curb outside. The curb was for unloading only; the place where the hunk-in-shorts delivery driver zipped in to unload boxes to the stores and the bakery next door and then zipped back out. This was not the hunk.

Amy watched as the man peeled himself from his car and then, when he grabbed his cane, she recognized him. Banjo Man. The man from the graveyard with the hobo tales. She inadvertently told him where she worked—and lived—but she was still surprised to see him. He was paying more attention to her than she thought.

It took him a while and she met him at the door of Tiddlywinks.

"Banjo Man," she said cheerfully. "What a surprise!"

He grinned a shy grin as she stepped aside to let him pass through the door. He carried a large book under his arm.

"I apologize," he said, without further pleasantries. "I come unannounced and uninvited. But I had something I wanted to show you, and I couldn't wait until we happened to chance meet again." He moved toward a chair and sat. "Is this a good time?" he asked, his expression full of hope and excitement.

"Well, sure," she said and pulled up the chair beside him. "I may have to interrupt and help customers if I get busy, but for now, I'm all yours."

He opened the book, and Amy recognized it as a scrapbook with yellowed pages, spotted menus, and pictures with the scalloped edges common to old Polaroid photos.

"Our conversation got me to thinking," he said, "so I pulled this out to show you some old hobo stuff. Since you were so interested."

That was an overstatement, but he was too pleasant for her to say otherwise.

"This is how my infatuation with hobos got started," he offered.

The first page of his scrapbook held a rectangular cutout from a box of Post Toasties cereal. She could see the cereal name across the top in bright red. The top edge had a piece of yellowed cellophane tape holding it in place on the page.

She laughed. "You sent away for a hobo decoder ring and a whistle!"

"You're making fun of me," he said, but laughed along with her. He lifted the bottom edge, the tape at the top acting as a hinge. "It's a hobo postcard," he said almost breathlessly, as if he still felt the awe all these decades later. "Hobos would cut up boxes they found in the trash to make postcards to send messages to people far and away. I guess they were keeping in touch with people they made friends with along the way. People who didn't travel the rails but stayed put in one place and grew old. Like me," he added, and grinned.

Amy leaned in. The message was written in pencil on the flip side of the decorative cereal box. The canceled postage stamp was two cents, she noticed, a picture of George Washington on a faded red background. The round postmark was dated November 5. 2 a.m. 1924, Fredericksburg Tex. It was addressed simply to Miss Della at 3 German Alley, Bluff Springs, Ark.

Amy read it aloud. "Fear knocked but faith answered. Your kindness filled my heart. Be ever watchful for the hand of God for he will make a promise. Please tell Miss M, I am beyond reach and blessedly grateful. Ever yours, Joe."

Amy looked at Banjo Man with surprise in her eyes. "And this is from a real hobo?"

He shrugged. "I like to think so. I found it with some old papers in my granny's attic. She went by the name Della, and she talked about hobos showing up to do odd jobs for a meal and a nickel. She never turned them away. Well, unless they were tramps and discourteous." He smiled and she saw that memory surface in his eyes. "She would be a hundred and twenty-three years old today if she were still alive."

He paused and then flipped through the pages.

"That's when I fell in love with the romantic notion of a life I couldn't live," he said. "I had a wife and three kids, a house and a mortgage.

"I wanted to show you some of these old signs hobos marked around town back in the day. Since I was always walking around town with my job, I made a point of looking for signs. It's something you have to look for. The hobos were crafty with their messages. But, for me, it was like a scavenger hunt. Something to keep the boredom at bay. I wanted to find as many signs as I could."

He opened the book to a double page of Polaroid pictures glued to the pages. The pictures were of the crude signs, often faded by age, with a description written below in block print as to where it had been found and what the symbol meant.

"Oh, wow!" Amy said, surprised. She recognized several of the signs immediately. They were the same as in the notebook in the dance card necklace. Not fraternity symbols like friendship, love, and truth. Hobo signs. A hidden language for a fraternity of a far different kind.

The older man tapped a photo. "This one was on the riser of my granny's front porch steps. It's a bit hard to make out if you don't know what you're looking at, but it's a cat." He nodded. "Cat was hobo for kind lady lives here. I've seen several around town."

Amy grinned. "What's this symbol?" She tapped the photo of two diamonds side by side.

"It means 'keep quiet,'" he said. "I'm guessing that's saying if they didn't know you were there, they won't be running you off."

She pointed to a picture of two circles that looked like wedding rings linked together. The circles were carved a little lopsided, but the etching was deep. "Does this say a married couple lives here?"

"Oh, no," he said and shook his head. "That means the local police are not friendly. Better keep your head down and your business to yourself."

"And what's this one mean?" Amy pointed to a picture of an etching that looked like a hashtag with one extra vertical line.

"That is not good," Banjo Man said. "That means a crime has been committed and no stranger is safe. I found that one near the old rail yard."

Amy stood up abruptly. "I have to show you something. I'll have to run up to my apartment to get it, but it won't take me more than a minute or two. If anybody comes in and asks, tell them I'll be right back."

He looked confused but she left him without any further explanation and raced down the sidewalk and up the stairs, taking some of them two at a time.

Amy returned out of breath; the necklace clutched in her fingers. She grabbed his hand and turned it over and then dropped the necklace into his palm.

"What do you have here?" he asked and fingered the metal.

"Open it," she urged. "Pull out the pencil. That's the hinge."

"Well, I'll be," he said, as the locket opened. "Isn't that something?"

"It's a dance card necklace. Women wore them to keep track of their dance partners at the ball. This notebook is full of hobo signs. I didn't know that before, of course, but now I do."

He let a thin finger thumb the pages gently. "You're right. These look like hobo signs. But I don't know what they are doing in a lady's necklace."

"I think it's a clue to a crime. Like a cold case murder."

Banjo Man whistled softly under his breath. "A murder."

Amy pulled out the chair, settled in to get comfortable, and started her tale. She told him about finding the necklace in the graveyard, about the newspaper account of the man shot after a poker game, and how no one had ever found the killer. Not that she had uncovered, anyway. The town authorities suspected an indigent named Hobo Joe. They suspected he shot Duncan, took his poker winnings, hopped the train, and was never seen again.

Banjo Man looked shaken. He raked a thin hand through his even thinner hair and closed his eyes. Amy fetched a bottle of water from under the counter, wondering as she opened it and set it in front of him whether his hobo hero ideals of life on the rails were crashing in around his shoulders. She wasn't sure how to comfort him. So, she let him be. She had her own feelings about who shot Duncan, and the fantasy she invented to go with it, all headed for its own crash landing. When customers came in, she was relieved she had something to do other than feel awkward. She helped them find what they were looking for, booked them into the escape room, and when she looked up, Banjo Man was gone, and the curb was empty.

What a fool she was! She was so eager to connect the crime to the necklace that she had lost sight of the fact that it belonged to someone. She had forgotten something old could have sentimental value that grew over time, not diminished. She was so eager to make a weird dream mean something that she had shattered the ideals of an old man and his love for hobo culture. Was that hubris? Was she that wrapped up in seeing the unknown and unpredictable, as if she were a crystal ball channel for the great beyond? What a fool. What a cruel fool.

The clock seemed to slow to a crawl after that. It seemed that everybody who came in the shop was after information, not games. They wanted to know if she had a restroom, the best place to eat dinner, what time the shops closed, and would the trolley pick them up at the curb. Same old same old. Today she was not in the mood.

She sprang for her bag a minute after five.

Bluff Street Jewelers was less than a block up the hill, and she nearly sprinted through the thinning throngs of shoppers, reaching it just in time.

"Well, hello, Amy," the woman said.

"Maggie," Amy breathed, trying to catch her breath. "I was afraid I would miss you."

She eyed the people on the street behind Amy and motioned her quickly inside, flipping the *Closed* sign in place as she locked the door. "I'm working on a set of custom wedding rings that need to be ready before the weekend," she said and smiled. "I don't have time for more curiosity shoppers."

Amy nodded. She knew what that meant. Shoppers who loved to look and ask questions but never seemed to buy. It was okay. It was part of the job of shopkeeping.

"What brings you here in a hurry?"

"This," Amy said and pulled the necklace from her pocket, dropping it in the woman's hand. "I was wondering what you could tell me about it."

"A dance card necklace," she said. "I haven't seen one of these in a while. Where did you get it?"

"Oh, I found it," Amy said, hesitating slightly.

"It's somebody's family heirloom. My grandmother had one much like it. Except hers was silver. It went to one of my cousins." She frowned slightly as if remembering a point of contention.

"Can you tell how old it is?" Amy asked.

The woman eyed it again and then raised the loupe from the chain at her neck. "Before the turn of the century, I'd say. Brass. Repoussage and chasing. These necklaces were popular in France and England in the mid-1800s. Are you looking to sell it? I might be interested."

"I was able to find a little about these necklaces with an internet search," Amy said, now breathing easy from her rush up the hill. "I don't want to sell it, but I am wondering how it got to Bluff Springs."

"By ocean liner and passenger train." The jeweler smiled at her attempt at humor. "After steamships made transatlantic travel more comfortable for the elite, the women of class brought all their best jewelry with them to the Americas. This particular piece isn't valuable, but pieces like this became the hold out for status and tradition."

Amy shook her head. "I'm not sure I know what you mean."

"In Europe, nobility was inherited which meant status was inherited. In America, nobility was a frame of mind. There was no inherited nobility. Items like this necklace and the etiquette attached to it became the way middle class emulated the upper class. Traditions," she added. "Jewelry was a visual centerpiece for those customs. This dance card necklace would be one of those traditions. The very act of asking a lady to dance was carefully orchestrated and there was an entire set of protocols."

"Protocols?"

"Oh, yeah, protocols," she repeated with a nod. "Like physical proximity, the proper bow and handshake, and yada yada. It was a big deal any time men and women were physically close. The Victorians were petrified of sex and obsessed with it at the same time."

Amy laughed. "Men were mesmerized by those bustlines they couldn't touch. But why would you need to keep track of a few dances?"

"A few dances?" Maggie laughed and shook her head. "More like dozens. The evening would start around eight with a concert, followed by dancing, a break at midnight for a light meal, and then more dancing until three or four in the morning."

"You're kidding! I can't imagine dancing until four in a corset."

Maggie laughed again. "Oh, gosh, me either.

"It was an unthinkable faux pas to miss a dance you had committed to, so dance cards were used to keep track," Maggie continued. "That's where we get the expression 'pencil me in.'. They pretty much went out of style around 1920, except at college dances, but college dance cards were made of paper and ribbon. They were more like souvenirs for a scrapbook. The dances were sponsored by organizations like the Masons and Templars so their single daughters and sons could meet people of the same social class. Bluff Springs had clubs that sponsored college dances. It's possible this necklace came here with one of the students. A family with old money and traditions.

"And here's another fact you'll never need. In leap years, the women were allowed to ask the men for a dance. That was a twist on tradition! Maybe that's where Al Capp got the idea of Sadie Hawkins Day for his Li'l Abner comic strip. I think that's still celebrated on Leap Day."

Amy looked at the locket still in Maggie's hands, now feeling appreciation for the history it held, not just as an heirloom but for the traditions that had come and gone and yet lingered in a meaningful way.

"Why do you know so much about the topic?"

"Fascination. Indoctrination. My grandparents used to take us to auctions when were little. The history was as important as the piece." Maggie laid the chain and locket on a velvet pad on the counter, arranging it as if she were creating a display by habit. "My family has been in the jewelry business in Bluff Springs for a very long time." She glanced at Amy with a sidewise look, smiling sheepishly. "And I love a good historical romance. It's my guilty pleasure binge habit."

Amy giggled. "I feel the same way about vintage games. I love finding the story behind them." She grinned. "And I love a good bodice ripper romance."

"If you change your mind about selling this necklace," Maggie said as she unlocked the door. "You know where to find me."

CHAPTER TWELVE

Amy glanced at her phone on the counter when it chirped.
"ROAD TRIP"
A group text from Rian.
"Details in a few…"
The phone was silent for several minutes, which didn't feel at
all out of character for Rian. Amy waited patiently, finishing her
internet search on vintage game values. Specifically, vintage Ouija
boards. She had postponed it long enough. If she had been on
top of it, she would have put them right on the Tiddlywinks shelf
when she bought them in time for all the Halloween shoppers.
But she had been busy with other things. And, she had to admit,
it's hard to make yourself do something you really didn't want to
do. So far, she had learned that the games were worth a lot more
than she paid for them. That was the goal, always, when shopping
for her store. If there was a market for old Ouija boards—and she
assumed there was—she would make a good profit on the boards
she scored from Camellia.

"Got us invited to a concert in the woods." Rian texted.

"Got us a cabin sleeps four. Zelda can drive us back tomorrow in time to open."

Text from Zelda. "Oh boy! A road trip and a concert!"

Genna's response. "Anybody we know?"

"Pack sensibly." Rian texted.

"That was for you, Zelda."

"Anybody we know?" Genna repeated.

"Yes. No. Maybe."

Amy typed. "You sound like a magic 8 Ball."

"Sending GPS."

The coordinates popped up next and then the link to the cabin. It was near the Buffalo River, one of their favorite places to visit. They hadn't taken a road trip together since their hunt for Rian's roots in Ireland. The Buffalo River wasn't the Cliffs of Moher, but it was as close as they would get in Arkansas. It wasn't convenient timing, but no one ever refused one of Rian's road trips. Well, almost never. Besides, the colorful leaves would be wrapping up in the low valley and there might even be frost on the pumpkins left in the field. Wide patches of bare trees would show off the stone bluffs along the river. They would have a breathtaking view, even if they didn't see much of it. It would be dark by the time they reached their destination, and they'd be on the road early to get back. Maybe they could talk Zelda into detouring to see the Elk roaming the valley at dawn.

"What's the rush?" Amy texted.

"Delivery." Rian answered.

"What are you delivering?" Genna asked.

"Porche. '69 911 Coupe."

"I'm riding with you." Genna added.

"Pick you up in 30."

Amy glanced at the clock. She and Zelda could close their shops early and head out if they wanted. It wouldn't take her long to feed Victor and throw some overnight necessities in a bag. That's all she really needed. They could be on the road by five if Zelda didn't dally with luggage.

Amy heard the *clip clop* of Zelda's mules on the old wood floor before she popped her head in the door of Tiddlywinks. "Meet me at my house and I'll drive from there."

"Pack sensibly," Amy repeated. "We're going to the woods, not the Taj Mahal."

Zelda huffed and put her hands on her hips. "Why is everybody always on my case about what I wear? What do you care if I'm overdressed?"

Amy shook her head. There was no foiling Zelda's intentions when her mind was made up. "At least wear sensible shoes," Amy offered. "Like hiking boots."

Zelda inhaled. "Hiking boots! Yes! I have just the right pair!"

The sun was already in the west when they loaded their bags into Zelda's SUV and Amy pulled up the destination details on her phone. The plan was to meet Rian and Genna at the rendezvous spot at the prearranged time. Rian would pass along the Porsche and then she and Genna would hitch a ride with Zelda and Amy to the party.

"I love our road trips," Zelda said. "If it wasn't for Rian and her car deliveries, we might never go anywhere."

"How can you say that?" Amy countered. "We go lots of places. We went to the Galápagos Islands for your birthday cruise. We just got back from Ireland."

"I know," Zelda said, "but those aren't road trips. Those are bucket list travels. Totally different thing. Road trips are not so much about the destination, they're more about all the fun that happens along the way."

"Oh, you mean when you were parading like a prom queen in the back of Rian's Fiat at forty miles an hour? That was fun. That was hilarious."

Zelda frowned. "That was not fun, not funny. Rian pulled that U-Turn on purpose, and I almost flew out of the car."

Amy grinned. "We would have come back for you if you did."

Zelda narrowed her eyes at Amy, but her indignation wasn't real. All four of them had some little road trip calamity they could conjure up for a laugh.

Amy pointed to the road. "Your next turn is just ahead."

Zelda nodded and turned right.

"I think you were supposed to go left."

With an exasperated huff, Zelda spun the car on the narrow pavement and went the opposite way. The pavement gave way to hard dirt pretty quickly and they drove for what seemed like miles. When they landed in front of the gate, Zelda stopped. The bull stood firm on the other side, horns ready to defend every inch of the road.

Zelda looked at Amy expectantly. "Well? Are you going to get out and open the gate?"

"Not with him standing there, I'm not."

"Do we sit here and wait him out?"

"And then what? Let him charge us at once we're on the other side of the gate?"

Zelda rolled down the window and flailed her arm, bracelets jingling. "Shoo, you! Shoo!"

The bull lowered his head and bellowed like an angry bear, hooves scraping the dirt.

"Shoo!" Zelda called and shook her arm with a loud clatter. He ambled a few feet closer to the gate. "He's going to charge us! What should we do now?"

"Back it up," Amy bellowed. "I'm not opening the gate and he's not moving. You need to back up."

Zelda huffed and thumped her hands against the steering wheel, bracelets clattering. "We can't be in the right place. We certainly aren't here at the right time. Wrong place, right time. Or maybe right place, wrong time. You need to check your directions, Sparks. Text Rian and ask where in the Sam hill we are. It's going to get dark soon."

Amy studied the map on her phone. GPS directions in the back country of Arkansas were suspect from the start. Amy realized her error. "We went the wrong way off the highway."

Zelda glared at her. "I was right. We were supposed to turn right. Now look. We're going to be late to pick up Rian and Genna and Genna's going to be steaming." She turned the car around and sped back toward the highway, dirt clouding the road behind her taillights.

"My bad," Amy acquiesced. "Don't tell Genna or she'll bring up Hags Head on the Cliffs of Moher."

Zelda snickered under her breath. "Boy, that was a road trip map snafu. At least we got a ferry ride and a karaoke cocktail out of it."

Amy grinned at Zelda. Genna got a t-shirt out of it, too. A gesture from her friends to make up for the mishap.

Back on course and about twenty minutes later, they found Rian and Genna at the roadside park, waiting. Rian was taking a siesta on a fallen tree trunk, her backpack under her head for a pillow. Genna didn't say a word.

"Don't blame me," Zelda said as they climbed in the car. "Amy was the navigator."

"That figures," Genna muttered, and shut the door with a bang.

The music was in full swing when they pulled up to their destination. It was an old Army Corps of Engineers campground with a raging fire pit in the middle and a wide ring of trees on the periphery. Someone had brought in a Port-A-Potty and a rick of wood, and Amy noticed that some of the guests came by horseback. The horses were tethered with plenty of grass to keep them occupied.

They slipped into the crowd and set up their chairs, unnoticed, just the way Rian would want it. A makeshift stage was lit by torch light, much the way the cemetery had been lit for their event. The music was fabulous. A little country twang, a little swing, a little Arkansas Bluegrass, and some powerful vocals. If the band weren't stars on the music scene yet, they sure would be soon. That's what these parties were about, Rian had told them. The host was involved in the music biz.

Zelda sniffed the air. "I smell food and I'm starving. Let's go see what we can find."

"Mind the brownies," Rian said quietly. "I imagine their potent."

Amy wished she had brought a flashlight to weave through the chairs and rocks and countryside. They made their way to a barbecue grill, the kind you pull behind a truck for parties and tailgate picnics. There was a line.

Zelda turned to the man standing beside her. "Has anyone ever told you that you look like Burt Reynolds?"

"Burt who?"

"Oh, please don't tell me you are not old enough to know *Smokey and the Bandit*. I think he was married to the *Flying Nun*. I could be mistaken. He was definitely married to Loni Anderson. She starred in *WKRP in Cincinnati*."

Amy noticed the confused look on his face. Even from her politically correct distance behind him she could see him struggle with the time warp.

"Sorry, but I don't know what you're talking about, ma'am."

"Don't ma'am me," Zelda scolded with a chuckle. "I'm not old enough to be your mom."

Amy snickered under her breath and caught Zelda's sidewise look.

The man looked pained for an appropriate response.

"Well, it's a shame that's all," Zelda said, smoothing her hair. "You look just like Burt Reynolds. And that's a good thing in case you were wondering."

He smiled and nodded. "Thanks, I guess."

The line moved forward, and Amy realized there was no grill master, and they would be roasting their own dogs over the flames. The grill grate was missing but the fire was just right for getting that golden char on a hot dog before slathering it in chow-chow and mustard. They were lined up four to the fire with their roasting sticks. Zelda stepped closer to her Burt Reynolds look alike.

"I like mine plump and toasted," Zelda said near his shoulder, "then nestled in a warm bun with nice toppings."

Amy nearly burst out laughing. She wasn't sure if Zelda realized the innuendo. Or maybe she did.

Burt Reynold grinned. "I like mine burnt to a crisp."

Zelda laughed and her hot dog dipped toward the flame. Suddenly a loud *whoosh* shot out of the grill. Everyone's hot dog ignited, and the fire blasted upward, licking the dark sky with flame and sparks and a loud scary roar.

"Oh no!" Zelda yelled, waving her fire engulfed stick perilously close to Burt's flannel shirt. The flames roared above them. Burt spun around and knocked into a woman standing behind him and she tripped and fell against Zelda, who lurched forward toward the flames.

Amy stood paralyzed by the sight. Zelda regained her balance and stepped away from the flames, her hot dog still sizzling on the stick.

"Fire!" someone yelled "The grill is on fire!"

A rustle sounded behind her and then a cloud of white blasted the grill as someone aimed a fire extinguisher at the blaze. The cloud covered the grill, and the flames died promptly.

When Amy turned to Zelda, she couldn't hold it together. Zelda's hair was peppered with what looked like white powder. She still held the roasting stick in her hand and her hot dog looked frosted. The band caught the commotion by the grill and broke into a banjo rendition of *Fire on the Mountain… Lightening in the air …* and everybody *whoop-whooped!*

Everybody except Amy and Zelda. And probably Burt Reynolds.

"Are you okay?" Amy asked her friend.

"Well, I'm not hurt, if that's what you're asking," Zelda muttered over the music. "But I think I've lost my appetite."

The music changed again as the incident settled and suddenly Rian and Genna were standing beside them. Genna was biting her lip. Rian pulled her ball cap over her eyes to hide her amusement.

"If you laugh, I'll never forgive you," Zelda spat. "And what is this stuff? Is it going to kill me?"

"It might," Rian said. "It might eat the skin right off your bones."

The look on Zelda's face was priceless. It was clear she didn't know whether to brush it off or run for the river.

"It's just baking soda," Genna said. "And maybe some flesh-eating additive."

Zelda dropped the stick and the hot dog she was still holding aloft. "I'm leaving. I'm out of here."

"We just got here!" Rian said. "They haven't even played their number one tune."

"And what is that?" Zelda snapped.

A hand reached out from the crowd holding a box of wet wipes and Zelda snatched the offering. She pulled a wipe and dabbed at her face and hair.

"Here," Amy said, taking another from the box. "Let me help."

There was no saving the hot dog, but the wipes were successful in removing whatever the powder was. She would need to wash her hair and clothes to get it all out, but it wasn't going to harm her. And, knowing Zelda, she had packed several changes of clothes.

Rian turned her attention to the band as the crowd cheered. "This song is going to make them famous," Rian said. "I'd lay money on that."

CHAPTER THIRTEEN

Zelda pulled her car onto the lane leading away from their overnight Buffalo River cabin. "All things considered, a good time had, but much too short," she said to the rearview mirror. "I don't know why you insist we have to be back in time to open our shops at ten on the dot." Zelda glanced at Amy. "Well, we should come here again," she added when Amy didn't respond.

It sounded as if Zelda had forgiven the incident at the grill.

The sun was barely above the horizon, the mist rising over the bluffs in blue hazy wisps like campfire smoke. The peace and quiet was alluring and the friends were silent as they left the gravel road. The colors were nearing the end of their fall season now that the November chill was here, but the oaks were still orange and the hickory golden brown. In a week or so, the fallen leaves would cover the roads in winding spirals of color. But for now, they were still coloring the mountainsides like a painting by a great master.

They passed a kayak hauler with empty racks, meaning early paddlers were already ferried in for a river run. They passed a farmer on his tractor. Dogs herding cows. A man chopping wood. An old barn stuffed to the rafters with hay.

Genna broke the silence a few miles down the road.

"I don't know how I missed it," she said quietly. "But in my defense, it was buried in the back pages like someone put the axe to it. It was only a few paragraphs long and I was looking for big headlines. It seems that Winslow Duncan's car was stuck in the snow-rutted road. That was a problem back then because the roads were full of rocks and mud, plus snow and ice at that time of year. It was January, remember?

"A witness saw this Hobo Joe helping him free the car and saw Duncan give him money for his help. Another witness said they saw someone rushing from the scene of the crime, but it was too dark to swear testimony as to who it was. The Rev. Hayes said the man in question had been in the company of himself and his wife, Evangeline, for prayer and supper and could not be in two places at once.

"Wait," she said, "let me quote this direct. It is too priceless to mess up." She flipped through photos in her phone, and landing on the right one, read on:

"The town of Bluff Springs is shocked out of its lethargy by the news that Winslow T. Duncan was indeed shot by an assailant unknown to us. Duncan was by all accounts a respected member of the community, a gentleman of stature, and as far as anyone knew, lived in harmony with his newlywed wife, Catherine. After questioning the parties in proximity to the incident at the time, it was determined that no eyewitnesses were present when the crime was committed. With no further suspects in regard to this heinous trespass, the conclusion drawn by all involved favor the opinion that whomever shot and killed Duncan did so for the money he had on his person and then fled the state, most likely by train. The incident will remain open and unsolved until the suspect or suspects can be identified and questioned by authorities."

"End quote," Genna said. "I can only assume the article was buried in the back pages of the Bluff Springs Weekly Times for good reason. No one needed a lynch mob loose in the wild Ozark Mountains looking for an indigent or anyone else who seemed fair game."

Amy stared out the windshield. That was a hundred years ago, and the case was still open. And it was still cold.

"This reminds me a little of Warren G. Harding," Zelda said brightly. She was in amazingly good spirits for as early as it was.

"Are you talking about American history?" Genna looked flabbergasted by the possibility.

"Oh, control yourself," Zelda said. "I was a history major until I got distracted. Some of that stuff sticks with you no matter how hard you try to shake it off."

Amy could imagine what Zelda was distracted by but now wasn't the time to go down that particular path of history.

"So, tell us about Harding," Genna encouraged.

"He was a bad boy," Zelda said. "He was greedy and corrupt, and he cheated on his wife. He probably cheated at poker. He paid hush money to his mistresses—yes, as in more than one— and he only got caught because he wrote some pretty steamy love letters that got him found out."

"What happened to him?" Rian asked.

"The history books say congestive heart failure, although at the time they thought it was a cerebral hemorrhage. A stroke. Some claim his death is still a mystery. A cold case mystery, still."

"A cold case!" Amy exclaimed. "Like this one!"

"The rumors claimed Harding's wife and his doctor poisoned him. On purpose." Zelda smiled with satisfaction. She loved delivering the drama. "He had just left a fishing trip in Alaska, and the national park named after the very man who gave Harding his start in politics. That man was William McKinley. He was a big wig newspaper publisher and editor, too.

"Like Frank Calhoun," Genna said.

"Yes, like Frank Calhoun," Zelda agreed.

"But why is Harding's death still a cold case?" Amy asked.

"Because there was no autopsy. There was no autopsy at the request of Harding's wife. So, no one knows for sure how he died. His wife said that if Harding had lived another day, he would have been impeached, and she couldn't bear to see that happen. She said she had no regrets."

"No regrets!" Amy exclaimed. "She and the doctor killed him!"

"That would be a worthwhile question to ask the Ouija, now wouldn't it?" Zelda suggested and Amy couldn't tell if she was joking or not.

"I think Mable Rose had a nice little business going with the Ouija parlor and her Spiritualism gatherings," Amy suggested. "Even if she charged a dollar a person, she was making a fair wage for that time. And if you add on her dressmaking clients, she was sitting pretty out there on Piney Top. I wonder what her house looks like."

"I have every confidence you will find out," Rian said. "You have snooping in your genes."

Amy grinned. She probably did have nosy genes. Snooping around in other people's business was more fun than she wanted to admit. It wasn't necessarily right, but it wasn't necessarily wrong, either. It was all in how you handled it. It depended on what you were snooping for. Zelda might call that discernment.

"I bet there's a table with four chairs there," she said absently, after a pause. "Alfred was pretty clear about a sitting for four at the Ouija board. I doubt Mable Rose played poker."

"Alfred?" Rian asked. "Who is Alfred?"

Amy moved her eyes to the top of their sockets and grimaced.

"You've had a snippet," Genna accused from the back seat. Amy felt Genna's breath on the back of her neck. "You promised you would share your snippets with us. Especially after those purple fungi and banshee screams in Ireland. You've got to stop being so secretive!"

Amy exhaled loudly. "It takes me a while to decide if it is a snippet or just a dream," she explained. "You would hate me if I told you every dream I have and would hate me even more if you thought every dream needed chasing down."

"Agreed," Genna said. "But Alfred is different."

Amy nodded. "Alfred is different."

"Who is Alfred?" Rian asked again.

"Alfred Hitchcock."

"Oh, puhleese," Genna said. "Sir Alfred Hitchcock was in your snippet?"

Amy didn't answer.

"Out with it," Genna demanded. She and Rian leaned forward from the back seat.

Amy told them about the table in the graveyard with Alfred Hitchcock sitting at the head.

"'*Good evening,*'" he said, "like he always did in his show. I heard him distinctly.

"He said, *'I would ask you to join me, but as you can see, the seats are all taken.'* But there was no one else there. Not that I could see."

"Ghosts!" Zelda exclaimed. "There were ghosts in the graveyard! I knew I felt a chill."

"Go on," Genna urged, ignoring Zelda.

Amy told them about the Ouija board in the center of the table and the items at each of the settings.

"The four queens!" Genna exclaimed. "I knew there was more to that than you let on."

"What else did Hitchcock say?" Rian asked.

"He said you can never believe what the deceased say. Especially on the Ouija board. Although he called it a talking board contraption. He said the deceased are inclined to spell out tales of deception. Harrowing tales," she amended, "of deception and murder."

"And then what happened?" Genna asked.

Amy glanced at Zelda, whose hands were gripping the wheel with more force than was needed.

"He put a bullet down on the table and said it was a remedy for insomnia. That it would cure insomnia permanently. Guaranteed to put you to sleep forever."

"A bullet," Genna echoed. "Winslow T. Duncan's bullet?"

"No birds?" Rian asked as if disappointed. "No *Dial M for Murder*? No Bates Motel?"

Amy narrowed her eyes at Rian. "Yes, I know we were just talking about all that, which is why I was not so clear about the status of the dream. It didn't really click until Genna uncovered the story about Winslow Duncan being shot after a poker game."

"A bullet and four queens," Genna said.

"That's a hard-to-beat poker hand," Rian added. "And a bullet is definitely permanent."

"Four queens. Was he talking about us?" Zelda squeaked.

"I don't know. But he did say I needed to be bold enough to ask. I presume he meant bold enough to ask the Ouija board. As in hold a séance to find out who killed Winslow Duncan. He said, *'you are the one.'*"

"Well, then that is what you are going to do," Genna declared.

"It's not at the top of my to-do list," Amy admitted.

"No kidding," Zelda quipped. "It will never make it anywhere on *my* to-do list."

"I can't do it alone," Amy added. "From what I've read no one should ever do it alone."

"One should not do it at all," Zelda added.

"I'm working up to it," Amy said finally. "What I've read about it makes it not as scary as you might think."

"I doubt that," Zelda spat.

"We see your sarcasm and raise you some sass," Genna said finally. "You're not a fan of the occult, Zelda. We get it."

"Ouija boards were advertised for a buck fifty a board back then," Amy said. "That's about fifty bucks in today's money. I sure won't feel bad about putting a hefty price tag on the boards I bought from Camellia. They are beautifully vintage, although some are in better shape than others."

"I can't believe you gave her twelve hundred bucks!" Genna exclaimed. "That was ludicrous."

"I don't agree," Amy responded abruptly. "I'll make my money back."

"Hmm," Genna muttered, and Amy hoped Genna wouldn't have the opportunity to prove her wrong.

"All the old advertisements I saw claimed the Ouija was a toy, but then they called it a magical device that answered questions about the past, the present, and the future with marvelous accuracy," Amy shared.

"No one would know what's accurate," Rian muttered. "Past, present, and future. It's malarky."

"True enough," Amy agreed, "but the US Patent Office testified it was proven accurate."

Genna snickered. "Oh, yeah, I can see that set up happening. *'We will give you a fistful of money if you say we talked to our late Uncle Beauregard on this magical toy.'"*

"Actually, her name was Helen, and she claimed to be a psychic. They brought her with them to the Patent Office just in case.

"You see, the inventors were sitting around the table trying to figure out what to name this talking oracle when the board spelled out *Ouija*. Helen, the same Helen who later went to the Patent Office, was wearing a locket with a picture inside. And wait, you'll love this, Genna. The picture in the locket was of a famous women's rights activist named Ouida. I guess the board didn't quite spell her name right."

"Kinda like yours, Rian. From O'Deá to O'Deis."

Rian nodded with a look of contemplative satisfaction. It was an act of dedication that led them to traipse Ireland looking for Rian's roots, even though she didn't belong to Irish royalty as Zelda had hoped.

"Anyway," Amy continued, "the inventors knew that if they couldn't prove the board worked, they wouldn't get a patent, so they brought Helen the psychic with them for good luck. The chief patent officer agreed that if the board could accurately spell out his name, which was unknown to them, he would allow the patent to proceed." Amy paused and turned her attention to the cows and hay bales in the pasture they were passing. It was difficult not to *moo* at the bucolic sight of cows.

"And?" Zelda said impatiently, her fingers tapping the wheel.

"And," Amy said, turning her attention back to her story, "the planchette spelled out the guy's name. They got their patent, and the board became a sensation. By 1920, the talking board was a favorite pastime for entertainment and recreation."

"They had to do *something* for entertainment," Genna interjected in her slow Southern style. "Radio theater wasn't around until 1924. There was no such thing as TV. Movies were silent and in black and white, and you couldn't go to a bar because Prohibition was in full sail."

"Well, at least they had baseball," Rian added. "My boy Babe Ruth was just making a name for himself. Twenty-nine home runs. They called him Bambino Ruth. He was sold to the Yankees that next season and the Boston Red Sox regretted that for another fifteen years!"

Amy laughed. Rian and her baseball stats.

"I think that was about the time they held the first Miss America beauty pageant," Genna added, "but there were only forty-eight states. No one had heard of Charles Lindbergh, yet. Plus, the words dump truck, bookmobile, parking lot, tossed salad, and zipper appeared in print for the first time. Imagine that."

"Bookmobile!" Amy exclaimed. "Reading was a big pastime. Agatha Christie was just making a name for herself at that time. Christie's Hercule Poirot and Tommy and Tuppence were just being introduced to the literary world.

"Maybe that contributed to the Ouija craze," Amy continued. "There were dozens of toy companies capitalizing on its popularity. They couldn't all call it Ouija, of course, that was trademarked, but people didn't seem to care what it was called or why it worked just as long as it did work. People really believed it was an oracle that pierced the veil to connect with the unknown."

Rian nodded, her head turned to the window and the countryside zooming past. "Isn't that always what people are after? Knowing the unknowable. That's what religions everywhere in the world seek."

"The unknowable to me is where we might find a station out here in BFA before we run out of gas," Zelda said. "I forgot to fill up before we left town yesterday."

Genna pulled out her phone. "There's one not too far, Zelda. There's a crossroads station in ten miles. Can we make it?"

Zelda glanced at the gauge and nodded. "But not ten more to spare. I knew there was something I was forgetting yesterday, Sparks. You should have reminded me. We were in such a hurry to get out of town."

Amy turned a knowing look to Zelda. They were lucky they found Rian and Genna at all. She shifted in the seat and turned to Rian behind her. "What I find interesting is that both the mysterious talking Ouija board and Spiritualism were approachable for the Americans of that era. It was totally compatible with Christian beliefs. You could hold a Ouija séance on Saturday night and have no qualms about going to church on Sunday."

"I bet the Reverend Cecil Hayes had qualms. His sermons were about the evils of anything fun," Genna interjected.

"Why would someone want to communicate with the dead?" Zelda asked. "I think that's creepy."

"It wasn't considered creepy," Amy answered. "It wasn't about opening the gates of hell or anything like that."

"Yeah, it was more about opening the gates of the American wallet," Genna offered.

"They sold millions of boards," Amy agreed. "They even used Ouija to solve crimes. Well, the police didn't, but desperate families did. And then almost overnight, it became a tool of the horror movies."

"Which is where I depart from the conversation," Zelda said. "I can't go anywhere near that topic."

"What happened to you?" Genna asked.

"I can't talk about it," Zelda said and snapped her lips closed.

"Can't or won't?" Genna prodded.

"Six of one, half a dozen of the other," Zelda answered. "Same thing either way."

Genna grinned and glanced at Rian, who shrugged and turned back to the window and the mountains and the colorful leaves falling in the curves in the road.

"Now Ouija is just a novelty," Amy continued. "Now it's all about spooky fun rather than a spiritual endeavor, and it's making a comeback like all the other vintage games. I think it's because people want to believe in something more powerful than themselves."

"What's the difference between a planchette, a dowsing rod, and a pendulum?" Genna asked and then quickly answered her own question. "Absolutely nothing. You're moving the thing yourself. It's all about the expectation. That's not magic. The mind can do seemingly amazing things."

"I agree," Amy said.

Zelda wiggled in the seat and flexed her fingers on the wheel. She glanced at Amy and declared, "You can be a walking advertisement for that talking board all you want, but you aren't going to get me anywhere near one. You are too obsessed with this stuff. Why do you want to move a piece of wood around on some board of alphabet soup?"

Amy was silent for a moment. It was a fair enough question, and it deserved a fair answer. Zelda glanced at her again and scrunched her nose. "Well? Tell me why."

"Because it's all about what's hidden in the mind," Amy said evenly, her thoughts forming with clarity. "I mean, it's non-conscious knowledge brought into the conscious. I think that's what my snippet dreams are about. I don't believe they are any more magical than the Ouija talking board. Or crystal balls. Or Tarot cards. I think it's just another way of seeing through the veil of hidden knowledge. You know, a way of bringing the unknown forward into the known. Kind of like being hypnotized and then you notice details you didn't remember seeing."

"That's heavy," Rian said.

"That's mystical stuff," Genna added.

"That's creepy as all get out," Zelda said, and Amy smiled.

True enough. Creepy as all get out. And yet, as much a part of her world as Victor the cat and her three best friends. Four queens. Four women. Four friends.

The car was silent for a long while as they sped away from the gas station headed for the final stretch home.

Genna snickered and then burst out into laughter.

"You should have seen your face, Zelda," she said when she could catch her breath. "You were holding that frosted hot dog like the Statue of Liberty herself."

CHAPTER FOURTEEN

She laughed all the way up the stairs to her apartment above Tiddlywinks. Zelda's hot dog fiasco was one for the books. The four of them would be laughing over this road trip for some time.

"Victor," she called, as she unlocked the door. "Mama's home, kitty boy."

The silence that greeted her was unexpected. When she left him alone to portion out his nibbles on his own, he was always sitting at the top of the stairs mewing with aggression about how hungry he was and how she had neglected her duty. His bowl would be empty, his water bowl spilled, and invariably the toilet roll would be attacked with mad abandon as if it were a hamster on a wheel. She never left him long without a keeper, and he was as spoiled as any cat on the planet who was lucky enough to have a home, a bed, and an indentured servant.

"Victor!" she called again, looking for shredded and tangled TP on the floor.

Silence. A clean floor.

Her heart thumped and she could feel the adrenaline all the way up the back of her hands.

"Victor!" she called again, this time more worried than stern. "Where are you?

She looked in the kitchen. No cat.

She looked on the bed. No cat.

She noticed the closet door was open an inch, probably pried open with kitty claws, but not open far enough for a fat cat to squeeze in and prowl.

She looked in the bathtub. Slim chance, but a known spot for chasing spiders. No Victor. No spiders, either.

Panic rose. A lump formed in her throat. "Victor!" she called again, and she heard something thump against the rug in the living room. The tippy tip end of his striped tail beat the rug with rhythmic impatience from his crouch behind the sofa.

Her sigh was audible.

"Victor, come out from there," she cooed. "I have yummies."

He whacked the floor again a little harder. Did he have something cornered behind the couch? Was he hurt? Probably pouting because he had to go without food for all of twenty minutes. She bent down and touched the tip of his tail. That's all she could reach. He drew his tail in quickly and disappeared.

She pulled a box of gas station shrimp tails from the fridge and rattled them in the box. "Shrimps, Vic," she called. "Come and get your shrimpies."

She retraced her steps to the kitchen and dumped the tails in his bowl. It was his favorite. There was no way he would choose a lingering pout over a bowl of shrimp.

She went back to the couch and peered over the back. She could barely see him, wedged between the wall and the back of the sofa. At least he was safe. He could pout until he got hungry and then when he came out she'd scoop him up and hug him tight. She plopped down on the cushions, glad to be home, glad to have a home to come to.

Her eye caught on the box on the coffee table. It was a wooden box she kept the odd items in, but the lid was askew and that wasn't a likely thing for her to do, even when in a hurry. She tentatively pulled the box to her, lifting the lid to peer inside. The rubber bands, matchbooks, and hair ties were there, but the necklace—the dance card necklace—was gone!

Did she return it after showing it to Banjo Man? Of course, she did. She showed it to Maggie after. Did she leave it there? She retraced her steps in her mind. She definitely remembered picking it up from the velvet pad before leaving the jewelers. She thought she remembered putting it back in the box on the table. She would have put the lid on straight, too. Maybe it was on her dresser. She got up to check.

The necklace was not there. And Victor was still crouched behind the sofa.

Suddenly aware of the possibilities of someone lurking in her apartment, she glanced around for signs of an intruder. That throw rug was bunched. But then Victor liked to use it as a surfboard. The lid of her earring box was standing open. The top drawer of her dresser was open an inch—that place where it stuck and wouldn't close until you gave it a good shove. She grabbed the umbrella in the stand near the door and swung the closet door open. Maybe the fact that it was cracked open had nothing to do with Victor's claws.

She pulled the light chain in the closet.

The closet was a mess. The boxes of shoes on the top shelf were dumped to the floor and the pockets of her jackets were turned out. Fear let loose to anger and anger rose in the back of her throat like acid. Someone had searched her apartment and threatened her cat!

But why? But who? And why? And who? How dare they!

There was only one thing missing that she could tell. The necklace. She plopped down on her bed and stared at the closet. The only people who knew about the necklace and didn't have an alibi was Banjo Man and Maggie. The rest of them were partying in the woods.

Somehow Banjo Man didn't fit. She couldn't imagine him climbing the stairs to her apartment. Or rummaging through her clothes. But he and the jeweler were the only people who knew she had the necklace.

She lay down on her bed and breathed in the scent of lavender linen spray.

Amy remembered how upset Zelda was when she went snooping in Zelda's house looking for clues. Zelda didn't know

Amy was the culprit at the time, but when Zelda called her to ask for support, Amy made an excuse why she couldn't come over. Not because she didn't want to be supportive of her friend. It was because she felt guilty.

Shoe on the other foot now.

What was she going to do? What *could* she do?

She could call the police and report the break-in. But it didn't appear that anything else was missing. What would she say? That somebody broke in and stole a necklace that wasn't hers. That somebody stole a necklace that she stole off a grave. Dumb question. Dumb answers.

Guilt pinged. She really should have run a want ad as Zelda suggested. She really should have tried to find the owner. The right thing to do was to take the necklace to the police station the same as if she found a wallet full of cash. At the very least she should have turned it over to the cemetery commission. Woulda. Shoulda. Coulda. She hadn't done any of it. And now the necklace was gone.

She closed her eyes and then felt the soft nuzzling push of a nose and whiskers.

"Victor," she breathed, as he nudged his way into her arms. "I am so glad you are okay, buddy," she whispered. "And I sure wish you could talk."

In minutes, the two of them were sound asleep, one snoring and one purring.

When she awoke she realized she had been dreaming again. Not about Alfred Hitchcock. The dream was a loud banging, like a hammer pounding a nail.

Victor jumped down and shot under the bed.

"Amy! Are you in there? What's going on?"

The banging continued. "Amy!"

"I'm coming!" she yelled. She stood at the door and listened as her name was bellowed once again.

"If you say land shark, Rian, I'll bean you," Amy said, unlocking the door.

Rian's face was flushed. "What were you doing?

"Sleeping." Amy answered.

"You mean we left early so you could come home and sleep?" Rian's tone turned angry. "If I had known that was the plan we would still be in the woods on the Buffalo River."

Amy gestured Rian inside.

"Somebody broke into my apartment."

Rian looked at the door and then around the room, first with concern and then with confusion. "How do you know that? The lock's not broken, and I don't see anything missing. Except maybe that fat cat."

"Victor is safe," Amy replied, "but he's spooked. And you didn't help matters. He dove beneath the bed with all your banging and hollering."

Amy motioned Rian to the sofa and pointed to the box on the table. "I had the dance card necklace in there," she said. "For safe keeping. I know I should have turned it into the police, but I didn't. And now I can't. There are only six people who know I had it, and four of us were in the woods."

Rian opened the box and looked inside, pulling out a wad of hair ties with a look of pure bewilderment. "Who knew about it?"

"Banjo Man."

"That old man from the cemetery? The hobo aficionado?

Amy nodded. "I told him where I worked. And where I lived, too. That was stupid, I know."

"You think he broke into your apartment to steal that necklace? And just that necklace?"

Amy shrugged. "Nothing else is gone. Not that I see. He knew it was here."

"And you're sure you put it back in this box?"

Amy stalled for a moment. She had questioned that fact herself. "Yes, I'm sure," she said with a confident nod. She remembered pocketing the necklace in her jeans. He must have come back for it. When she didn't answer her door, he jimmied the lock and snooped until he found it.

Rian scanned the room again. "Tell me why you think someone broke in."

"Victor was so spooked he was hiding under the couch. He didn't even budge when I loaded his bowl with shrimp tails."

"A Sherlock kind of deduction," Rian mumbled.

Amy told her about the closet and Rian followed her into the bedroom.

"That could have been Victor trying to climb up on the shelf."

Amy turned a warning look to Rian. "And then he turned all my pockets inside out. That's a talent for a cat."

"I agree," Rian acquiesced. "Someone wanted that necklace. And who knows why? It can't be worth much."

Amy closed the closet door. "The necklace is a clue to the crime, Rian. The clue to a murder. That's its worth. And just because everybody back then thought Hobo Joe shot Winslow Duncan and ran off with the poker cash, I don't. And I think someone else doesn't think so either."

Rian whistled softly under her breath. "You're talking about Alfred and your snippet."

Amy nodded. "The necklace wasn't one of the objects on the table, so I don't know how it fits in. But the snippet came right after I found it, and I can't get rid of this feeling that we haven't solved the crime. Even the newspaper left the murder of Winslow Duncan as a trail gone cold. A cold case that was never solved."

Rian retreated to the living room and dropped onto the couch. She put the hair ties back in the box and replaced the lid. "Tell me again what objects were on the table in your snippet."

Amy closed her eyes, picturing Alfred at the table with his three invisible guests. "The thing I saw first were the playing cards. Four queens."

"Definitely a winning hand if you're playing poker," Rian added.

"Which he was," Amy said. "Winslow Duncan was playing poker with friends. He won the hand, and he won the pot of money along with a deed that Langford wanted back. All that came from the newspaper articles Genna found in the archives," she added.

"There was a thimble and a handkerchief," Amy continued. "You know like the thimble playing piece in the Monopoly game."

Rian nodded.

"There was a bottle. I don't know what the label said, but I do remember thinking it was a medicine bottle. An old pharmacy bottle."

Rian sat back against the cushion and absently twisted a curl with her finger. "The RX," she said quietly. "I wish we knew the nature of Oscar St. Claire's addiction. As a druggist he had access to just about everything."

"Are you thinking the medicine bottle is part of this?" Amy asked.

"It's your snippet, I'm just trying to make some sense of it. St. Claire was at the card game. St. Claire owned the drug store."

Amy nodded, grateful for the collaboration.

"You said the newspaper mentioned the players—Duncan, St. Claire, Langford and… anybody else?" Rian asked.

"It didn't name Frank Calhoun, but I figured he was the anonymous witness in the newspaper article. Or maybe that was the Rev. Cecil Hayes. I think he's involved somehow, and he wouldn't have wanted his name connected to a poker game in the paper."

"If Duncan represents the cards in poker," Rian continued, "and St. Claire is the pharmacy bottle, then Langford has to be the Monopoly game thimble. Sort of like the properties on the game board. He was gambling with something he shouldn't have. Maybe even his family home."

"I never thought of that," Amy said, encouraged.

"That's motive for murder," Rian added. "But they didn't finger Langford for the crime."

"No, because Langford said he saw Hobo Joe at the scene."

"Very convenient for Langford."

Amy nodded. "I can't make sense of it. Who did the necklace belong to? All along I thought it was Catherine Duncan's, only because of the Mrs. Teddy Duncan frilly bit written on the page, like she was designing her wedding monogram. I don't even know if women had monogrammed hankies back then. The lady at the museum said Catherine was forced to marry Duncan, so why would she spend time doodling his initials?"

Amy went on. "Hobo Joe's name comes up every time I turn a corner. He was seen at the scene of the crime. And then he went missing. It sounded like he was on good terms with people in town, for a hobo; at least it seemed they liked him. They fed him. He even sent a postcard to say he was safe if I can make that leap. You wouldn't sign *Hobo Joe* to a postcard if you were running from the law for murder."

Ever yours, Joe. That's how it was signed. Affectionate but not too sappy.

"Why would Banjo Man want the necklace?"

"It was full of hobo symbols, and he collects hobo memorabilia." Amy snapped her fingers. "What if the necklace belonged to his granny? What if he recognized it and knew it was connected to his grandmother and his grandmother was connected to the crime?"

"That's a stretch," Rian answered.

"Not if he's the one who dropped it in the graveyard! In my mind the chain was broken when it was yanked from someone's neck as they were running away. Maybe that didn't happen in the past. Maybe it happened more recently."

"Are you going to call the police?"

Amy shook her head.

"You want me to call *my* police?"

"You mean Ben?" Amy chuckled. Rian's now-getting-serious boyfriend was a cop in a county over. They had played it low key for a long time because he was a cop and, well, she grew weed. They joked about the pair of them being Dudley Do-Right and Belle Starr. Belle was a famous outlaw who spent some time in Bluff Springs back in the late 1800s. Dudley Do-Right was a Canadian Mountie with a dimple and a big heart.

"No," Amy said finally. "I'm going to hunt down Banjo Man and see what he has to say."

"I can come with you," Rian said. "I could be the muscle to rough up your old man."

Amy laughed again. She knew Rian was joking, but that wasn't a scene she wanted to picture in her mind.

CHAPTER FIFTEEN

Tiddlywinks opened late because of her morning disruption. No one but Rian and Zelda complained. The day went quickly. Sales were flat. The fall visitors had thinned to a slow crawl after the Halloween rush, and she realized that she welcomed the lull before the Thanksgiving hustle.

Victor was still hanging low in the apartment, and she decided he could wait an hour or two before his evening meal. She locked up and headed for her car. Parking was a premium in Bluff Springs, and she felt grateful the old building came with three private parking spots. One she reserved for Sammie at Crumpets and Cones bakery and one for Zelda. Rian had other options. The parking spots were behind the building and across the creek, with a crumbly looking bridge connecting the two. The bridge was barely high enough to escape high water during torrential rains, but amazingly, the ancient concrete was still holding sound. She crossed the bridge now, watching the water swirl over the rocks beneath her. On impulse, she turned and looked back at the building. Victor sat in his favorite seat in the windowsill. She waved and then felt silly.

She pulled on the hat and gloves she always kept handy in the car, wrapped the scarf tight, and put the top down on the Miata, all hoping to catch a few last-minute rays. The sun was already low in the sky. She wanted to reach the graveyard before dark, and she made her way quickly, meandering through the maze looking for the spot where she and Banjo Man had met. She found it without much effort.

Banjo Man said his name was Charles. And now, looking at the headstone, she also had his last name. Gray. It was already etched in the granite beside his beloved wife. When the time came, he would spend eternity as Charles Gray, not Banjo Man, and she wondered how he felt about that.

She left the cemetery satisfied. The road was a little rough on her Miata, but 7 Piney Top was not as far down as she thought it would be. She noticed it was almost directly across from the path near the back gate of the graveyard.

Amy pulled off the road and parked. There wasn't really a driveway, but a car was jammed into the opening between two overgrown hedges. Camellia was right. The place was so overgrown it was almost hidden from the road.

She made her way to the porch steps.

Camellia met her at the door. She stood behind the screen that separated the dark house inside from the growing dark outside.

"Oh… hey!" Camellia exclaimed, sounding surprised. "What's up? Why are you here?"

"Just being neighborly," Amy answered. Just being nosy was more like it. "I was visiting the cemetery and thought of you. I wondered how your project is going." She motioned to the house, which, as she took in the structure was as Ozark as they came. While many of the houses in Bluff Springs were grand painted ladies with decorative gingerbread trim, some were much more modest. Others were downright sparse. This was one of those. The siding boards were a dull gray, having lost their whitewash decades ago. The porch planks had holes where rain dripped year after year and rotted them through. She also noticed the porch was swept clean and an old rocker sat on one end. It wasn't a porch rocker with wide arms and a wicker bottom, the kind that sat on her own great aunt's porch. This rocker looked like a parlor chair from inside the house, with its polished wood and an intricately embroidered seat. There was only one chair. Camellia wasn't expecting to sit with company.

"It's going okay, I guess," Camellia said. "I still don't know why you're here."

"I wanted to know if you found any more cool things," Amy ventured.

Camellia opened the screen door and stepped through. "What kind of things?"

Amy raised a brow. "Like more old games. I'll buy any you find." She smiled, hoping to put Camellia at ease. She hadn't been invited to drop in unannounced and some people considered that a problem.

Camellia cocked her head. "Oh. Well, okay. If I find some, I'll let you know."

"I'm always interested. And Zelda, too. She loves vintage kitsch for her shop. Ceramic bunnies and such." She grinned. "Seriously, you could make some money while you're figuring out what you're going to do."

Amy was dying to get inside and take a peek at what *"abandoned but not empty"* looked like. It was clear the invitation wasn't going to come on its own.

"I know I've come unannounced," Amy said, "but I don't have your phone number, and I wanted to ask you something." Amy peeked around Camellia's shoulder at the interior of the house. It had grown even darker in the last few minutes as the sun slipped behind the ridge, and there were no lights on inside. Either Camellia didn't get her invite-me-in signal, or she wasn't receiving, as they said in the proper South. She shuffled her feet, and Amy noticed Camellia's feet were bare, her toenails painted marmalade orange.

"It's a strange request," Amy said finally, realizing the conversation would happen on the porch or not at all. "I need another person to do the Ouija board with me. My friends are too busy." Too not-on-your-life too busy if she was honest. "And I was hoping you would be willing."

"Me?" Camellia seemed perplexed. "You want me to do that Ouija board thing with you?"

Amy nodded.

"But I thought you said—"

She waited and then realized Camellia wasn't going to finish her thought. "I said they spooked people, and that's true, but I've been dared by someone to use the Ouija to ask a question. And, well, a dare is hard for me to pass up. We could do it here if you like." Amy looked in the darkness behind the door.

"Here!" Camellia exclaimed. "You want to do the Ouija here?"

"It's not like it hasn't happened before."

"What are you talking about?"

"Oh, come on, Camellia, you're a smart woman. I know you figured it out. Your Aunt Mable Rose ran a Spiritualist Ouija parlor out of number seven Piney Top. This place. Your place. Your Aunt Mable Rose was the person people came to when they wanted messages from the beyond."

Camellia stepped back quickly, and Amy thought she might flee the porch and disappear into the dark house.

"That's not true," Camellia said hotly and crossed her arms. "She was a dressmaker. She made clothes."

"A dressmaker who had an ear turned to every woman in town," Amy suggested. "She was someone they could trust. A confidant. Another woman to tell their secrets to while being fitted for a new frock. They knew their secrets would never leave the room. And when they wanted to know if their husbands were cheating on them or if they were having a boy or a girl, they consulted the oracle. The Ouija. And Mable Rose was there for them."

"That's a wild assumption," Camellia spat. "Why would you say that?"

"The widow wore a mourning dress with just the right touch of chic in a panel of crepe on black taffeta."

Camellia looked up. "What did you say?"

"It was a line from an obituary in the newspaper. A detail only a woman would notice. The kind of detail only a dressmaker could provide."

Camellia sighed and dropped her arms to her side.

"You knew there was a reason she had a dozen Ouija boards," Amy said quietly.

Camellia nodded slowly. "I'm reading her diary. Actually, there are many diaries. The words are hard to read with that spidery writing and I've only read through some of it, but I guess you're right. She was, she was—"

"She was the secret keeper," Amy interjected. "She was the person who knew the dark secrets of just about everyone in town."

The quiet of dusk closed in around them. An owl hooted somewhere nearby, and Amy was reminded of her grandmother's tale of the owl's cry warning children to hurry home before the *bogeyman* came out of hiding. That particular superstition claimed that owls carried messages from the haints to the living. The very messages that the restless took to their graves. Amy wondered what secrets Mable Rose took to hers.

"I don't know how to do the Ouija board thing and I'm not sure I want to," Camellia said after a long pause. "Maybe you shouldn't either."

"At least think about it." Amy turned to leave. "Hey," she said turning back toward the house. Camellia was still standing on the now dark porch. "Did you find that money tin, yet?"

Camellia looked startled. "Money? No, but I did find a tin."

"Keep looking," Amy offered as she made her way to her car. "One is bound to turn up."

CHAPTER SIXTEEN

She circled the block and then parked across the street, eyeing the front yard with doubt. A plastic wagon and a Big Wheel were parked on the sidewalk leading to the front door. Banjo Man hadn't said anything about grandchildren. The topic never came up. She checked her notes. This was the address listed in the phone directory for Charles Gray.

Only one way to find out.

A rather haggard looking woman opened the door and looked her over with suspicious eyes. "You're not the regular delivery guy," she said. The woman looked at Amy's empty hands. "Where's the pizza? You don't have my pizza."

"Is Banjo Man here?" Amy asked before the woman could shut the door.

"Who?"

Amy heard babies bellowing in the background. "Mr. Gray," Amy said quickly, knowing her window was closing fast. "Isn't this his address?"

"Are you a bill collector or something? Look, I forward all his mail that comes here just like he asked. If he's not paying his bills, it's not my fault."

Seize the moment, Sparks. "Could you give me the forwarding address? That would be helpful."

The woman's eyes narrowed.

"And then I would be on my way and out of your hair."

The woman shut the door and Amy stood on the stoop wondering what just happened. No goodbye. No go away. No nothing. Just a door closed in her face. She was turning away when the door opened again.

"Here," the woman said, thrusting an unopened envelope into her hands. "This came a few weeks ago and I haven't had time to put it back in the mailbox. The address is on it. You could deliver it yourself."

Amy glanced at the envelope. A forwarding address was hand lettered beside the cellophane window.

"You tell him we hope he's doing okay," the woman said with sudden compassion. "It sure was a nice thing he did."

Her curiosity peaked. What nice thing? Amy opened her mouth to ask but the woman was already closing the door.

Amy retreated to her car just as the pizza delivery pulled into the driveway. She studied the envelope the woman gave her. There were no brand markings to identify the sender, but *Forward to Happy House Retirement Village* was clear enough. It wasn't far. In less than fifteen minutes she was parked in the lot and headed toward the front door.

"Mr. Gray is not available," the receptionist said brightly as she checked her computer. "I will be happy to leave a message."

"When he will be back?"

The receptionist looked at her and smiled. "Are you a member of his family?"

"No."

"Well, then you will have to wait until he returns. We aren't allowed to give out information on our residents. And that goes double for their medical details. Happy HIPAA, you know." The woman seemed satisfied with her protocol and turned her attention to her computer screen.

"Can you at least tell me how to reach him by phone?"

The receptionist looked up again. "You can leave a message." She slid paper and pen across the counter. "It would be easier if you write it. I'll be happy to make sure he gets it when he returns. I know he will be happy to hear from you, Miss—?"

Amy didn't reply.

"I see, well, I know he will be happy you stopped in to see him."

Amy noticed how many times she said *happy*. Happy House Retirement Village seemed eager to earn its name.

Amy stared at the blank paper in front of her and then back at the woman behind the desk who looked like she was nearing retirement age herself. What should she write? *You broke into my apartment and took my necklace, and I want it back. I know who you are, and I know what you did. How dare you scare my cat!*

None of that seemed appropriate and in the end she simply wrote. *Need to talk. Call me.* She started to write *Please* and stopped herself. More urgent without it. She added her name and her cell phone number, folded it, twice, before handing it to the woman.

The receptionist looked at the folded paper before making an exaggerated point of taping the edges closed. "Signed, sealed, and as good as delivered," she said with a bit of reproach in her tone. "I am *happy* to do my job."

"Oh, and here's this." Amy handed her the envelope. "I intended to forward it through the mail, but hand delivery is better."

The woman looked at the envelope and frowned as if it posed an issue not covered under her duties as receptionist.

"Are you sure you can't tell me when he will be back?" Amy urged. "I could wait a little while."

"Oh, goodness," the woman said. "You'll be waiting a long while." She paused and then reached for a card on her desk. "If you want to send flowers, here's the address."

Flowers? Amy looked at the card in her hands. United Hospital. Hospital? What happened to him? Just a few days ago the two of them were looking at his old scrapbook.

"Why hello, my dear, so happy to see you," the woman called from the porch rocker as Amy passed on her way out. Amy turned and smiled. "I hope you're having another happy day," the old woman said. Her hair was white and cropped to her head, little sprigs of curls bouncing in odd directions. "Sit a spell," the woman urged and patted the arm of the chair beside her. On impulse, Amy sat.

The porch was adorned by glass windows and potted palms that made it look more hospitable than it was. It was a pleasant enough place to sit and watch the world go by.

"Who are you here to see? No, let me guess. Everyone comes to see someone and I'm happy to see them all."

"Are you a resident?" Amy asked.

"Are you?" the woman queried in return.

Amy laughed gently. "No, but I came to see a resident. He goes by Banjo Man."

The woman clasped her hands in front of her, delight filling her eyes. "Banjo Man! What a dear he is. Too bad what happened to him."

Amy stopped rocking and leaned forward. "What happened?"

"You don't know?"

"No, but I hope you're going to tell me."

CHAPTER SEVENTEEN

Amy sat at the counter of Tiddlywinks with her head in her hands. Her trip to the Happy House Retirement Home was not so *happy.* She learned a lot from the visit, even though the receptionist tried to keep details from her, but a resolution wasn't one of them.

"Why are you so glum?" Zelda asked. Amy looked up, surprised. She hadn't even noticed her approach.

"You look like someone ran over your cat," Zelda said and then gasped. "Oh, no! No one ran over your cat, did they?"

Amy laughed at her friend. "No, he's safe upstairs. But he's not happy and neither am I."

"What's going on? You always tell me everything."

Amy sighed. She did tell Zelda *almost* everything on her mind when her thoughts were crowding in on her. And right now, that was exactly what was happening.

"Well…" she started, and that's all it took. Amy repeated the front porch gossip as best as she could remember. The conversation had derailed a number of times in a number of directions, but the gist was there. Banjo Man had taken a fall and went by ambulance to the hospital. He had broken his wrist. Or maybe it was his hand. Or it might have been his elbow. But whatever he broke he was being kept for observation and would be released in a few days. And then he would probably be giving up his apartment and moving to Florida like everybody else.

"She said, 'They drop like flies if they don't move to Florida or Arizona first.' She claimed that every time she trained a good pinochle partner, they up and left and she had to start all over again with someone who didn't know how to play." Amy giggled at the thought.

The woman had gone off on another tangent about the musician who came every week and played their favorite songs and how he and Banjo Man played together until they got so loud the manager shut them down and ruined it for everybody.

"That was when this woman came out to the porch, and I figured the receptionist had ratted me out because she glared at me over her glasses and said, 'Don't believe everything you hear. Not all of our residents know the facts.'

"I knew what she was saying. But still, at least I got the 411 on what happened."

"Well, your Banjo Man couldn't have been the one who broke into your apartment and scared the cat," Zelda declared.

"Not if the front porch gossip was accurate. He was already in the hospital by the time we left for the woods."

"Let me see those pictures again," Zelda said. "The pictures of the necklace. Something has been pinging at me since we talked about it last."

Amy fished out her phone and opened the photos.

"Uh huh," Zelda said as she swiped through them. "Yes. I thought so. Uh-huh."

"What is all this '*uh huhing*' about?"

"See these numbers written by the names. You were thinking they were telephone numbers or had something do with the dances. But look." She turned the photo for Amy to see.

"Calhoun 32 30 38 - 60 - 120."

Amy felt confused.

"32, 30, 38—these are not phone numbers. They're measurements. Thirty-two inch bust. Thirty-inch waist. Thirty-eight-inch hips. Sixty inches. That's five feet tall and one hundred and twenty pounds. I would venture to say those were Maude Calhoun's measurements."

"Zelda!" Amy shrieked. "You're a genius! How ever did you come up with that?"

Zelda grinned. "Well, genius works for me. But really, it's because of Vito. You know, the tailor who made our costumes. We've been looking through lots of old pattern books and I noticed he listed our measurements in much the same way. Not that my measurements looked like that, mind you. I haven't been that slim in a long time. Or you either, Sparks. If I may say so."

Amy hugged her friend. "You can say whatever you want about my muffin top," Amy said. "I can't believe you figured this out! You know what this means don't you?"

Zelda shook her head.

"It means the necklace didn't belong to Catherine Duncan. It didn't belong to Banjo Man's grandmother. It belonged to Mable Rose!"

"Camellia deRossier's Mable Rose?" Zelda asked.

"The same."

Zelda inhaled sharply and then laughed. "I knew I had seen that necklace somewhere when you first showed it to me. I couldn't place it then, but I can now. Camellia deRossier was wearing it that day we met at Tiddlywinks. I remember admiring her collection of necklaces. That necklace was one of them. I am almost sure of it."

Amy wanted to hug Zelda again. She didn't; but it wouldn't have mattered to Zelda either way.

"It seems to me that your Mable Rose was the town's dressmaker. If that's true, she would be the one to set the style for the whole town. I wonder if she was any good."

"She claimed to be a First-Class Dressmaker," Amy said. "That's what her ad in the newspaper said. *Skilled and discreet.*"

"Does that mean she helped hide pregnancies when the need arose?"

"It's possible," Amy said, "but I don't think that's what she meant by *discreet*. Genna and I figured out this was her calling card for announcing her séance parlor sessions."

"You're talking about that Ouija stuff again."

"Genna and I suspected she was the town medium. The ad in the paper was a code to let women know a session was on the calendar. All they had to do was call on her to make an appointment and they would find out when the next séance would take place."

"And in between she made their frocks," Zelda declared. "Infinitely more interesting to me than whatever you're talking about. Fashion is my love language. Some people can speak it fluently and some never will. Vito is fluent. I've been talking to him about creating a whole new line of 1920s fashion. I might even get one of the dress shops to carry it. Of course, I don't have the boyish figure that was stylish back then, but that's what pleats and sashes are for.

"Oh!" she exclaimed suddenly. "And maybe we can have a fashion show and raise money for something. Who haven't we raised money for yet?"

Still rambling, Zelda said, "I was just thinking about a new 'do, too. And an eyebrow lift. In that decade, they wore their eyebrows in a sophisticated thin arch that said we are whimsical and fantasy prone. The butterfly look. I think I could pull that off."

Amy wiggled her brows.

"You've got a lot to work with there, Amy. A good pluck would do you some justice. I'm happy to help."

There was no way she would put her brows in the hands of Zelda's tweezers, but she wasn't going to say so.

Amy scanned through the photos on her phone. The numbers made sense now. Each name that had a set of numbers was similar to Maude Calhoun's. She noticed then that some of the names had symbols drawn, too. Now that she knew what she was looking at, she recognized them as hobo symbols. But why did Mable Rose know so much about hobos? Or at least their symbols. And how was this secret language used with her clients?

Amy flipped through her photos. Cat—as in Catherine Duncan, she presumed—had a donut looking symbol under her name. Evangeline's entry bore a cross. There was a diamond looking shape with a tail much like a short-tailed kite on another page. Two vertical bars were drawn on several pages.

She made a mental note to ask Banjo Man what these symbols meant when she saw him again—if she saw him again. He might be on his way to Florida.

Amy looked up to see Zelda watching her. "What are you looking at?" Amy asked.

"Your eyebrows," Zelda said. "You really would look good with butterfly brows."

"No," Amy said. "And I think you should think twice about that yourself. Just because they wore that look in the 1920s doesn't mean it would work now. Today's eyebrow is all about power and authority."

"They are about power, aren't they? They truly are. I liked Camellia's eyebrows," Zelda added. "In fact, I liked her whole ensemble. Very well put together."

"Minus a necklace," Amy added. "The chain must have broken when the tree limb broke. I'm talking about the limb in the graveyard that crashed right beside me."

Zelda nodded. "I remember."

"She's lucky she didn't land under that limb, or she would have been hurt," Amy continued. "I thought it was an animal running off, but it was Camellia. It was so dark I couldn't see much more than a shape running away."

"Camellia climbs trees?" Zelda looked astonished.

Amy nodded. "Camellia climbs trees. And she likes hanging out in the graveyard. I thought she was looking at old gravestones, but I bet she was trying to find the necklace. She knew she dropped it somewhere. And then I all but told her I found it when I described the notebook and strange symbols."

Her brow furrowed. "But how did Camellia know I was going out of town?"

"Oops," Zelda said. "That was me. I ran into her that afternoon and I told her we were going on a road trip. I would have mentioned we were going to be hearing the next great band to make Arkansas famous, but I didn't know that part yet."

"She's the one who broke into my apartment and took it! I just know it!"

"And why would she do that?" Zelda queried. "Couldn't she just ask for it back? You would have given it to her, right?"

"Of course I would," Amy answered. "But I told her it was a clue to a crime. I told her it was a clue to a murder."

"Don't believe everything you hear," Zelda pointed out. "Poor thing was probably scared to death that she's going to get mixed up in that murder right after getting to town. Even if the murder is a cold case that happened so long ago no one remembers."

Amy looked at Zelda and frowned. "Somebody in Bluff Springs remembers. I am almost certain of that," she said quietly, wondering if that someone was a restless haint.

CHAPTER EIGHTEEN

Amy stewed in anger all the way to the cemetery. After all the generosity she had shown Camellia, the return for her effort was a double-crossing B & E. Break and enter. Scare the cat. Steal the goods. And then act like nothing ever happened. She had stood on Camellia's front porch chatting about this and that like neighbors and all the while Camellia was hiding the truth.

What a little thief! What a little actor!

Amy slammed the car door.

To be fair, she hadn't actually told Camellia she had the necklace. She hadn't mentioned the necklace to Camellia at all. There was no lie involved on Camellia's part if she was honest with herself. But that didn't assuage her anger. There was no need to break into her apartment to steal the necklace.

She pushed through the gate at the back of the graveyard and headed toward Camellia's house on Piney Top, her gait fueled by anger. From here it was a short walk on a dusty road, and she was glad her Miata was safe on the pavement and hidden from view. She was after the element of surprise. Camellia wouldn't know what storm was coming. Little thief!

She noticed the car was gone from its place between the hedges as she climbed the front porch steps, careful to avoid the rotten planks. The solid door was closed behind the screen door, which made a whisper-soft squeak as she opened it and rapped on the wood.

No one answered. She didn't hear any heavy Doc Marten footsteps making their way to the door. She didn't hear bare marmalade toes padding over the floor, either. She rapped again harder and waited.

She turned to the worn spot where Camellia's rental car had been parked. Maybe Camellia had left town. Maybe she decided to sell the property and start a new life elsewhere. Maybe she had gotten all she wanted from this old homestead on Piney Top, including a necklace that was a clue to a crime and her 1200 bucks to boot!

"Camellia!" she yelled, giving up on the element of surprise. Still, there was no answer. "Camellia! It's Amy!"

She reached for the doorknob, finding that it turned in her hand. She gave it a gentle push and it opened effortlessly. The dark interior lay before her, beckoning.

Tit for tat. Snoop for snoop.

She swung open the door and stepped inside.

It was dark, but not as dark as it looked from the outside. The windows had been cleaned of their grime, and a soft autumn light was filtering in, dancing with the dust in the slanted beams across the bare plank floor.

As her eyes adjusted, she saw that the interior was anything but gloomy. The furniture was old and mismatched, but it was gleaming with fresh polish. The wallpaper was peeling from the walls, and someone—Camellia, she guessed—had begun pulling the old pattern in long thin trails, leaving patches of yellowed wall behind. A small fireplace anchored one wall, and a pretty vase of purple fall asters brightened the sooty looking mantle.

In the center of the room was a round table. The table skirt that went all the way to the floor was a faded shade of gray, the kind of gray that led her to think at one time it had been purple. Or maybe it had been red. Amy crossed to the table and touched the surface and then the faded skirt.

The Ouija table. Was this the parlor where the ladies met for their spiritual encounters?

There were several odd chairs about the room, and Amy saw immediately that they would be drawn around the table to accommodate the guests when the time came to call the spirits.

The thought gave her a start.

In the corner was a round wood stool about two feet high. The perfect stool for a seamstress to mark the hem of a dress. She didn't dare venture further, but she could see a tiny kitchen off to one side and a bedroom on the other, the furnishings and decor as if taken right out of a 1920s Good Housekeeping magazine. How did it survive the times? It looked like Mable Rose walked out of the door to run an errand, only to never return. Except that now, generations later, a last living decedent stepped into a time warp to polish the furniture and place flowers on the hearth.

Amy heard a shuffle outside and the sound of heavy footsteps approaching. Camellia! She had not left town! She was headed this way!

Darting into the kitchen, she glanced around the room and noticed the door next to the sink. Grandmother Ollie had one just like it in her country kitchen. A door to let in deliveries, toss the dish water to the herbs growing by the stoop and the food scraps to the chickens in the yard. Amy pushed it open and hopped down the stairs. She darted behind a bush and then to the other side of the hedge by the road. Out of breath now, partly because it had been a big hop and a fast run, and partly because of the exhilaration, she hid behind the hedge to catch her breath.

She noticed him then. He looked up to see her scrambling and out of breath. A surveyor with his bright orange jacket and tripod set up a few hundred feet away. She lifted her hand to wave, and he nodded in his helmet. How embarrassing. It was one thing to snoop. It was quite another to get caught.

She waited until her heart stopped pounding and then she made her way back to the front door, her mission still ahead.

This time when she knocked, Camellia answered.

"What now?" Camellia said, her tone sharp. "What are you doing here?"

"You know what I'm doing here," Amy spat. "You broke into my house!"

"You left your door unlocked. Your cat was howling, and I thought he was hurt!"

"You rummaged through my closet!"

"Your cat jumped up on the shelf and knocked all those boxes off!"

"You turned out my jacket pockets!"

"Only one of them! The rest were like that already."

"You stole my necklace!"

Camellia narrowed her eyes. "It's *my* necklace."

Amy stepped back, realizing that she and Camellia were standing nearly nose to nose. "You could have asked for it, you know."

"That's what I was trying to do," Camellia answered. "You weren't home. Your cat was howling, and the door was unlocked."

"So, you helped yourself to a little snoop!" The moment she uttered those words she felt foolish. Wasn't that exactly what she had just done?

"Where is your car?" Amy demanded.

"Where is yours?" Camellia returned.

Amy paused and the humor of the moment struck her. She let out a little snort of a laugh. And then she let loose.

"I don't see what's so funny," Camellia said, fighting a smile.

"What's funny is that you and I are birds of a feather," Amy said. "I might have done the same thing if I were in your shoes."

Camellia looked down at her dusty Doc Martens and then motioned to the bicycle leaning against the porch. "I turned in my rental car for that bike," she said and smiled. "I found it in the basement. I had the tires and chain replaced, but for as old as it is, it's in good shape. It's not so easy to ride on these hills but it's a lot cheaper than a rental car. The guy that fixed it said it's worth some money. It's a collectible antique," Camellia continued. "Maybe even worth a couple grand if I want to sell it. The basket's been chewed through by squirrels or something, but I'm going to find a replacement so I can carry groceries. I forgot how much fun it is to ride a bike."

Amy snickered. "And climb trees, too."

Camellia looked at Amy with a guilty look. "So, you figured out that was me. I didn't realize that branch wouldn't hold me when I stood on it."

"It's a good thing you weren't hurt."

"It's a good thing you weren't standing beneath me."

Amy nodded.

"Is that where you found the necklace?"

Amy nodded again.

"I knew I dropped it. The chain broke."

A broken chain. Something struck her at that moment, like a stirring beneath the surface of a pond. Nothing you could see. But it was there, nonetheless.

Camellia shuffled her boots, kicking at an acorn that had fallen to the porch. "Why do you think it's a clue to a crime?"

Amy didn't answer. She wasn't sure how to answer, not without sharing more detail than she was prepared to give. There was no rhyme or reason to her belief, except for the dream. Her snippet. A snippet like any other snippet, and yet, never the same. How many had she had in her life so far? She'd lost count long before she even started counting.

"You were looking for it that day," Amy said instead. "The day I met Charles the Banjo Man and discovered there are far more secrets in the cemetery than I ever imagined there to be."

Camellia's nod was brief. "I knew you found it when you started talking about those symbols in the pages. I couldn't make sense of them."

"The language is quite sophisticated," Amy said. "Although it's a language anyone could learn, anyone can use, and yet, it remains a secret language. A language for the people others don't even take notice of when they walk by them. It's a language of people they consider lesser-than just because they are homeless and full of wanderlust.

"But, Banjo Man—he saw something else," Amy went on. "He saw art—outsider art, maybe—but art that paints a path most people aren't brave enough to follow."

"You still haven't answered me," Camellia said pointedly. "Why is the necklace a clue to a crime?"

"Mrs. Teddy Duncan," Amy said slowly, pronouncing the name precisely. "You saw it. The lettering was all fancy curlicues as if she was trying it on for size. As if she were practicing for when a romantic dream came true."

"I don't get the connection," Camellia said. "Mable Rose never married and as far as we know. I mean, I've seen pictures, and she was…" Camellia paused, "well, she was kind of plain."

"They didn't wear makeup in the country," Amy said, feeling like she had to defend plain women everywhere. "And that doesn't mean she wasn't marriage material, even so."

"Hey, I didn't mean anything by that," Camellia defended. "I just meant that Mable Rose didn't marry, and she never had children."

Amy looked Camellia in the eye. "And you know that for a fact?"

Camellia's eyes widened. "Yes. No. I don't know. That's what they said about her in my family. Not that she came up in conversation very much."

Amy eyed Camellia. "I thought the necklace belonged to Catherine Duncan. Or rather Mrs. Winslow T. Duncan."

"You mean the one your friend played in the Silent City?"

Amy realized Camellia had been listening to their speeches while perched in her tree. Whether she was trying to get out of paying twenty bucks for a ticket or just preferred a bird's-eye view didn't really matter.

Amy nodded and went on. "Her husband was shot after a poker game and the killer was never found. Whoever killed him took the money and ran. Rumors said it was a man called Hobo Joe. But I have my doubts about that."

"Wow," Camellia said quietly.

"Since Catherine Duncan went on to do great things for Bluff Springs after her husband's demise, we thought maybe she was the one who shot him. He was a rake. He gambled. He probably cheated at cards. He probably cheated on her as well."

Camellia shuffled in her Doc Martens.

"We've encountered black widow societies in the past," Amy added. "Well, at least we *thought* we were encountering black widow societies," she amended. "Somehow we seem to run into women who would be better off without their crappy husbands."

"That still doesn't answer my question."

"I'm getting to that," Amy said, her impatience showing. "It's not an easy question to answer."

Camellia held up her hands in surrender and then zipped her lips in a pantomime.

"Six months after Catherine's husband was murdered, Frank Calhoun had a heart attack in his sleep. His wife, Maude, became the publisher of the Bluff Springs Weekly Times. And then, not quite a year after that, Oscar St. Claire died of an accidental overdose. He was an addict," Amy added, "or so we think, but the thread we've picked up is that all three of these widows went on to do big things in Bluff Springs once their husbands were gone. Coincidence? We're not sure. There was a fourth death in 1926. But the Mrs. Reverend Cecil Hayes doesn't really fit our pattern, so we've concluded that he was just the odd duck out."

"We?" Camellia ventured.

"Zelda, Rian and Genna. You've met Zelda. You'll meet the other two tomorrow."

"Tomorrow?"

"For Ouija. I'm calling a Ouija session. I'd like to use your Ouija parlor table," Amy said, motioning to the interior of the house. "But we don't want to invite ourselves to your home."

Camellia glanced nervously at the interior of the house and then narrowed her eyes. "How do you know I have a table?"

"About that," Amy said. "I apologize. I went looking for you to make sure you were okay when you didn't answer the door. Kind of like when you went looking for *me* in my apartment when *I* didn't answer the door." Amy smiled briefly.

"You went inside my house?"

"It looks cozy," Amy offered as an answer. "The house has good bones. All it needs is a few grand and a carpenter."

Camellia exhaled and Amy could tell she wasn't sure which infringement to respond to first. Amy's snooping or her scrutiny. "I see you're already marking your property lines." Amy motioned toward the man in the orange jacket.

"What? That's not me. That's the neighbor. He wants to make sure I'm not taking up any of his space."

"Oh," Amy said and shifted her feet.

"I'm still confused," Camellia said, after a brief silence had come between them. "What does any of this have to do with that necklace?"

"That's what we are going to find out," Amy said. The idea had just concreted itself into her thoughts at that very moment. "We are going to ask the Ouija board that question. What do four women have to do with the necklace? And what does the necklace have to do with the crime?"

CHAPTER NINETEEN

She glanced at her watch and realized her friends would arrive soon. The sky was already dark. Night came early in autumn.

She lit the candles she placed around the room and then turned off the lights. Too dark. Too creepy. She turned on the overhead lights that lit Tiddlywinks. Too bright. Too glaring. She turned off the lights and turned on the lamp on the counter—an old piece of furniture from a hotel lobby Zelda had found at an auction and insisted Amy buy. As usual, Zelda was right. It was the perfect anchor piece for Tiddlywinks.

The lamp made the atmosphere better, but it was still too flickeringly creepy. She dragged a floor lamp from the escape room and plugged it into the corner. Much better. Maybe perfect.

She watched as the candle flames danced and the colorful images glowed on the outside of the tall glass jars. These prayer candles, the *veladoras* of Mexico, were only two bucks each at the local *mercado*. She was glad she thought to buy them. They made the room feel less lonely. They made her feel less vulnerable.

She walked about the room where she spent nearly every day and knew every inch, but noticed how the candles made it look different. Spidery shadows danced on the old tin ceilings and the shelves of familiar games all but disappeared in the dark. She passed by the candle of *Saint Clare of Assisi* who brought clarity and insight. The mysterious *Santa Metro* offered protection against adversaries and those seeking justice. The *Virgin of Guadalupe* brought maternal protection and unconditional love. And last but not least, the *Sacred Heart*. Each table held a group of three candles, and while she didn't know all the images or their meaning, they were all welcome. And somehow, she knew they all needed to be present.

She felt a trickle of sweat drip beneath her bra, and she realized she was more anxious than she thought. She touched the Celtic knot at her throat.

What was she doing? What madness was this?

She remembered Rian's comment when she'd bought the Ouija boards, first met Camellia, and inadvertently met Mable Rose. No one thought twice about sharks until the movie *Jaws*. No one was afraid of birds—or phone booths, for that matter— until Alfred Hitchcock. And no one had considered Ouija anything but a parlor game until the movie… she couldn't finish the thought. These boards had been found in an attic, too, and the thought made her stomach flutter.

She swore off séances as a teenager when an old palm reader had scared her silly. She had never played with the Ouija board. She had enough spooky chatter in her head as it was. She could have taken Zelda's approach and just say no. No arm twisting, no guilting, no bribing had moved Zelda an inch. Zelda had said *no*. Just *no*.

But here she stood, open to inviting the invisible. Ready to call spirits in from the beyond. Yes, this was madness. Yes, she knew it was something she had to do. She closed her eyes and pictured the dream. Alfred Hitchcock's table was set for four. Four queens. She heard him again in her memory: *"You can never believe precisely what the deceased will tell you. Especially on one of these popular talking board contraptions. They are often inclined to spell out the most harrowing tales of deception and murder."*

These talking board contraptions. Was it merely coincidence or was there really a tale of deception to solve?

She draped the table in a purple pashmina scarf selected from her closet for the color and set the Ouija board in the center. She chose one of the smaller tables so the four of them could easily reach the center and the planchette. Their fingertips would rest lightly on the wood surface as they awaited a message from the beyond.

She placed a candle in a jar at each of the places. Black for protection. White to attract good energy. Blue opened the door of communication. And purple enhanced psychic powers. She exhaled deeply and the candles flickered beneath her breath.

Amy watched as a car pulled up to the curb outside Tiddlywinks. She recognized Genna's BMW, although the nearby streetlamp made it look more silver than blue, and when Genna cut the engine and the headlights went out, it nearly disappeared into the dark.

In moments, the bell over the door jangled with familiarity.

"What a perfectly stunning séance atmosphere," Genna said in greeting. "What restless spirit could possibly resist this charm?"

Amy handed her a goblet of wine, noticing that Genna was wearing her witches of Eastwick outfit from Halloween. The silver moons and stars on the dress flickered in the candlelight as she moved.

"This is not a costume party," Amy scolded playfully, but she had to admit the shimmer effect was enchanting.

"Your invitation didn't say what attire was required. If you wanted us to dress a certain way, you should have said so. I've never been to a Ouija séance."

"Me either," Amy agreed. "I read up on it, though. I think I'm ready. As ready as I'll ever be."

"Is that sage I smell?"

Amy nodded. "Just a precaution."

The door jangled again and Rian sauntered in.

"Well, this is appropriately creepy," she said as she accepted a glass of wine. "Mother Superior would not approve." Rian grinned. "All the more reason to be here."

Amy laughed and the sound echoed in the room. Tiddlywinks was used to laughter and chatter and the sounds of people exploring a good time. The empty dark space was a totally different vibe, and Amy could tell they all felt it. They hadn't been in the dark at Tiddlywinks since the demise of the wine merchant. The streets had been empty that night, too. They had taken comfort in the dark after the harsh reality of how the evening ended. The memory gave her a chill and she shivered and reached for a glass of wine.

"I thought you said there would be four of us," Genna said.

"I invited Camellia deRossier," Amy responded. "I wanted to do this at her house, at Mable Rose's Ouija table, but I couldn't persuade her. She finally agreed to join us here, although it took some arm twisting. I hope she'll show up."

"I gather no amount of arm twisting worked on Zelda," Genna added.

Amy shook her head. "Her heels were dug in like a mule."

"So, who is this Camellia deRossier?" Rian asked. "What do you know about her?"

"Not much," Amy answered. "Except that she inherited an old house that belonged to a relative who lived in Bluff Springs a hundred years ago. The necklace I found belonged to her. Camellia dropped it in the graveyard when the chain broke."

"She's the one who broke into your apartment?" Rian looked surprised.

"She claims the door was open and Victor was howling. She thought he was hurt and needed rescuing."

"A likely story," Rian countered.

"You were right all along," Amy replied. "The cat did knock off the boxes in the closet and my jacket pockets were turned out because of that superstition about the fairies. I had forgotten I turned them out when we got home from Ireland. I have picked up too many pennies in my lifetime to ignore that warning."

Rian laughed. "I won't say I told you so, but I did point out the lock wasn't broken."

Amy nodded. "And Banjo Man had an alibi because he fell and broke his ankle. Or he broke something. That was never made clear by my source."

"Your sources are always suspect," Genna claimed. "Weird dreams and raccoons and fuzzy mushrooms. You're not exactly getting your facts from the most reliable sources."

Amy didn't have a witty comeback. What Genna said was true. And she wasn't all that certain that Mr. Hitchcock was any more reliable than the others. He was, after all, one of the masters of deception.

"I don't think she's coming," Rian said.

"Just the three of us, then?" Genna asked. "Are you ready to summon the spirits and ask them who killed Winslow Duncan?"

Amy frowned. "I wanted there to be four of us, but three will have to do."

They put down their empty glasses and Amy motioned them to the table at the back of the room. The floor lamp in the corner lit the Ouija board like a spotlight center stage.

They settled into the chairs at the table and Amy was acutely aware of the empty space. She couldn't shed her disappointment. Camellia was part of this puzzle of a mystery she was trying to solve. She knew that as sure as she knew this Ouija board stuff was folly. Amy touched the peridot necklace at her throat and a familiar warmth rushed over her.

"Okay, what do we do now?" Genna asked.

"We're going to put two fingers on the planchette," Amy instructed. "Like this." She placed her index and middle fingers lightly on the wooden planchette. "I will ask a question and then the planchette will move around the board to answer." She looked at Genna and then at Rian. "No cheating. Either one of you. The planchette moves on its own or not at all. Got it?"

"Got it," Genna said. Even with that, Amy was still doubtful that could be possible.

Rian rolled up the sleeves of her flannel shirt. "What are you going to ask?"

"You're supposed to start with something easy," Amy answered. "Something a spirit can answer yes or no. If they have something more to say, then I guess they'll spell it out."

Rian snorted. "I can't believe I agreed to this nonsense. I feel like a school kid hiding from the nuns."

Amy placed two fingers on the planchette and felt the smooth surface beneath her fingers. "Are you ready?"

They nodded and placed their fingers beside Amy's.

"We are here to call upon the spirit world," Amy said softly, her eyes glistening in the light of the candles. "We wish to talk to the spirits of Bluff Springs who lived before us. We welcome the silent voices of those who wish to speak. We open this channel to positive energy and only positive…"

Genna's phone rang, and they all jumped.

"Turn it off!" Amy commanded. She had already turned her phone off and left it at the counter. "Rian?"

Rian shrugged. "Left mine at home. It's not like I have to be connected 24/7." She eyed Genna with mock disdain. "Not like some people I know."

Genna shut down her phone without saying another word.

Amy's heart was racing, and she took a deep breath, exhaling slowly. "Okay. Seriously now."

Genna and Rian nodded.

"We wish to talk to the spirits of Bluff Springs who lived before us," Amy began again. "We welcome the silent voices of those who wish to speak. We open this channel to positive energy and only positive energy. Is there anyone who wishes to speak?"

They waited in silence. The planchette stayed still beneath their fingers. "Are there any spirits who wish to come forward?" Amy urged. The silence continued and Genna let out a deep sigh.

"No one's home," Rian whispered. "The lights are out, and the dead are sleeping."

"Sshh," Amy warned. "They won't respond if you're going to be rude."

The planchette began to slide under their fingers. Amy held her breath, using all her courage not to pull her fingers from the wood to make it stop.

WT

WT? Winslow T? Her heart skipped a beat. Had they reached the very victim of the murder itself?

WA

WTWA? What? Amy glanced at Genna, who was staring at the planchette under her fingertips. Rian's eyes were closed.

IT

It?

The planchette moved again.

W

A

I

T

Wait? Wait for what?

The planchette stilled beneath their fingertips.

Amy cleared her throat and whispered. "Is there someone here who wishes to speak?"

The planchette jerked.

YES

"Will you answer our questions?" Amy whispered.

YES

The planchette moved again slowly.

W

A

I

T

Wait. It was becoming clear that whatever was moving the planchette beneath their fingers wanted them to wait. But wait for what? She glanced at Rian and then at Genna. Both women shrugged.

"I don't know what to do," Amy whispered. "Do you think there's something wrong with this talking board? Should we try another one?"

The planchette moved again.

NO

Rian and Genna exhaled loudly at the same time. "Holy Moly and Mary," Rian muttered. "I'm not moving that thing. Are you moving it, Genna?"

Genna shook her head, her eyes wide, her braid haloed in the light from the lamp.

The door jangled and Amy jumped.

"Yikes!" Genna yelped and jerked her fingers away.

Amy turned to face Camellia deRossier who stood in the shadows just inside the door. Her silver hair looked ghostly in the flickering lights.

"Camellia!" Amy said and rose from the table. "You're here!"

"I'm here," Camellia said quietly. "I almost didn't come, but some feeling kept nudging me out the door. And before I knew it, here I am."

Amy beckoned for Camellia to join them.

Wait. The Ouija had been waiting for Camellia.

CHAPTER TWENTY

No wonder Aunt Mable Rose had so many Ouija boards. Eight fingers was a lot to fit on one planchette. Amy could imagine her using every surface in her small parlor when she held their Spiritualism meetings. More than three sets of fingers on the planchette was too many and too tempting. Someone could find it irresistible to influence the planchette with a gentle shove.

Genna offered to take notes and grabbed a score pad and pen from the basket on the next table over.

"Chicken," Rian quipped.

"Bawk, bawk," Genna answered.

Amy eyed Genna's pad of paper and hoped that Patience Worth wasn't looking to come through and channel another novel. In her research on the going price of old Ouija boards, she had come across the story of a woman who lived but a few hours north in St. Louis in the 1920s. She published several books she claimed were channeled via Ouija planchette from the long-dead Patience. Psychologists of the day had a lot to say about that. And none of it was good.

Amy returned her attention to the mysterious oracle of the Ouija and once again invited the good spirits to come forward. She had barely uttered the words before the planchette began to move. Camellia drew in her breath sharply.

Genna scribbled the words as they formed slowly one letter at a time. "You are the one," Genna read.

Amy frowned and she and Rian exchanged looks. She remembered those words. They had been haunting her for days. Hitchcock said the same thing.

"You are the one. The one to tell. If you were bold enough to ask."

She was being bold. She was outside her comfort zone on every level. And so were her friends. She glanced briefly at Camellia, whose eyes were wide and staring at the planchette under her fingers.

"Who killed Winslow Duncan?" Amy asked, her verve reengaged.

"Heart," Genna read as the word spelled out slowly.

"He was shot in the chest," Amy said. "That's what the newspaper claimed."

"Heart," Genna repeated as their fingers moved again across the board. "Less," Genna added and the planchette paused. "Heartless," she murmured. "It's saying heartless!"

"Heartless? He was heartless? The killer was heartless? But who killed him?" Amy asked urgently, hoping the momentum would continue and they would have all the answers they needed.

The planchette was still and Amy heaved a sigh. "Are you still there?" There was no movement beneath their fingers and then finally…

YES

"Who killed him?" Amy repeated. "If you know you must tell us!"

The planchette jerked across the board.

LOVE

They didn't need Genna's interpretation to read that.

Camellia inhaled sharply. "Love," she breathed and the candle at her elbow flickered.

"Who are you?" Amy asked.

There was no answer.

"Are you Winslow?"

The planchette lay still.

"Are you Hobo Joe?"

There was no answer.

"Are you his killer?" Amy whispered.

The planchette moved again quickly under their fingers and Amy held her breath. Was this really a spirit talking to them, or were they somehow moving the planchette without knowing it? Was it going to spell out a name to bring justice to a cold murder? Was she ready to believe the mysterious talking board really could talk?

"You are the one," Genna said finally when the piece came to rest.

Rian had been silent during the scurry of activity. She looked at Camellia now, her brown eyes even darker in the candlelight. "You are the one," she said quietly. "It's you. Not Amy. It's you."

Camellia startled, but she kept her fingers on the planchette. "What do you mean, it's me? What does that mean? I haven't done anything! I've been here less than a month! I don't know anything about Aunt Mable Rose and her mad obsessions!" Camellia glanced at Amy. "She had so many Ouija boards. Wouldn't you call that an obsession?"

A bell rung in the silence.

A male voice said, "Good evening."

Amy shrieked and they all jumped in their seats. The overhead lights flicked on, and the room filled with harsh light.

"Ben!" Rian called. "What are you doing here?"

"I was driving by on my way to your house when I saw the flickering lights," Ben answered. "I thought the place was on fire! I could ask you the same thing. What are you doing? Are you having a séance? Is that what's going on here?"

Amy glanced at Rian and thought her cheeks looked flushed. From embarrassment? Probably. This was pretty far outside of Rian's routine and *mea culpa*.

"I forgot," Rian said.

Ben looked wounded. "You forgot we made a date for tonight?"

"Wait," Camellia said as Amy started to rise from the table.

Rian had left the table already and was headed out the door with Ben. Amy felt a bit shaken by the turn of events. Ben's choice of words were still ringing in her ears.

Good evening.

"Wait for what?" Genna asked.

"We have to say goodbye." Camellia pointed to the Ouija board now illuminated by the overhead lights. "If we don't, the channel will stay open, and we don't want that to happen."

Amy looked at Camellia. "So, you do know more about the mysterious Ouija than you said." Amy was beginning to realize there was more to Camellia than she let on.

"I read it somewhere," Camellia said. "There are twenty-one rules. Saying goodbye is one of them. The consequences can be disastrous."

Amy nodded and then she and Camellia put their fingers back on the planchette. "Do we move it to that spot or wait for the planchette to move?"

"I don't know." Camellia shrugged. "I hope it's not too late. We've already broken the circle."

"Well," Amy said, lightly pulling the planchette to the bottom of the board with her fingertips. "This will have to do."

AU REVOIR

CHAPTER TWENTY-ONE

Victor complained about her tossing and turning by jumping off the bed in a noisy pout. He wasn't his usual cat-confident self these past few days, and she was sure Camellia deRossier's intrusion into his conclave played a part. She'd been leaving him home instead of bringing him to Tiddlywinks, just to be on the safe side—ghouls and goblins and whatnot—and he looked a little bored with the windowsill. And maybe a little chunkier if that was possible. He made a point of punishing her for uprooting him from his warm spot on the bed by crunching as loudly as any cat could crunch. She could hear him all the way from the kitchen.

She tossed in her lavender sheets, trying to block out a busy mind and a noisy cat. She finally gave up. She showered and dressed, had three cups of espresso, and a big bowl of yogurt. She shared her yogurt with the cat, hoping to win favor. His licked her spoon and with his tail straight in the air, went back to bed.

Amy backed her Miata from her parking space. It was a few minutes of eight. Plenty of time to run errands before opening the shop.

It was clear Camellia deRossier was more complex than Amy realized. So often the case when an older woman beheld a younger one. It was easy to fall into the stereotypes. An older woman might be considered out of touch with the trends. Often seen as irrelevant. A younger woman could be seen as carefree and incautious and hasty in her decisions.

There was some truth in all of that. Older women did have *a been there done that* point of view. They had more experience with life's challenges. Some women were jaded by that. Others were empowered. Younger women were still looking out at the world with fresh eyes and an optimism that no matter what they imagined for their lives, they could bring it into being simply by wanting it. There was no clear path or equation for how you handled bad marriages and failed dreams. There was no manual for surviving the school of hard knocks, the winner's circle, or the nerd club.

At fifty she saw herself in the middle of that spectrum. Neither old nor young. Neither irrelevant nor optimistic. Fannie Flagg's book, *Fried Green Tomatoes at the Whistle Stop Cafe* came to mind, and how Evelyn lamented that she was too old to be young and too young to be old. How true that seemed. And how much difference a decade on either side made.

How much difference an era made.

The heroes of Fannie Flagg's story, the Threadgoods, lived in the 1920s, the same era of their roles in the *Tales from the Silent City*. Evelyn lived in the 1980s. Amy and her friends—Zelda and Rian and Genna—had been there done that, too, and were now living well into the new millennium. All these ideals about who people were and who they should be were still as cumbersome as ever.

The misconceptions that old was bad and young was good seemed unfortunate because both ages could benefit from a deeper connection. She felt that way about Camellia. She felt invested in Camellia. Not just because of their exchange of goods and money, but because she felt a magnetic pull toward the younger woman looking for a new start. She wanted her to succeed. She wanted her to thrive. She wanted her to reach for her dreams and achieve them. Whatever they happened to be.

She really felt that fostering a friendship with Camellia would be meaningful. That was especially true if Camellia was going to take on that old house and become a member of the community.

All that played into the realization that Camellia had hidden certain facts. She knew Amy had the necklace. She knew more about Ouija than she claimed to know. And she had connected with the comments the spirits of the planchette had spelled out. Or maybe it was their collective unconscious that spelled it out. She was still on the fence about whether spirits really did tell tales. Either way, she remembered Camellia's reaction. She had been startled, yes, but she had also looked awed with surprise. As if she was expecting the news. Whoever killed Winslow was heartless. And love the reason he was dead.

If Camellia had hidden all those facts, what else was she hiding?

She shifted gears and realized she had driven off course from her errands. A senior moment, Zelda would call it, even though neither one of them were seniors. *Yet.*

She planned to hit the Post Office and mail a game a collector had bought from her new Tiddlywinks website. Instead, she found herself in the lot next to the town lawyer on the opposite side of town. No time like the present. She parked and went inside.

"Hello, Amy," he said. "Do we have an appointment today? I didn't realize that. I can't seem to keep track of my days without my right hand. She's on a river cruise in Europe and won't be back for another week."

Amy shook his hand and sat where he indicated.

"Did we have an appointment today?" he asked again.

"I just need some information," she said, skirting the obvious answer. "I've met Camellia deRossier and I was hoping to get references on her behalf." That seemed as wide-swooping as possible. He could fill in any gaps he wanted. She would take any information he offered.

"Who did you say?"

"Camellia deRossier," she repeated and then spelled the surname she had written on the check. "She inherited a house out on Piney Top. Number seven? You handled the estate, didn't you?"

"Oh, right, deRossier," he said. "Mable Rose deRossier's property. The one we spent forever and a day tracking down the heirs. But I don't know a Camellia," he said. "Could you mean Rose Compton? Are you looking to hire her at your shop?"

Amy paused briefly. "Yes," she lied.

"She seems responsible enough," he said. "But, of course, I can't speak to her character. I don't know her. Never met her. We transacted all our business by Federal Express."

"Do you know where she came from? Perhaps I could get references from her last employer."

He eyed Amy with caution. "I couldn't give an address without her permission," he said. "But then, you could get that information directly from her now, couldn't you?"

Amy nodded. That would defeat the purpose of snooping, but she couldn't share that here. Why would Rose Compton go about town as Camellia deRossier? What was she hiding?

The phone on his desk rang and he looked flustered as it continued its shrill ring, and no one answered. "Yes?" he asked finally as he picked up the receiver. Clearly, he was not used to this end of the protocol. He glanced at her with an apologetic grimace. Her cue to move on. She mouthed, "thank you," and slipped out the door.

Were Rose Compton and Camellia deRossier the same person? If so, why the name change? Mable Rose deRossier was a woman who didn't marry and didn't have children, according to Camellia. Rose. Whatever her name was. Had she taken the family namesake as part of her new start in Bluff Springs? Or was there something more to it than that?

Amy backed her Miata onto the road. Was Rose Camellia Compton deRossier really the great great great niece inheriting the estate after all these years? Or was her relationship more direct than she let on? Maybe Zelda was on the right track about a hidden pregnancy. If so, Mable Rose could be more than aunt. And Camellia deRossier could be more than niece.

Her heart fluttered with excitement. So many questions!

Amy dialed Genna but her voicemail answered.

"How would I find a birth certificate from the 1920s?" She asked into the phone without any prep or introduction. "Where would I go to look?" She started to hang up. "This is Amy," she added and then felt stupid. Of course, Genna would know her voice. Just as Genna would know where to find the information she was looking for.

She passed the clothing store that Zelda would pester until they carried her new 1920s collection when it was ready. And then the thought occurred that she could go to the mouth of the horse himself. Maybe he could shed some light on a dressmaker in the 1920s.

A bell much like the one over the door of Tiddlywinks announced her presence and a bent little man with specs on the end of his nose rose from behind his sewing machine. They exchanged greetings.

"I'm Zelda Carlisle's friend," Amy offered. "You made our costumes for the fundraiser."

He nodded. "An appreciative customer, our Zelda," he said kindly, and Amy knew he meant profitable.

"She has such wonderful ideas. She envisions an entire vintage twenties inspired line for our over-forty curves. Something as stylish as the pencil thin boyish look of the day but more flattering for our fuller figures." He patted his small paunch. "It is such an ambitious goal, I admit, but I am truly looking forward to the design challenge."

She hadn't realized how serious Zelda was about this new line of clothing. Zelda very well might bring the roaring 1920s fashion forward into the raging 2020s. If not single-handedly, as she claimed, at least with the help of Vito the tailor using her abundant cash flow.

"What is it I can do for you today?" he asked, peering over the top of his glasses.

"I am looking for information on dressmaking," Amy offered.

"Oh? What kind of information do you need?"

"I'm not sure," Amy said and frowned. The idea had seemed so much more definitive in her mind. "How would one become a First-Class Dressmaker back in the 1920s?"

He scratched his thin beard and pushed the glasses onto the top of his head. "First-Class, eh? Well, one could apprentice under a tailor, I suppose. Or work as a seamstress in a factory. But I doubt either would give you cause to call yourself First-Class. No, I should think you would need a certificate from the Woman's Institute of Domestic Arts and Sciences."

"An institute," Amy repeated with reflection. "Here in Bluff Springs?"

"Oh no, it was based in Pennsylvania. It was a correspondence program. A mail-order school. Founded by Mary Brooks Picken. Anybody who's anybody in fashion knows of Picken's contribution to the industry."

Amy noticed his enthusiasm for the topic as his volume got louder. "Pickens was the veritable authority on fashion. She wrote nearly a hundred books on dressmaking, design, and needlework. Oh, and so much more. Her institute graduated three hundred thousand women at its peak in the 1920s. Quite the trend for that time period—women going to school to learn a trade, that is. My grandmother worked in a factory, and she taught me everything I know. Well, that and four years of costume design off-Broadway. Off-off Broadway, mind you." He tilted his head and smiled at his admission.

"It really is timely that you should ask," he added. "Because I have only just purchased a collection of Pickens *Fashion Service* magazines. Students enrolled in the dressmaking program were sent magazines twice a year. I acquired these just the other day." He clasped his hands with a light clap. "They are absolutely wonderful. Priceless. A treasure to an old fool like me."

"Let me guess," Amy said. "Camellia deRossier sold them to you."

His eyebrows raised. "Why yes! You know her, then?"

Amy nodded. Not that she knew *much* about her. That was becoming obvious.

"I also acquired a lovely tin of buttons," he went on. "I won't ask if you want to see them." He looked at her with hopeful eyes. "I know not everyone gets as excited about old buttons as an old tailor." He smiled apologetically.

"She offered me a tin of beautiful jade buttons, too," he added, "but I told her that while I would love to have them, they might be more valuable than either of us realize. I couldn't take advantage of her, so I offered to hunt down a more knowledgeable source to value them. I do hope she will give me first dibs and I hope I can afford them."

"Did she leave her phone number?"

He scratched his beard once again. "No, I don't believe we exchanged numbers. She said she would check back with me. She asked if she could bring a coat by for me to look over and make some repairs. She was wondering if it was real fur and wanted to know if I could tell. She wanted to know if it would be troublesome to wear it. I told her old furs were back in vogue. Especially when refashioned into cuffs and collars. She seemed rather pleased to hear that. It's going to be a cold winter," he added. "The persimmons are full of spoons. That means snow, you know. A coat like that will be worth its weight in comfort in the cold."

Amy glanced around his shop, noticing the dress forms and mannequins in various stages of dress. Some of them looked ancient and all of them looked well used and well loved.

"How long have you lived here, Vito?"

"Long enough to know winters are cold and spring is wet," he answered rhythmically and smiled. "Something my grandmother used to say. Why do you ask?"

"I was wondering if your grandmother lived here in the 1920s."

"Here? In Bluff Springs? Oh, no. She was a North Carolina mountain girl through and through. I doubt if she ever stepped foot outside the state her entire life. Probably never even made it to the ocean. Hard to imagine that. Living so close to the sea and never diving in."

Somehow Amy couldn't picture Vito diving into the ocean, either. She thanked him for his time and the great work on their costumes and left his shop remembering that Camellia mentioned finding a tin. Too bad. She was thinking it would be an old saltine tin can full of money not buttons, but buttons made more sense for a dressmaker in the Ozarks.

She glanced at the clock on the Miata's dash. It was time to head to Tiddlywinks and she was almost late to open. She skipped the Post Office and decided to ship the game tomorrow. She would stop by her insurance agent then, too, and ask about purchasing life insurance. She didn't need insurance, but Banjo Man had talked about life insurance salesmen and the gravestones of the Woodmen of the World. If her agent didn't know anything about how policies worked back then, she might at least know who to ask.

She was headed to work when she passed the local antique shop where two men were carrying a heavy piece of furniture. She made a U-turn and pulled in the parking lot. What would another half hour delay matter at Tiddlywinks on a Wednesday?

She was no stranger at this particular antique store. She often prowled the shelves looking for vintage games still priced low enough to sell. Even if they didn't leave room for a great mark up, the games added inventory to Tiddlywinks. And usually, the owner was willing to make a deal to move an item off the shelf. Sometimes even a ten percent markdown made it worth her while.

"Good to see you, Amy," the woman called over her shoulder as she directed the incoming furniture. "Lots of good browsing today."

Amy acknowledged the owner with a wave, then perused a couple of aisles not too far from the checkout counter. She grabbed her opportunity when it came.

"You didn't you find anything special today?" the woman asked warmly as Amy approached the counter.

"You know me, I would buy everything if I could," she answered, knowing that wasn't exactly true. It drew a warm, appreciative smile and that's what she was after.

"Actually, I was wondering if you recently bought anything from Camellia deRossier. She's inherited her great aunt's place on Piney Top."

"Oh, yes," she said, as if delighted by the question. "I bought several items as a matter of fact. Something you might be interested in?"

"Could be," Amy answered. "Depending on…" She let it hang.

"Let's see." The woman put on a pair of readers and pulled a heavy leather-bound ledger from the shelf below the counter. "Some clothes," she said scanning the page with a fingertip. "Vintage stuff that sells surprisingly well these days."

Amy shook her head.

"No? Well, let's see—two boxes of glassware. Nothing extremely exciting as far as glass goes, but worth the purchase. She wasn't willing to consign any of it, but I agreed to her price. A nice young lady. Said she didn't know if she was staying in town long." She smiled and glanced back at the book. "Oh, and a writing desk. A wonderful Ozark-made desk."

"Hmm," Amy said. "Nothing that speaks to me today."

"You're always welcome to stop in for a look. I suggested that to the young lady, too. She asked if I had any old photos of people who lived here in the past. That's exactly what booth forty-nine collects, so I sent her down that aisle. She didn't buy anything, but she spent quite a while back there looking."

"Did she say who she was looking for?"

The woman shook her head.

Amy frowned. Of course not. Why would she?

"Do you know if there's any Mayor Duncan memorabilia in any of the booths?"

The woman cocked her head. "Memorabilia?"

"Well, you know, scrapbooks and school yearbooks and stuff like that."

"Mayor Duncan? Oh gosh, I passed all of that on to the museum some years ago. It was a trunk full of clothing, mostly, and I knew it would be important to our museum. Oh yes, that was a long while ago now. Years."

"Do you remember her scrapbook?"

She nodded. "Oh, yes. And cards and letters. It was such a tender keepsake of memories, I recall thinking at the time."

"You looked through it."

"Well, of course, I did. That's how I knew it needed to go to the museum. The trunk was full of Bluff Springs photos and souvenirs and keepsakes. A slice of history in Catherine Duncan's private life. History that belonged in the museum."

"And the clothes? Were they hers?"

"No, I seem to remember the trunk was mostly men's clothes. Suit coats and hats. Although there were dozens of embroidered lace handkerchiefs. I think she must have had a fondness for violets. I gave all of it to the museum."

Amy felt her hopes slip. That trunk could still be sitting there, piled on the bottom in the upstairs room with all the other old suitcases and trunks. If she did get permission to plunder through them, it could take her months to go through each one. And for what? What was she looking for? She didn't even have a clue. Something, anything that made her feel closer to Catherine Duncan—wife, widow, mayor. The old woman's comment came to mind. *'If you don't know what you want, you'll never find it.'* Well, she wasn't going to find it, then. Unless she could talk the museum into letting her see Catherine Duncan's scrapbook. What reason did she have? Alfred sent me?

She started toward the door when the woman spoke again. "Wait, the young lady didn't leave her phone number, and I don't know how to reach her. Do you?"

Amy nodded.

"Oh good. When you see her, give her this, will you?" She reached into the cash register and pulled out a piece of paper. "I found it wedged in the back of a drawer in the writing desk. All those old pieces have secret drawers if you know where to look.

"It's still sealed," she added. "It looks as if it could be something important. It's always very exciting when you find something hidden away."

Amy accepted the paper. It was old and a little crumpled on the edges where it was stuck in the drawer and was tugged free. The wax seal was dark and crusty, but there was no way to know what was written inside. She fingered the paper. No. Just no, she told herself. There was no way to read what was written without breaking the seal.

CHAPTER TWENTY-TWO

She managed her morning chores at Tiddlywinks without a second thought. Victor was still camping out in the apartment instead of his usual spot on the armchair in the window at Tiddlywinks. She missed him being in the shop. He could be great company. He could also disappear altogether only to show up at closing time. He had uncanny timing for that hour, but Amy guessed it had more to do with his supper than anything else.

Repeat visitors had gotten used to seeing Victor in the window. If they were lucky, they were afforded a brief petting. He wasn't unfriendly, but like most spoiled cats, he didn't need their admiration as much as they needed his. She decided his bad behavior this morning warranted another day left at home.

She thought about the morning's mission and wondered where they fit in Alfred Hitchcock's snippet. Camellia was a newcomer on the scene, so she couldn't offer any insight to the crime. But Camellia did have insight into something because she was parading around town as one person when she really was another.

Rose Compton. Camellia deRossier. Had she taken the family moniker to fit into Bluff Springs history? Maybe the family was fond of flower names. Rose. Camellia. Perhaps there was a Daisy in there somewhere, too.

It was obvious that Camellia was cleaning out the old homestead and purging items in the community for cash. No doubt she was keeping some of the items for herself. The fur coat Victor mentioned was a possibility and she had noticed the corset looking piece Camellia wore over the top of her shirt the other night at the Ouija gathering. That night she carried an old, beaded evening bag instead of her marmalade sling. If she wasn't mistaken, Camellia had traded her Doc Martens for a pair of well-worn women's calf-high boots with lace up eyelets and pointed toes. If Zelda had seen her, she would have called it a good look. It was certainly a mashup of fashion.

But why was Camellia looking for old photos? Who or what was she looking for? And what was in the letter?

Amy couldn't shake the feeling that settled over her now. It wasn't dread. She knew that feeling well enough. Dread is what settled over her after nearly every snippet, like a cold wet blanket weighing her down. Dread was knowing something bad was going to happen but not knowing when or where or to whom. So, what was this feeling?

The remnants of their Ouija gathering were cleared away before she left Tiddlywinks last night, but now she took time to return the floor lamp to the escape room and put away the washed glasses. The box o'wine had finally run out and she tossed it in the garbage in the kitchen, which was more of a closet with an Ikea cabinet and a dorm fridge. She glanced at the stack of Ouija boards she bought from Camellia. What was she waiting for? Why hadn't she cleaned them and put them on the shelf for her buyers to see? What was keeping her from that simple task?

You are the one to ask.

"It's you. Not Amy. It's you," Rian had said as the planchette moved across the board. Rian had been looking at Camellia.

That was it! That was the feeling. Alfred Hitchcock had led her astray. Things had seemed one way and were deceptively another. He suggested she was the missing piece of the puzzle. The one to solve the crime.

She was not the one.

It was Camellia. And Camellia knew more than she was sharing.

Amy pulled the boards from the shelf and carried them to the counter. Today she would work on getting the games on the shelves. Today, when she delivered the letter to Camellia, she would just come right out and ask. Who are you really?

She was no closer to solving the murder of Winslow T. Duncan than the town constable was back in the day. Towns the size of Bluff Springs didn't have detectives at that time, and while they had staff now, it wasn't something she could take to them with the wild idea that Sir Alfred had told her so. He might carry some weight, but not *that* much.

The police would have nothing to go on anyway. Crime scene collection was not a procedural thing in the 1920s. Forensics was just beginning its shaky foothold. Few were equipped or trained to investigate; a reality she could certainly identify with. Most old crimes were solved on a hunch. She could identify with that, too. A hunch could be a dangerous guessing game for an innocent person with no way to clear his or her name. Like the hunch that put Hobo Joe at the scene. Innocent until proven guilty might be the law of the land, but it was often the other way around. People were often tried by gossip and their futures ruined. With Prohibition in full swing, the Roaring Twenties revolution afoot, and criminals taking over cities like Chicago and Hot Springs, it was unlikely that Bluff Springs was prepared to deal with a crime of any kind.

On the fact side of the issue, she knew the particulars of the Duncan homicide. He was shot with his own gun in his own car in his own town. In her mind that made it likely he knew the person who pulled the trigger. The wad of cash he had won in the poker game was gone, but that didn't mean the killer had stolen it before, during, or after the murder.

She knew several players attended the game, and that Duncan and Langford had an angry spat over the promise note, which the latter had put up as cash. It was never disclosed in the newspaper what property the note was for or even for how much. The matter was left for readers to make whatever assumption they chose. And, she realized now, the newspaper had never said whether the promise note had been recovered.

Also on the fact side of the issue was that Langford served as pallbearer. That made his culpability seem slim. Or slimmer, at least. He stood out as the most likely suspect at the start, but either his alibi was iron-tight, or his character was, because who could kill a man and then carry him to his grave?

Langford was also the witness who saw Hobo Joe at the scene helping Winslow free his car of the icy slush in the road. And while that put the hobo at the scene of the crime as well, it didn't mean he pulled the trigger. Why would he? For the money? What would a hobo do with a wad of cash? There was simply no need.

The last thing that came to mind was the Rev. Cecil Hayes' comment about having Hobo Joe in for supper and prayer. The indigent seemed known to the townsfolk as someone to be trusted. Or at least someone they didn't fear.

Which left *whom* to pull the trigger?

And therein lies the rub.

She thought of the hobo postcard in Banjo Man's scrapbook. *Ever yours, Joe* was probably Hobo Joe. He probably took to the rails immediately after the incident, but he had taken time months later to write about his safety. He had taken time to remember the women who helped him. Della was Banjo Man's grandmother. And Miss M? Who was she? Maude Calhoun, perhaps.

Had Maude known something about the crime and helped him get away? She buried the story on purpose if Genna was right. With the prime suspect missing, the crime went cold.

Pulling a piece of paper from the counter, Amy drew a grid much like a Tic Tac Toe. The hobo symbol came to mind. One very similar symbol meant a crime had been committed and no stranger was safe.

She remembered the look on Banjo Man's face when she told him about the murder and the suspect. He'd found this mark at the rail yard, but there was no way to know if Hobo Joe was the one who carved it. But if he was, he had taken time to etch the warning for others hopping off the train behind him while waiting to hop the next train himself. Had that been after shooting a man dead and taking his cash?

Banjo Man was shaken by that news. Was that because the ideals of his childhood hero were falling away? Or was there another reason?

She wrote WTD in the center of the grid. Winslow T. Duncan was the center of the mystery. That much was certain. In the box above it, she wrote HJ for Hobo Joe. As she made her way around the grid she filled in the initials. FC for Frank Calhoun. EL for Langford. OC for Oscar St. Claire. That left four spots open. She pondered whose initials went there. Langford had a wife but she had never learned the name.

Opposite Oscar she wrote B for Bella. Next to Winslow's initial she wrote C for Catherine. M for Maude across from Frank. Someone's initials went in the empty spot. But whose?

That was the puzzle. What did she know about any of these men? Especially about their secrets. She didn't even have a bad hunch. Not a wild guess. Except that, somehow, they were connected like the boxes on this grid.

What she knew about Frank Calhoun was that he ran the newspaper. He was a member of the Odd Fellows. He played poker. Well, that was a guess not a given.

Frank went to sleep and never woke up a mere six months after Duncan left this earth. The newspaper claimed it was a heart attack, but it didn't say who determined that cause of death nor how they knew for sure. If the owner of the newspaper died unexpectedly, it seemed the news would make the front page. Instead, all Genna found was the obituary that mentioned that Frank hadn't been sleeping well and sought a remedy to give him some peace.

Permanent peace.

Was this the insomnia Alfred mentioned? Or was he alluding to Oscar St. Claire, the druggist, who would be the one to prepare such a remedy?

Oscar was gone not long after that. Was that guilt?

Rian had said Oscar's death was an accidental drug overdose. Maybe Frank's was accidental, too. Like Rian said, there were many dangers hidden in the drugs in those days. Accidental could mean a good many things.

She needed to hunt down more information about these men. She needed background on Winslow, too. They called it something on those true crime shows. Victim something. *Victimology.* That was it. Looking at the victim to find out how they connected with the criminal. If she could understand Winslow's characteristics and habits, she might understand his connection to the killer. And if she looked at Frank and Oscar, she might discover how they were part of the plan. Or not.

Victimology wasn't so much *who* but rather *how* and *why*. And once you had how and why, you might find who.

But how would she accomplish any of this? They were all long gone. There was no one left to ask.

If Winslow was targeted by the killer it could be happenstance, a victim of opportunity. After all, he was alone with a stash of cash on a cold winter's night. The newspaper claimed there was *"an assailant unknown to us"* but was he really overtaken by someone he didn't know? Or did he open his car door to someone he knew? Someone he invited into the warm car. Well, probably not a very warm car. It was a Model T after all. In the dead of winter.

She pictured him leaving the poker game in his fur coat with a wide lapel and a wool fedora, a smug and satisfied smile on his face. He may have worn a wool coat better suited for rural life, but somehow Winslow seemed like a fur coat kind of guy. That signet ring in the picture said he was a man with status. At least he was a man who wanted to appear to have status.

None of this information was mentioned in the newspaper articles Genna uncovered. Even if they could access city records and police files, those details wouldn't be included there, either. So, what could she find out about Winslow? Where would she even begin to look? And what about Frank Calhoun, the small town newspaper magnate? Or Oscar St. Claire and his bad habits?

She wished Rian was here to bounce all these ideas. Ben had swooped in and stolen her attention, but then Rian wouldn't give him her attention if she didn't want to. Amy knew the two of them shared many interests and activities. Cannabis wasn't one of them, but Ben was drawn to the new vineyard down in the Arkansas wine country. Rian mentioned several times he was going to make a great grape farmer. He had to know about Rian's plans to make cannabis wine.

She wanted Rian to go with her when she confronted Camellia again. Rian promised to be the muscle, not that it would come to that, but two against one was always better odds. Especially in an information ambush. She would have to wait. In the meantime, she would bounce her ideas off Genna or Zelda. Or both if they were available.

When she pulled out her phone, she saw a missed call from Genna and then saw she had left a message.

"Of course, I know the answer to your question," Genna's message started. "You contact the state Vital Statistics Bureau for birth certificate information. You have to be a relative, though. I'm not sure how you prove that. So, whatever you're up to, you'll probably hit a dead end. No pun intended." Genna laughed briefly. "You should know that Arkansas didn't start requiring birth certificates until 1914, but it was well and good into 1930 before they got all the counties in line. So, anything prior to 1930 is iffy.

"Can't wait to hear what bone you're dogging.

"Speaking of bones, I've finally dug up Pastor Hayes. Well, not actually dug him up. But I know something you don't."

That was it. The message ended as Genna hung up.

CHAPTER TWENTY-THREE

Amy decided to try anyway. She hunted down the number to the Vital Statistics Bureau in Little Rock and dialed.

"I'm trying to find a birth certificate from Bluff Springs," she said to the woman who answered.

"What year?"

Amy stalled. She hadn't thought that through. "1923 or 1924 maybe?" she said finally.

"Oh, we don't have access to birth certificates that old here. I assume you're doing ancestry research?"

"Uh, yes," Amy answered. "I am." *Sort of.*

"There is a link on our website for genealogical requests," the woman said blandly as if she has said the same thing a million times before. "You will need to provide your name, address, date of birth, driver license number for identification, and the appropriate proof of relationship to the person in the documents you are requesting. And a form of payment," she added. "Twelve for the record, five for the processing, two dollars for verification. If they don't find the record you're looking for, there is no refund."

She rattled off the url address, but Amy didn't bother to write it down. She didn't have what she needed to make that search.

"Interesting," the woman added casually. "You're the second request this week for a Bluff Springs birth certificate for that year."

"Really? For what name?"

Amy heard a polite scoff on the other end of the phone.

"I know," Amy said before she could be scolded further. "You can't give out that information."

"Thank you for calling," the woman said politely. "Good luck on your search."

Thwarted in that train of thought, it was time to tackle the Ouija boards. All twelve boxes stacked in a cardboard-spine pile made an impressive stack. She pulled out the measuring tape she used when she needed to ship boxes. The bottom Ouija box was 20 inches long and 14 inches wide. The others nestled neatly on top, a mere inch or two difference in either length or width.

She turned to her computer and began her search.

Somehow William Fuld was considered the founder of the Ouija. It couldn't be further from the truth, but accuracy didn't seem to be the goal of marketing tactics back in the early nineteenth century. The first board was patented by the Kennard Novelty Company. She had shared with her friends on their road trip that factoid along with Helen the psychic's trip to the patent office.

Kennard became Ouija Novelty, and at some point, fell into the hands of Fuld, who made Ouija boards for the next fifty years.

She keyed the information into the search bar and whistled softly under her breath. This board, with its honey-colored maple was circa 1922. It was well-worn but in good shape, and if the listing was accurate, the online auction seller expected a bid of $1100. If she sold hers for half that, she'd be happy.

She considered how old Mable Rose would have been in 1922. She guessed in her late-twenties, or perhaps a little older. It didn't really matter, she probably succumbed to the talking spirit craze and phenomenon as most of her peers had—a trendy parlor game that amused millions. For whatever reason, the practice had stuck with this dressmaker turned Ouija guru. With twelve boards in her possession, Mable Rose had her pick of whatever kind of talking spirit she wished to invite to speak.

She pictured Mable Rose and her friends around the table at her house on Piney Top, their fingers lightly atop the planchette. How would a woman in her twenties own such a home? That wasn't the norm. Perhaps she inherited from her parents. She realized she didn't know much about Mable Rose deRossier. She didn't know anything more about her than she knew about the men at the poker game.

The door of Tiddlywinks jingled, and an elderly couple poked their head in.

"Welcome!" Amy called. "Come in and browse! We have games from every era."

The couple nodded and smiled politely and then retreated without saying a word.

Oh well, games were not everybody's passion. People didn't think they were being rude when they left without speaking. It happened all the time. People were used to shopping at the impersonal big box stores. She happily returned to her task.

Throughout the game's history there were dozens of manufacturers. Ouija fell in and out of favor. It was now gaining nostalgic interest but Mable Rose's boards, as she was discovering, were all made before 1930. As she cleaned the boxes and researched as best she could, she discovered that every maker had its own spin on the talking board. Some designs echoed the pyramid theme, which matched the trendy fixation on Egyptian culture. That made sense since Tutankhamun's tomb in the Valley of the Kings was discovered around that time.

Some boards depicted swamis or mystical places printed on the surface. Some had pictures of Halloween scenes and black cats. None of these were in her possession and she was a little disappointed. It seemed that Mable Rose was a purist. In today's lingo, a Ouija snob.

What made Mable Rose stop buying Ouija boards in 1930? Had she simply grown tired of the talking board? Grown too old and skeptical? Had her interest in the occult changed? Or had she fallen out of favor with the Ouija along with the rest of the country? Was Mable Rose even alive after 1930?

Another trip to the cemetery, she decided. This time for another name on a headstone. Tomorrow, maybe. She'd ask Rian to go with her and they could deal with two birds at the same time—Mable Rose deRossier and Camellia.

As she reached for the last box in the stack, she realized she had quite a tale of history ready for the shelf at Tiddlywinks. Most of the old talking boards were long gone, she learned, either tossed in the trash or burned in the grate after only a few scary rounds. The boards she possessed not only represented her fascination for games in general but true American art from that era as well. She was delighted to have them and a little part of her wanted them to stay put in Tiddlywinks as treasures. Maybe she would mark them up and out of reach for anyone but a true collector.

This last box was made by Wilder Manufacturing of St. Louis, MO. She knew of them. They manufactured paper kites and Tiddlywinks, the game after which she named her shop. The company made many games after their 1914 start, but they jumped on the Ouija bandwagon in the 1920s, when spirit-communication paraphernalia was all the rage. They launched their version as *Mitche Manitou* and the *Mystic Hand* and its finger pointing planchette. She found the hyperbole in the advertisement on the box amusing. The board was striking, although now quite moldy with age, with its stylized letters and the distinctive diamond-shaped logo center.

What struck her most in the game's advertisement was the word drawn by the pointing finger of the planchette. Love.

Hadn't that been the words the planchette had spelled for them?

She had asked the Ouija who killed Winslow T. Duncan. The Ouija had answered LOVE.

Camellia had drawn a breath of surprise.

Was it surprising? Or was it something more?

She finished cleaning the board and box and replaced the lid, realizing that she had left out the finger pointing planchette. She picked up the box and something rattled inside. She opened the box. There was nothing there other than the board and it fit snug. She shook the box and again something rattled.

She took out the board she had just cleaned and stared at the bottom. There was nothing there but old age. She shook the box again, and sure enough, she heard it. Her heart quickened. Something was rattling inside.

She pressed gingerly on the cardboard with her fingertips, noticing as she did that there was a slight spring to it. She brought it closer for inspection and realized a seam had been cut on the narrow end. She pushed on the edge and a wisp of musty air puffed up from beneath.

She shook the empty box. There was definitely something there.

Grabbing a letter opener, she gently edged the point into the seam. Opening slightly, like a breath drawn, it popped up under the pressure.

Amy gasped. Hidden in the space were four envelopes. The paper looked ancient.

"*Dearest,*" it read. "*No amount of willpower I possess can keep me from dreaming of you. Of dreaming of us. Of dreaming of the life you promise we shall have. It will be mere months from now that our lives will change forever. I anticipate this moment with every breath I take. And I shall be content to live all my remaining days as your loving wife.*"

She exhaled slowly.

It was signed, "*Rose.*"

Amy realized her hands were trembling.

Mable Rose. She called herself Rose to her beloved. And who might that have been? There was no date on the letter. There was no postmark on the envelope. She sniffed the page and age tickled her nose.

Reaching for the next letter, she opened it, wondering what tiny glimpse into this woman's life this letter would reveal.

"*Dearest,*" it read. "*I have no words to describe the pain I suffer. It is greater than any being should endure. Your silence cuts me through as the knife edge cuts beeswax, and though both yield with no resistance, neither can remain the same. I beg you to consider the consequences. Rose.*"

Amy opened the next; her heart pounding in her chest.

"Dearest, I have consulted with complete confidence in someone who understands the rigors of a life unfulfilled. No matter as great as this should be left to chance. I will be ready when the time arrives as all necessary details are being arranged. Joe will meet you to convey this message and you may reply by same. Rose."

And the last one.

"Dearest, I can bear no more."

It wasn't even signed.

Amy felt crushed, empathy swelling her chest. Mable Rose was in love with someone. And that someone was cruel in return.

CHAPTER TWENTY-FOUR

"A life insurance policy? That surprises me. Most single women don't bother with one unless they have family they want to provide for. Is that your situation, Amy?"

She smiled at the agent whose name she could never remember correctly, too many vowels in odd places. "Not exactly," she said. "But I would like to learn more about how life insurance works."

The woman's face creased with confusion. "I don't think I understand. Are you looking to insure your life or someone else's because there are very strict rules?"

"You're talking about a policy for someone who is not your spouse," Amy said.

"Precisely. Or someone related to you. The rule of thumb is whether that someone would suffer from your, uh … demise." She shuffled the pile of papers at her elbow and looked back at Amy. "You can take out a policy on yourself and name any beneficiary you want, but if you are considering a policy on someone else, all parties need witnessed consent. Stranger-owned life insurance policies are illegal." She steepled her fingers. "In other words, you couldn't insure a race car driver on the off chance he didn't make it around the last lap."

Amy laughed. "Sorry," she said. "I guess that's not a laughing matter, but I had forgotten your passion for NASCAR."

"I go every year I can." She glanced at the credenza beside the desk, full to the hilt with memorabilia. Cups and model race cars, ball caps, and foam koozies cluttered the surface. "Maybe someday it will be worth more than I paid for it, but for now it's worth the memory. I can tell you what race every item came from."

"I get it," Amy said. "I feel that way about vintage games."

"Oh yes, your game shop. How is that going?"

"Good. No complaints."

Amy wiggled in the club chair opposite the desk. She hoped their pleasantries had been satisfied. "I was wondering how life insurance worked back in the 1920s?"

"1920! Well shoot, surely the policy conditions have been met if it's that old." She eyed Amy carefully. "What are you really after?"

"I guess you could say we've been bitten by the history bug since our fundraising gig. Did you go? I don't remember seeing you."

"Of course I went. I am one of the event sponsors. I waved to you, but I didn't want to be rude and call out from the crowd."

"I really couldn't recognize anybody," Amy said. "The lantern light was in my eyes."

The woman smiled. "You and your friends did a fabulous job. The costumes alone were worthy of a ticket. I took friends visiting from out of town and I know they enjoyed it because they talked about it all night. They didn't know the history of these women in Bluff Springs. Very impressive. Someone should write a book for the museum."

Amy nodded. "Genna could write that book. She spent a lot of time researching for the scripts."

"I always enjoy that event and this year's was no exception." Her eyes lowered to her desk. "There was a little hiccup though, somewhere in the program."

"That was me," Amy said and grimaced. "A tree branch fell very near to where I was standing."

"Oh goodness, you could have been hurt."

"Lucky me," Amy said brightly. "I guess you can see why I am interested," she began. "I understand a lot of life insurance policies were written in Bluff Springs back in the 1920s and I was wondering how that worked. If a husband who had a policy died, did his wife get the money?"

The agent leaned back in her chair and steepled her fingers. "That is an interesting question," she began. "There was a surge in policies written in that era. To your point though, the wives and children may have been named as beneficiaries, but in fact, most women were prevented by law from benefiting from their husband's death."

"You mean they couldn't collect?"

She nodded. "I would like to say how much I disagree with that law," she said. "And I am very grateful the industry has changed."

"How was that even legal?" Amy asked.

"The first problem was that the policy required the beneficiary to have a *'specific monetary interest'* in the deceased." She drew air quotes around her comment. "Neither wife nor child were considered *'adequate'* evidence of an insurable interest. Since the policy was part of the husband's estate, the proceeds could be claimed by creditors until nothing was left."

"Is that still happening today?"

"Oh, thank heavens, no. Back then a married woman couldn't enter into a legal contract on her own behalf, and she couldn't take out a life insurance policy on herself."

"What about an unmarried woman? Could she take out a policy on her own?"

"Doubtful, although I guess it's possible, depending on how unscrupulous the selling agent was. She wouldn't be buying anything of value, but she wouldn't know that. Insurance marketing was very aggressive at that time and so were the agents who traveled city to city, working solely on commission."

"Hypothetically speaking," Amy said, "if an unmarried woman did have a policy that was never collected, would it be valid now? If a relative could be found, could the proceeds from the policy be collected?"

"Oh, you're in way over my head. That's a deep legal question I can't answer. But I would venture to say that if a person is listed as a beneficiary on the policy, the terms are valid."

"And they would be owed money."

She nodded. "Hypothetically."

Unless the Mayor of Bluff Springs made radical changes in this arena, and that was highly unlikely, neither she nor Maude, nor Bella, nor Evangeline were likely to benefit from their husband's life insurance policies. Not motive for murder. And a very real shame as a standard for an industry that promised to stand by you when times were tough. Another benchmark in the evolution of women's rights, she considered, as she left the office.

She had been thinking all along that perhaps Winslow T. Duncan was in over his head in trouble. Maybe he had gambling debts. Or his car dealership wasn't as lucrative as he planned. She was considering that one well-placed shot to the heart of a man with a life insurance policy would free his widow from a financially troubled life. But none of that fit. The idea didn't fit what she knew about Catherine, nor did it fit the legal scenario of the time. Catherine probably wouldn't have benefited, even if her husband did have a life insurance policy in force. Besides, who wanted to impugn the mayor's reputation now? Who wanted to have a heroine turn out to be a killer? Especially a hundred years later? She sure didn't want to be the one to do that.

So, what was the rub that got Winslow rubbed out?

She set out to solve the mystery of the locket found in the graveyard and now wondered if she had uncovered a series of murders in Bluff Springs. At least, there was more than one husband who didn't make it out of his marriage alive.

She had found no proof nor evidence of a serial murder, but that was not completely out of the question. Insurance or not, money didn't seem to be the motive, except for a pot of money from a poker game. And that couldn't have been much, could it? A few hundred, maybe. Was a life worth a few hundred bucks? It was if you were desperate enough. Was Hobo Joe that desperate? The Great Depression hadn't hit yet, and the economic bounty of a post-war country was in full fling. No, money didn't seem to be the motive. A windfall circumstance, perhaps, but not the reason Winslow was dead.

Genna's comments about Reverend Hayes and his gossip came to mind. If money wasn't the motive, blackmail went out the door with it. But if he was blackmailing Duncan for some reason, Rev. Hayes would have been the target. Not the other way around. In the deaths of the four husbands, Hayes was the last one out.

Money, revenge, love, power, and the threat of death. Those were motives for murder. Or at least the ones she and Sam Ford had talked about in their conversations about tracking down the guilty. His PI work was mostly centered around insurance fraud, but he knew a lot and he was willing to share it. So far, she had uncovered no one with those apparent struggles. The fact that the passing of these husbands paved a more fortuitous path for their widows could be pure coincidence. Or it could be a master plan. She would have to dig deeper if she was going to find a motive.

There was a truth in there somewhere. She knew that. Alfred Hitchcock said you couldn't believe precisely what the deceased had to say. He was talking about the Ouija board and its talking planchette, which meant LOVE might be a detour from the truth. His comment seemed to fit this cold case victimology as well. She couldn't know for certain if the trail she was following had merit or if it was a trail of deception.

Gossip could be an angle if money wasn't, she decided as she drove through town. She was feeling a little guilty about her own gossip. She figured the surveyor at Piney Top was the result of her telling Langford about Camellia inheriting and moving in. She shouldn't have done that. She passed the building where the People's Drug had been. It was a gift shop now, but it made her wonder who in town in 1924 would have gossip? Not the innocent kind of gossip shared at the Coke counter at People's Drug. Not the gossip about who had a new boyfriend or the latest color in lipstick. Gossip about things that got you killed.

If gossip could get you killed, the pastor was on the list. In his role as a spiritual advisor, however misappropriated, gossip would be a naturally occurring part of his job. He would hear things.

People would confide in him. If Hayes was on the list, so was his wife. Even if he didn't bring her into his confidence, she could be listening at the keyhole. If she knew who met with the pastor and then listened to his sermon, she would know what sin went with which sinner. It was a flawed assumption, but possible. She decided to ask Genna to find the last sermon Rev. Cecil Hayes gave his congregation.

The dressmaker was next on her mental list of people who had gossip. Mable Rose would have an intimate and captive audience of the women of town. While they were being measured and fitted and draped, Mabel Rose would be the ear they would gossip into. She would be the one who let out a seam when a patron started showing. She would be the one sewing the wedding dress or adorning the household linens with needlepoint skills she learned from her mail order school.

And then, when Mable Rose shifted roles and brought out her Ouija boards, her parlor might ring with even darker secrets. The kind of secrets that only get spoken in the dark. Amy pictured the scene.

"Does he love me?"

"Is he having an affair?"

"Will I have a boy or a girl?"

"Does anyone know what I did?"

There were secrets behind all these questions. She could imagine Mable Rose and her querent at the table posing those questions to the talking board, fingers on the planchette. Even their presence at the table was a secret most would choose to keep. Mable Rose might know who the killer was.

Amy thought of Maude Calhoun who inherited Frank's newspaper when he passed in his sleep. Maybe Maude didn't own the monetary value of the business, but her moniker M.A. Calhoun owned the pages. Even before her husband's death, she was an active writer. It was she who wrote the stories about the town and its people. She was the one who influenced what stories and articles made the pages and what didn't. It was Maude that people might confide in when they witnessed something untoward, and it was she who would either print their story or not. Plus, Maude would have access to the Monday sermon before everyone else.

Was it Maude Calhoun, then, who buried the story about Hobo Joe as the suspect in the murder of Winslow Duncan? Did she bury it because she knew who the killer was? The words in the newspaper articles Genna uncovered came to mind.

The town's complaisant lethargy…

Heinous trespass…

No further suspects…

Maude may not have been talking about the murder with her veiled and cautious words. But if she deliberately buried the story so the crime would remain unsolved, was she the "M" that Hobo Joe wrote about in the postcard? He wrote about being out of reach and grateful. Most likely he was talking about the long arm of the law.

Could it be? Could it be that a hundred years later, in the graveyard, in the Silent City of Bluff Springs, Maude Calhoun's hainted spirit was speaking out for resolution for what she had done. And what had she done? Buried a story? Covered up a crime? Shivers went up Amy's spine. She reached for her necklace and found it warm to her fingers.

Maude was best friends with Catherine Duncan and Bella St. Claire. And probably Mable Rose deRossier, too. Any one of them could have gossip they wanted to hide. Any one of them could have known Winslow's killer. Any one of them could have killed him and then one by one got rid of their husbands to hide the truth. And perhaps Mable Rose knew what they had done.

She pulled into her parking spot and jammed the gear into first. Was she ever going to find enough facts to land on one suspect? Or was she going to have to juggle all of them until the very end?

CHAPTER TWENTY-FIVE

Amy stirred the dominoes on the table. Zelda had baked a pan of spinach and feta popovers as her penance for winning the last game. This was a long-standing rule. The winner made food. The losers brought wine. The pastries were not homemade, Zelda had already pointed out, but they were better than nothing.

"Better than Vienna Sausages," Zelda quipped with a mischievous glance at Amy.

Amy glared back, daring Zelda to bring up her kidnapping in the backwoods of Arkansas while she was trying to save Zelda's immortal soul from the gallows. She was about to say so, when Genna spoke up. Amy would have to wait to tell them about the letters in the false bottom of the Ouija box.

"The Reverend Cecil Hayes," Genna said with an amused grin, "was a man who liked to gossip. He used his pulpit to preach his gospel, and he used his sermon to oust folks caught in the rumor mill of inappropriate deeds. Well, at least that's my take on it," she added. "If one reads between the lines. I promised you I had dug up Pastor Hayes," she added and nodded to Amy.

Genna pulled her tiles from the pile in the center and painstakingly organized them in front of her, knowing full well, Amy was certain, they were waiting for her news to drop.

"But that is the least of it. I only found it because I was looking," Genna offered, as the game began. "Our reverend has not always been a law-abiding man of the cloth." She paused for effect and played a tile without scoring. "He and his wife moved to Bluff Springs from a little town in Missouri after much hubbub about money missing from the church coffers. He was courting Evangeline—the church choir director—when the upset began. According to the news article I uncovered, there were accusations but no charges, and Hayes left town stealing Evangeline and the congregation's funds for a new Sunday School.

Rian laughed. "Why does this not surprise me?"

"Because you are a jaded woman," Zelda said.

"A self-made jaded woman, if you please," Rian amended.

"*Touché,*" Zelda replied. "A magna cum graduate from the school of hard knocks."

"From the school of Mother of Mercy," Rian countered and smiled. "Best education, ever."

"Back to Cecil," Genna said. "I hunted down his sermons available in the Bluff Springs Weekly Times. I am still reading through them, but if you wanted to know what was happening behind the scenes of Bluff Springs, you had only to read his sermon on Monday. He didn't name names, but I could tell he was calling people out. People in town might know who he was talking about. His most common themes seemed to be about greed, alcohol, and forbidden love. Forbidden love. Nothing new. I'm guessing the Roaring Twenties was a hard time for someone pretending to be pious."

They hadn't given much credence to the passing of the good reverend when they were connecting the death dots earlier. But now it was hard to leave him out of the picture. Rev. Hayes could have been at the poker game. No one said he was. No one said he wasn't.

If Evangeline was the fourth queen, why did she want her husband gone and out of the way? At some low point in the marriage, why did any wife want her husband gone?

And then poof! They were gone. A wish come true.

Revenge, love, fear, greed, power. She couldn't say how these fit into the lives of the victims here. Especially in a society where one sex coveted power and aggression, while the other sex was stuck with whatever they got. Stuck with what they settled for. Or whatever was arranged for them by their parents. Stuck. Just stuck.

The truth was the truth. Divorce was no option for a woman of that era. That made murder a perfect dead end, no-return solution. A permanent solution just like Hitchcock said. Homicide, as the constable had said, and it was certainly possible that four wives had plotted this atrocity. It was possible, but was it true?

Catherine became mayor. Maude took over the newspaper. Bella became the town druggist. What about Evangeline Hayes? What happened to her?

By all appearances, the not-so-honorable Rev. Hayes abused his power by filtering other people's business and beeswax into his sermon like honey drizzled on toast. A bit of honey sweetens the burned spots. But if Hayes put too much fire, brimstone, and contempt in his sermons, did it get him killed?

"I found a false bottom in one of the Ouija boards," Amy announced before anyone else could take the floor. "There were love letters hidden in it. Four of them. From Mable Rose deRossier. She signed her name Rose."

Three pairs of eyes turned to look at her.

"Well, that's a zinger," Zelda said. "Go on. Tell us what they said."

"She was in love, and they had plans to be married. I think they were going to elope. No wedding was mentioned, but something happened, and she was crushed by the news. She sounded lost and hopeless. The letter was really quite sad."

"Aww," Zelda said. "That makes my heart hurt."

Amy nodded. "The love letters were in the Ouija box with the special pointing finger planchette. I couldn't help but see the love connection. It would make that board easy to identify in a stack. But what I don't understand is why these letters were still in her possession. If she sent them, how did she still have them? Wouldn't she have the response letters sent to her in return?"

"Good questions," Genna offered. "What's your explanation?"

"I don't have one. I was hoping you might."

The three of them shrugged.

"One letter did mention a Joe and I wondered if she was talking about Hobo Joe. If so, he was more familiar to her than we knew. The letter said something about using this Joe to receive her message and to send the reply. *Convey* was the word she used. Such a wonderfully old-fashioned word."

"Maybe the letters in the box were duplicate letters," Genna offered.

"I guess," Amy said, "Why hide them in a false bottom of a box?"

"Duh," Zelda said. "So, no one would see them."

Amy shook her head. "Then why not destroy them?"

Genna huffed. "Why duplicate a letter and then destroy it?"

"Maybe she never sent them," Zelda continued. "Maybe she wrote them and never had the nerve to *convey* them to their intended."

"I don't know," Amy said after some thought. "I checked the other boxes, but there were no false bottoms in any of them. There must be more letters somewhere, and I have a feeling that Camellia knows more than she has been willing to share with us. For starters, her name isn't Camellia. It's Rose. That might not be a coincidence."

"Hmmm," Genna said. "The plot thickens. Is that why you were asking about a birth certificate?"

Amy nodded. "I was looking for a 1923 or 1924 birth certificate."

Zelda gasped. "She *was* pregnant!"

"That's where I went in my thinking, but we're not related and that means we're not privy to any birth certificate. Like you said, Genna, they didn't always keep track of births back then. Especially if it was out of wedlock. There might not be a birth certificate on file." The thought struck her then, and she gasped. "The letter in the drawer!"

Zelda leaned forward. "A letter in what drawer?"

"Camellia sold a desk to the antique store owner who found a letter wedged in one of the drawers. She gave it to me to give to Camellia."

"I hope you opened it to see what it said," Genna declared.

"No, I did not."

"Well, why not?"

"It was sealed."

"So?"

"Genna! I can't open someone else's sealed letter!"

"How would Camellia know it was sealed when you got it?"

Amy paused long enough to consider it. "No, Genna," she said finally. "That is just not right."

"What if the letters in the secret box were returned unopened to Rose?" Rian asked when the chatter eased. "What if the letter was refused and returned to sender?"

Amy nodded. "That would explain why she had them. It would explain why she kept them. It would also explain why she was so wounded." Amy paused to gather her thoughts. *"'Your silence cuts me through as the knife edge cuts beeswax…'"* she quoted. "That has to be it! Whoever he was, he dropped her like a hot potato!"

"Men!" Zelda exclaimed.

"Men!" Genna echoed. "One of the sermons from Rev. Hayes was about resisting the sins of the flesh. He talked about turning away from the *lust of the heart in a time when spiritual chaos walked among them hand in hand.* I think I'm quoting him right. I bet he knew something. I wonder if he *was* the something. His words may have been what cut her heart. He could have been the secret Mable Rose kept in the box."

The room drew quiet. Eerily quiet.

She had already gone there in her head. It was interesting to see that so had Genna. Rev. Hayes had a history of stealing women's hearts. At least one heart, anyway. That could be why Hobo Joe went to dinner and prayer at the Hayes home. Maybe he went to deliver her secret messages and return with a secret reply, all right under his wife's nose.

That could be why he was so full of fire and brimstone. His own guilt egged him on.

The group was so quiet, Amy wondered where they had all gone in their thoughts. What secrets of the heart were they thinking about? Everyone knew lust at some point in their life. Everyone knew chaos. At some point in everyone's life, they plotted revenge, were wounded by love, retreated in fear, and coveted someone else's money and power. And love, well, everyone knew the ebb and flow of love. The eerie silence continued without so much as a clank of the dominoes on the table.

"Imagine if you will," Rian broke the silence with her best Rod Serling imitation and a gleam in her eye, "…a place on the corner with glass and mahogany shelves filled with jars labeled in Latin. *Euphrasia officinalis, Oplopanax horridus, Acetylsalicylic acid.*" Rian glanced at Genna and added, "For the Latin disadvantaged, that's eyebright, ginseng, and aspirin."

Genna narrowed her eyes. "I would have figured that out on my own."

"With a copy of Latin for Dummies," Zelda quipped. Genna let it go.

"You could also be ripped off by Fatoff Obesity Cream, Make-Man Tablets, and Dr. Bonker's Celebrated Egyptian Oil."

"Dr. Bonkers!" Zelda laughed. "I love that!"

"The People's Drug at the corner of Mountain and Main in Bluff Springs was the community gathering place where anybody could drop in for some measure of cure."

"Or some measure of murder," Amy added.

Rian nodded. "Plenty of that available. Arsenic, strychnine, morphine, mercury—they all had their household uses. You didn't even need a prescription. Codeine, nitroglycerin, and alcohol tonics were sold to cure just about everything. Or at least help you forget you were suffering. Opium and cannabis tinctures were popular. And completely legal."

"Do any of these mimic a heart attack if overdosed?" Amy asked.

"Probably all of them. Under the right circumstance."

"Any of them used for insomnia?"

"Definitely," Rian answered with a nod to Amy. "Laudanum, which was a tincture of opium, was available by prescription."

"I've heard of laudanum," Genna said. "Wasn't that Edgar Allan Poe's favorite recreational drug? It's no wonder he heard ravens knocking, knocking on the floor."

Amy laughed. "Rapping, rapping at my chamber door."

"I never understood that poem," Zelda said. "It's no wonder it didn't make sense to me. He was blotto."

"The poem was about love and loss," Genna explained tirelessly. "It was about grief and sadness and dark thoughts. And yes, probably some pretty heavy-duty drugs."

"I am grateful a raven didn't show up in the lamp light at the graveyard," Zelda added. "It was spooky enough as it was. And then Amy had to scream. I nearly peed my bloomers."

They laughed and Poe's dark poem faded, but Amy wondered if the People's Drug at the corner of Mountain and Main had a hand in the deaths of Frank Calhoun and Oscar St. Claire. And maybe the Rev. Hayes, too. It would have been easy for Bella to gather whatever was needed to aid her friends in the execution of their crimes. But then, it would have been easy for just about *anyone* to gather what they needed. There were drug registers, surely, but they were long gone now and obviously that line of inquiry went unchecked back then. No one would believe three upstanding women would murder their husbands. Was Evangeline Hayes the fourth? Did she know about the affair? Was she seeking her own revenge?

"Speaking of bloomers," Rian continued, breaking into Amy's troublesome thoughts, "at that time Johnson & Johnson was mostly known for their Band-Aids and surgical dressings, first aid kits and hygiene products for women. Their ad campaigns encouraged the local drug store as the first stop in primary care, health advice, and cure-all remedies."

"And Kotex," Zelda added.

"Different brand," Rian countered, "same concept. They simply repurposed and repackaged war wound dressings."

Zelda made a face.

"If your town was lucky—and Bluff Springs was lucky," Rian continued, "customers could sit and sip a Coca-Cola for an afternoon pick-you-up. The two main ingredients in that were kola nut and coca leaf extract. In other words: caffeine and cocaine.

"It was Prohibition, so you couldn't order a G and T. A Coca-Cola was the next best option. It was actually marketed as a temperance drink, an alternative to alcohol, and a patent medicine for whatever ailed you."

"How much was a Coke back then?" Amy asked.

"A nickel," Rian answered quickly. "It was always a nickel. Until 1959."

"What happened in 1959?" Genna asked.

"Inflation and greed, I guess. Well, that and probably the cost of advertising."

"The Cola Wars," Genna added with authority. "The war against Pepsi-Cola."

"I can't drink Pepsi," Zelda said. "It gives me a stomachache."

"I wonder how much that nickel is worth today?" Genna looked at Rian, as if expecting her to know that tidbit, too.

Rian shrugged. "A couple bucks, maybe?"

"I bet you could catch up on all the gossip at the Coke counter, too," Amy interjected. "I wish we could eavesdrop back in time. I bet we could solve this murder if we could eavesdrop at the People's Drug."

"Prohibition was a waste of energy, anyway," Zelda said, then stuffing another spinach pastry in her mouth.

"It was about society trying to control its masses," Rian said tersely.

"That's the truth," Genna agreed. "The idea behind Prohibition was that if alcohol was not available, saloons would disappear, and men would be forced to go home to their wives. That didn't work out so great."

"Men and their bad habits," Zelda said, licking the crumbs from her lips. "We're always pointing a finger at men and their bad habits."

"I feel like I just sat through a history lesson," Genna added.

"It *is* history," Rian added. "That's my point. I couldn't stop with the script on Bella St. Claire, I had to know more. It wasn't a fad, all these drugs and remedies in society. It was a human condition. It *is still* a human condition. As a whole, people like altering their state of being. They like the feeling they get from herbs, drugs, and alcohol. And the humanities—art, music, literature, theology—they are all rewarded because of it.

"Society is the guard dog. A fickle one," Rian continued. "Depending on the era and the political ethos, the pendulum swings this way and then the other. This altered state of being is either seen as a sin and disease to be morally and medically addressed, or it's considered a reality of choice and made freely available.

"I don't have the answer," Rian added. "I'm not trying to find one. But I was pulled into the history of why we have this love-hate relationship with ourselves and our natural tendencies. Whatever those tendencies may be. I admit some are dark. And the more they are kept in the dark, well…"

"The darker they become," Amy finished in a near whisper. She glanced at Zelda, knowing the secrets Zelda had kept in the dark, even from her best friends. She couldn't say that circumstance turned out for the better for all, but it turned out for the better for Zelda. That could be the case for Catherine Duncan, Maude Calhoun, and Bella St. Claire. Maybe Evangeline Hayes should be on the killer list, too.

"Boy, y'all sure know how to ruin a good bottle of wine," Zelda quipped. "Why aren't we talking about where we're going on our next bucket list trip? Why aren't we talking about my up-and-coming vintage clothing line? Why aren't we talking about dominoes and how Genna is skunking us in this game, and no one is paying any attention. We'll be eating baked tofu cubes next game if Genna wins."

Genna laughed. "Tofu is good for you."

Zelda scrunched her nose.

"I've always wanted to see the pyramids of Egypt," Amy suggested. "Maybe sail the Nile."

"I've always wanted to eat my way through Paris," Zelda claimed.

Genna said, "I've always wanted to see Antoni Gaudí's *la Sagrada Familia* in Barcelona."

"See what I mean?" Zelda interjected. "Barcelona is in Spain. We should definitely put Spain on our bucket list."

"What about you?" Amy asked, turning to Rian.

"I've always wanted to fly over Albuquerque. In a hot-air balloon."

"Oh!" Amy said. "That sounds fun."

"Fun," Zelda echoed.

"A whole lot of fun," Genna agreed. "Let's add that to our bucket list!"

CHAPTER TWENTY-SIX

Amy grabbed the "Be back in an hour" sign when she saw Rian pull to the curb in her truck. They had determined that Piney Top was not a destination to reach in either Rian's Fiat or Amy's Miata. This was a truck kind of adventure, they decided, when Amy made the call to Rian.

"I need my muscle," Amy had said on the phone.

Rian had answered, "When and where?"

Amy hung up the sign, locked the door, and jumped into the truck at the curb.

"Who are we roughing up?" Rian asked with an excited smile.

"You know that's not why I wanted you to come," Amy said.

"I can fantasize, can't I?"

Amy laughed. "You're a pacifist. Why are you pretending to be so tough?"

Rian slapped her chest with an open hand. "Wounded!" she exclaimed. "I am absolutely wounded."

Amy laughed again, grateful to have Rian's company on the errand. Rian was like a bunny rabbit with some bulk. She was a pacifist who didn't kill spiders or flies, but if the need should arise, Rian would come to her rescue. She had seen it before.

"Why are you afraid of her?" Rian asked as she U-turned into the narrow street, expertly dodging parked cars and aimless pedestrians.

"I'm not afraid of her," Amy spat back. "You're coming because I want a witness. You're coming because I want to intimidate her a little."

"Intimidate? That's your sleuthing style now, huh?"

"I want to know why she's pretending to be Camellia when her real name is Rose. I want to know if she has found any more love letters in the attic. And I want to know what's in this one." She pulled the letter from her bag and shook it. "It's still sealed. As you as my witness."

Rian glanced at the letter in Amy's hand and back to the road. "What if it's an electric bill or something as benign? You're going to feel silly."

"Who seals an electric bill with wax?" Amy countered. "It has to be something secret."

It wasn't a long drive but the last of it was dusty. The usual fall rain had skirted north of the city and the dirt roads were full of loose grit. A cloud of dust trailed behind them.

"Camellia parked her rental car between those two hedges," Amy said pointing ahead.

Rian nodded and pulled off the road a good fifty yards from the hedge.

"Why are you parking way back here?" Amy asked.

"Muscle arrives unannounced," Rian answered with a grin. "Why advertise your presence by parking out front? We can walk from here. Hey, watch your step." Rian motioned to the wooden stake stuck in the ground, bright orange vinyl tape tied at the top and blowing in the wind.

"This wasn't here the other day," Amy said, "but I did see a surveyor. The property probably hasn't been surveyed since the house was built."

"And maybe not even then," Rian said. "I think most properties went by legal description alone."

They approached the house on Piney Top from the other side of the hedge. The same hedge she had hidden behind the last time she visited Camellia. Was she afraid of her like Rian had claimed? Or was she just being sneaky?

"Pretty impressive stand of Rose of Sharon," Rian said quietly as they passed through the opening in the hedge. "*Hibiscus Syriacs.* Looks like it hasn't been pruned in eons. "

"Eons," Amy echoed. "Could be a hundred years."

They climbed the porch steps and knocked on the screen door. Amy noticed a new screen had been stapled in place. The solid door was shut and there was no answer to the knock.

"Do you think she's hiding from us?" Rian asked.

Amy shrugged.

"Let's go around the back," Rian suggested. "Let's just see what we can see."

The grass was thin and autumn brown as they passed on the south side of the house. "Look at that," Rian said as they passed a decrepit trellis falling away from the wall. "*Datura stramonium*," Rian said. "Jimsonweed. It's still blooming."

Amy looked to where Rian pointed and saw a wrangle of branches and large lavender-white flowers shaped like trumpets hanging from the leaves. The flowers were nearly closed, and she bent forward to lift the bloom and sniff the fragrant perfume.

Rian grabbed her arm. "Don't! They're toxic."

Amy pulled her hand away quickly. "Toxic?"

"Like send you to sleep forever toxic," Rian said, pointing to a spot in the leaves. "See those little spiky balls? Those are the seed pods. One seed could send you into another world altogether."

Amy exhaled. "You mean like a hallucination?"

"Like magic mushrooms. If it didn't kill you first."

Amy stepped back from the plant. "It doesn't smell lethal."

"Of course not," Rian said. "That's nature's way. Lure you in and kill you."

Amy shoved her hands in her jacket pockets and followed Rian around the back of the house. Rian climbed the old stairs that led to the kitchen door; the same one Amy had escaped through when snooping unannounced. This was becoming a habit, this snooping around unannounced and uninvited. But how else would you find out what people didn't want you to know?

"There's the door to the basement," Rian said, as she hopped off the stairs with ease. She lifted the rusted metal plate from the loop and pulled at the door. It jerked open and the smell of musty dirt wafted out. Rian peeked in. "Dark as Hades in there," she said. "Maybe there's a light pull cord somewhere."

They heard the screen door slam above them and Rian quickly pushed the door back in place, securing the hasp lock. If there was a padlock on it previously, the lock was long gone.

They retraced their steps, jumping behind the hedge as Amy had done before.

"You again," Camellia said abruptly, when they knocked, and she answered. "How is it that you always seem to get here right when I do? I think you're the one stalking me!"

Camellia looked at Amy and then at Rian.

"We have impeccable timing," Rian said.

"Well, what do you want?" Camellia said rudely after a long pause. "I'm busy today."

"I know you've been going around town selling items from the house," Amy began.

"It's my house. It's my stuff to do what I want. I told you, if I find more games, I'll let you know."

Holding her ire in check, Amy fingered the letter in her back pocket. "The antique dealer found a letter stuck in the desk you sold her." Amy stepped forward and the porch plank squeaked. "I believe this belongs to you," she said and extended the sealed paper. She wanted to tighten the grip on the letter instead.

Camellia eyed the envelope with concern for a brief moment. "I hope it's not bad news. I don't think I can take any more of that. You see all those stakes?" She motioned in the direction they had just come from. Amy nodded. "They're springing up everywhere. Front and back. The guy who owns the property next to mine got some hair brained idea that I'm trying to steal his land. He's having it surveyed to prove his point. He's got a bug up his butt because I wouldn't take his offer. It was a low offer. A really low offer. I told him I wasn't planning on selling, but if I did, he'd have to come up with a lot more than that!" Camellia looked disgusted. "I may be young but I'm not stupid."

"That's good news and bad news," Rian said and stuck her fingertips in her jeans pocket. "No one wants a jerk for a neighbor, but if he's paying for the survey, you're saving yourself a chunk of money if you decide to sell. And you don't have to sell to him, anyway."

Camellia nodded. "That's good to know."

Amy swallowed the lump forming in her throat. One of the Langford brothers was Camellia's neighbor. And she had blabbed to the other brother about Camellia's inheritance. What had she stirred up? She said she would pass on the phone number, but she had completely forgotten. Looks like they had connected anyway.

"You hear that?" Camellia asked, and they turned toward the sound. It was a horrible screeching, metal-eating wood kind of sound. "That's some mammoth machine back there chewing up the brush. He says he's going to clear all the way to his line."

Camellia huffed. "And I was really liking Bluff Springs, too, but I don't like being bullied."

Amy winced. She had come prepared to intimidate Camellia out of some information. Not intimidate, exactly, but she was prepared to insist. Now she felt responsible for Langford's noisy invasion and complicit in dragging Rian with her for support. She felt even more guilty than before, but she wasn't sure about what.

"Maybe everything would go smoother if you explained a few things," Amy said cautiously. "Maybe you could be more forthcoming."

Camellia narrowed her eyes. "Forthcoming? What does that even mean?"

"I mean your name is not Camellia. It's Rose. Rose Compton. And you told me your name was Camellia deRossier. As in Mabel Rose deRossier. The same person who owned the necklace you stole from my house."

"Not that again," Camellia whined. "I told you what happened. You would have done the same thing."

"Why would you pretend to be someone you're not?"

"What business is that of yours?"

"I thought we were going to be friends, and now I'm not even sure what your name is. I can't get over this feeling that you're hiding something."

"I am not hiding anything," Camellia said sternly. "And it's none of your beeswax if I was."

"Is that why you were looking for a 1924 birth certificate?"

"What? Where was I looking for a birth certificate? I don't know anybody born in 1924. I don't know what you're talking about."

Amy look startled. "I don't know what to believe. I thought we were friends. I thought we were opening our community to you. I even mentioned you to my banker. I put in a good word in case you needed a banker you could trust. Now I just don't know…"

Rian stepped forward. "We're trying to sort out a few details that are hanging in the wind. And I know your neighbor. I could probably get him calmed down a little. Why don't we go inside and talk? It's too noisy out here."

Camellia looked at Rian and frowned. Amy watched her closely. Maybe she was remembering Rian's comment at the Ouija table. *You are the one.* Or maybe she was remembering the way the Ouija had spelled out *LOVE* and she had let out a gasp. Maybe she was somewhere else entirely with the sound of that machine chewing up her thoughts.

"My name *is* Camellia deRossier," she said quietly, her eyes shifting back to Amy. "Rose Compton is my sister. She wasn't able to make this trip. So, I am here instead. The lawyer doesn't know the difference between me and Rose. He's never met either one of us. We look enough alike anyway. Or we used to. I brought her passport just in case I needed to sign a document or something."

Amy felt dumbfounded and she knew it showed on her face.

Camellia looked off in the distance once again, and Amy thought she saw a quiver to her chin. "My sister is sick," Camellia said. "I'm here to get the house ready for when she can come." The quiver turned into a tremble. "We both need a second chance. We both need a new start."

Amy sighed, guilt taking hold with hard, cold hands. "I'm really sorry to hear about your sister. And I'm sorry for what I just said."

"She's going to make it," Camellia stated brightly, glossing over Amy's apology. "She's stronger than she thinks she is." Hope filled her eyes.

Amy stood silently. She didn't know what else to say. Only pure will and love could hold out hope like that. She opened her mouth and Rian stepped on her toe, adding a nearly imperceptible shake of her head. She wanted more answers, but it wasn't really any of her beeswax as Camellia had said. Camellia could explain or not. It was her story to tell. And the letter was her business.

"You know it's kind of weird," Camellia said dreamily. "When I read my great aunt's diaries, I hear my sister's voice in my head. It's like Rose is reading to me."

She glanced at the letter in her hands.

They waited silently, and when it was obvious, she wasn't going to open the letter and share its contents, they turned and walked away. When they got to the truck, Amy turned and looked back. Camellia was still standing on the porch looking lost in thought.

"That was unexpected," Rian said with a chuckle, as she turned the truck in the narrow dirt road. "Did you get what you wanted?"

Amy was quiet. She still didn't know what was in the sealed envelope. The only thing she did know was why Camellia told the lawyer she was Rose Compton.

"If you hadn't stepped on my toe and stopped me, I would have asked if there were more love letters," Amy said.

"Which is why I stepped on your toe," Rian answered. "There is a time and place. That was not it."

Amy acquiesced. Sometimes wanting to know the answer overcame propriety. Timing was everything. Her PI friend, Sam Ford, had told her that, too. Pushy pushes back, he told her. He was right and she was still learning. Sometimes it was hard to know the right time and place. Sometimes she got caught up in the hunt instead.

"Hey," she said as the thought struck her. "If Camellia wasn't the one looking for the birth certificate, who was?"

Rian shrugged.

"Let's take a detour to the graveyard. I want to check something out."

Rian nodded and turned in the direction of the front gates of the cemetery. "You want to look for Mable Rose deRossier's grave?"

"That's a good idea," Amy said.

"Well, what were you thinking?" Rian asked.

"I suspect Banjo Man knows more about the murder of Winslow T. Duncan and Hobo Joe than he wants me to know," Amy answered. "Maybe he's the one looking for a birth certificate and I'm hoping on the off chance that he'll be playing his banjo at the grave."

"At Winslow's grave?"

"No, but that's not out of the question, either."

There was no twang of a banjo in the quiet of the graveyard. They walked to the area where the event had taken place. There was the Duncan plot. There was the Calhoun's. Another row over was the St. Claire's and dozens of residents in between. But not another living soul. And no Mable Rose deRossier headstone.

"I wonder how we find her grave," Amy asked, when they had circled back to the truck.

"Graves R Us," Rian quipped. "Seriously, I don't remember what it's called but there is a registry of graves online. If she's buried, she's in it. Where to now?" Rian added.

"Back to square one," Amy said quietly. "I need to see that scrapbook, even if I have to break into the museum to get it."

"Yes! A clandestine snoop. It wouldn't be our first time," Rian said with a grin.

She parked outside the museum and Amy pulled a map from the glovebox, rehearsing the plan in her head. It wasn't much of a plan, but she was hoping for the best. She recognized the clerk at the counter as one of the players from the Silent City. She had played the town gossip who ran a café and fed everybody for free on the town's birthday anniversary. Amy sighed with relief that it wasn't the stern old lady from their last visit to the museum.

"Well, if it isn't Maude Calhoun and Bella St. Claire," the woman said brightly. "What are you two up to now? More Petticoat shenanigans?"

Amy laughed. "I needed to bring this back," she said and waved the map in her hand quickly enough that it would go unrecognized. "It belongs in Mayor Catherine's scrapbook. I'll just return it now if that's okay. Can you tell me where it's kept?"

"Oh," the woman said and frowned. "I didn't realize…"

"She let Genna borrow it for research," she added quickly, regretting that she hadn't asked the old woman's name. "She was very stern about returning everything to its right place."

The young woman nodded and motioned with her head. "It's in the third drawer on the left. The key is on top of the cabinet." She shrugged. "I know. Why bother, right? It makes sense to some. I'd help you but I have to stay here at the register."

Amy nodded, more than relieved. Bending the truth wasn't all that bad when no one was harmed, right? She and Rian disappeared behind the curtain.

Amy stuffed the map in her back pocket and retrieved the key. In moments, they were looking at the pages of Catherine Duncan's life. "I'll turn the pages, and you take the pictures," Amy whispered to Rian and handed her the phone. "We don't have much time."

CHAPTER TWENTY-SEVEN

Amy was looking through the photos she had taken of the scrapbook when the bell above Tiddlywinks jangled, and she looked up to see Zelda standing in the doorway. She was dressed in emerald green and cream, a flowing pants ensemble straight out of tailor Vito's vintage *Fashion Service* magazines.

Zelda twirled in the doorway, her shoes clicking on the wood floor.

"Lovely," Amy ventured.

"Stunning is more appropriate," Zelda said. "The dress shop has already placed an order. And since when do you and Rian go off to who-knows-where without telling me? The Pot Shed was closed, and Tiddlywinks was locked up tight. People have been wandering down the hallway all morning looking like lost souls."

"Sorry," Amy muttered. "We should always check in with you first."

Zelda seemed to miss the sarcasm her best friend was trying to deliver. She stepped aside as a group entered the shop.

"Hello and welcome!" Amy called out. "We have games from every era. Something for everyone. Come in and browse!" The group moved toward the shelves and Amy noticed that one of them was very pregnant.

Zelda put her hands on her hips. "See? You would make money if you would stay put and stop gallivanting off on a wild goose chase. Genna said she passed y'all turning into the graveyard, but you didn't notice her wave. What is so all-fired-interesting about that place? Didn't you get enough of it when you were pretending to be Maude Calhoun and getting whomped on the head with a tree branch?"

Amy laughed. "Almost whomped," she said. "We went to see Camille and then to the graveyard to see if we could find Mable Rose deRossier's grave. And then to—"

"What for?" Zelda interrupted.

"What for," Amy started and then glanced at her patrons, who were now eyeing a shelf of Y2K games. "What for is something I will have to tell you later."

Zelda nodded, swirled the emerald caftan dramatically and clip-clopped out the door to Zsa Zsa Galore Décor.

Amy turned her attention to her customers. The shoppers had a lot of questions, and she had all the answers. Amy thought they were going to open every box on the shelf. Part of her wanted them out of Tiddlywinks so she could make the call she was eager to make. Hopefully, Banjo Man was back from his hospital stay and available to come to the phone. The other part of her—the business owner part—was happy to have customers interested in spending money. In the end, they bought the *Pretty Pretty Princess* game, for nostalgia and the baby to be, Amy guessed. One of them looked at the Ouija boards, then chose *13 Dead End Drive*, a Y2K version of *Clue*.

"Farewell and fond memories," she called after them as they left the store laughing and headed across the way to Crumpets and Cones.

Finally, a break. Amy dialed the number.

"It's a *happy* day at Happy House Retirement Village," the woman said brightly. "How can I make your day better?"

Amy stalled.

"Hello? Is anyone there?"

"Hello," Amy said finally. "I'm trying to reach Charles Gray."

There was a silence on the other end of the line.

"They call him Banjo Man," she added, and then realized that was a silly thing to say. Of course, they knew his nickname. He lived there.

"I'm *happy* to help. Just a moment," the woman intoned.

Amy waited.

The line reconnected. "Are you a relative?"

Not again. She was going to get booted off the phone the same way she got booted off the porch in a not so *happy happy* manner.

The woman cleared her throat. "I'm *happy* to help but…"

"I'm not a relative," Amy said quickly, "but I am a friend." She grimaced. How much of a friend remained to be known. "I was hoping to get his phone number. Is that possible?"

"That information is not available outside of family members."

Amy frowned. All because of *happy* HIPAA. "May I leave a message?" The one she left before had no effect. Banjo Man had not called her back. She gave the woman her name and number. "Please mark that *urgent*," she added and hung up.

Well, shoot. Dead ends everywhere. Dead End Drive. She smiled in spite of her predicament. No Banjo Man. No secret letter. No clue as to who from 1924 had shot a man and taken his money and then—maybe—bumped off three other husbands just because they could.

She returned to the photos she took of the scrapbook. She was disappointed that nothing seemed particularly useful to the crime, but she enjoyed the sentimental journey. The photo of the four women used at the museum's mayor exhibit was in the front of the book. She looked over the photo carefully, her first real visual study of the characters in the Silent City program. Catherine looked like a woman who had everything. Good looks and personality, good family and education, a bright future ahead. Bella looked like a woman who worried a lot, and Amy noticed the dark circles under her eyes. It could have been a shadow, but there was something troublesome in her expression even as she was caught in a laugh. Maude Calhoun looked like a straightforward, no-nonsense kind of gal. She wore a pair of wire-frame glasses on her round little face, her hair looked oddly out of place, as if the confluence of old style and new style wasn't as smooth a transition. Mable Rose, if that was her, looked old-fashioned compared to the others. Her hair was curled under instead of bobbed in the trend of the day. Her face was shifted slightly from the camera angle as she looked elsewhere, but Amy could see a tender smile and the intensity in her gaze.

There was a picture of Catherine and her teammates. The college tennis club by the look of it. She scanned through the photo, but she didn't recognize anyone else, and the only reason she recognized Catherine was because someone had written "Catherine the All-Star" above her head.

In another photo, she stood with her mates in the Thespian Club. Rian had snapped a picture of the cover of the drama playbill in the museum.

The Bat

Based on the novel, <u>The Circular Staircase</u> by Mary Roberts Rinehart. Adapted for stage by Mary Roberts Rinehart and Avery Hopwood.

An arson, a bank theft, a mastermind villain, and a maid hunting for stolen cash.

"One of the best plays of the year."

There was a graduation photo. Catherine was summa cum laude and valedictorian. Beneath the black drape of her graduation gown was the familiar string of pearls the mannequin in the museum still wore. Catherine was an overachiever.

Amy studied the photo of a Valentine's dance card with its hand drawn cupids and a red velvet bow tied to wear at the wrist. The dances for the evening were listed on the card, and even though the cursive was hard to read, she wouldn't recognize the songs, anyway. Another photo in a newspaper clipping showed a group of them dancing. Amy strained to see the men in the background. Was that Winslow in the frame? She brought the photo closer. It sure looked like Winslow Duncan, with long legs and a big mustache, dipping someone in his arms.

There was a wedding portrait and a honeymoon picture. They made a stunning couple, Winslow and Catherine, although neither of them looked all that head over heels in love. There was a picture of the couple standing beside a Model T. His head was cocked with supreme pride. Catherine smiled broadly, a handkerchief in her hand as if waving goodbye. He wore a fur coat, and she wore the fur collar she still wore at the museum. A piece of paper had been wedged into the seam of the scrapbook and she had opened it so Rian could take a picture. Now she saw that it was a receipt. Two fur coats and a fur collar purchased from the Leppert-Roos Fur Co. in St. Louis. The bill was $192. Special delivery paid.

That was a lot of money back then.

There was a series of poems pasted to a page. It looked like one of the poems had been removed and a sprig of violets were pressed in its place. A birthday card with hand drawn bluebirds on a nest of violets wished Catherine happy birthday. The handwritten message said, *Dirty Birdy Look Who's Thirty* followed by a short row of XXs and OOs. It was signed, *Your Friend Always, MR.*

Mabel Rose, Amy wondered?

The rest of the book held newspaper clippings; some she had already read. Others were of the mayor's success at the helm of Bluff Springs. There was a page of recipes for a tea party clipped from the *Ladies Home Journal.* Lemon Sponge Cake, Hawaiian Surprise, Mayflower Salad, and French dressing made with the newly introduced Mazola oil.

Amy spun through the pictures on her phone again, watching as Catherine peaked in her prime and then grew older, until finally the contributions to the scrapbook stopped. She yawned as the door of Tiddlywinks jangled again. She huffed with impatience. Zelda was right, if she wanted to make a living, Tiddlywinks needed to be open for business. She looked to the door, surprised to see Camellia deRossier standing there. The look on her face was heart wrenching and Amy couldn't help but rush to her and throw an arm around her shoulders.

"What's the matter?"

Camellia shook her head, tears welling in her eyes.

Ushering her to a chair, she asked, "What's going on? Are you okay?"

"I shouldn't have been so snotty to you," Camellia said and sniffed. "You were just trying to be helpful. I was a brat."

Amy patted her arm. "We can all be brats no matter how old we are."

"It's overwhelming," Camellia said finally after several minutes of quiet as she fought back tears.

"What's overwhelming?"

"Everything!" Camellia motioned dramatically with her hands. "That guy is trying to bully me into selling. Now he's threatening to shut off my water. He says the well and pump house are on his property! And now he says I owe him for half of the survey. He says he will put a lien on my house if I don't pay. How can that be true? I didn't agree to anything."

She took a breath and rattled on. "The taxes will be due in another four months. I don't have it. The house is a wreck and it's going to take a lot to fix it up—with money I don't have. And if there was money it should go to my sister's care. But we need a place to live and…"

She paused in frustration and Amy tried to offer a sympathetic smile. She felt guilty about the water. And the bullying. And the survey. None of it was her doing, but it was her fault.

"And," Camellia added with a burst. "Aunt Mable Rose was a looney bird. I don't believe she started out that way, but I'm reading her diaries and she's just getting weird. The things she writes!"

"Like what?" Amy urged, eager to hear.

Camellia sighed with a groan. "Like all this dark spirit stuff. About how everybody who comes to see her for spiritual counseling takes a little piece of her with them. How they leave a little piece of themselves behind. And how she feels she's losing herself to the place between the two worlds. She doesn't know how to make it stop."

Camellia took a deep, shuddering breath.

"She writes that the *boogeydog* barks," she added and rolled bloodshot eyes. "She says the *boogeydog* barks all night long. What is that? What does she mean?"

Amy shook her head. Grandmother Ollie talked about the *boogeyman*, but she had never heard of the *boogeydog*.

"The worst part is that when I'm reading her diary it all sounds like my sister in my head!" Camellia put her hands to her ears and shook her head until her earrings swung wide. "It's creeping me out. And you know what else? You were right, there was a baby born in 1924."

Camellia reached into her sling bag and pulled out the letter Amy had delivered from the antique shop. The wax seal was now broken. Amy looked at the letter Camellia placed in her hands and for some reason her heart thundered as if she were about to open an ancient secret tomb. She glanced at Camellia's overwhelm and tears and she could feel the weight in her hands. Not the weight of paper, but the weight of something hidden away for decades. A secret that someone didn't want found. And yet, the words had been committed to paper as if someday all would be revealed.

She opened the page, surprised by how few words were written. It was a birth announcement. Nothing official, there was no stamp or seal. A handwritten note, the kind that might be stuck in a family Bible to record the comings and goings of the family tree. No wonder Camellia felt so overwhelmed. She felt it herself. Who wouldn't? It was not uncommon back then to lose an infant. But that didn't ease anyone's suffering.

Born January 2, 1924. Died January 8, 1924.

A baby who had come and gone within days of drawing its first breath.

Amy studied the ornate cursive. There was no mother listed. No father listed, either.

Teddy was all it said.

Born and buried but days before Winslow was shot.

Mrs. Teddy Duncan. The name in the necklace, drawn in pencil with curlicues. But hadn't the necklace belonged Mable Rose? Zelda had figured that out. Had Catherine given her the necklace as a gift? Amy pictured Mable Rose making needlepoint designs for little baby Winslow. Maybe she was making matching sleeping gowns with fine needlework stitches for her friend Catherine, whose infant would not survive long. How very sad!

Had Catherine endured a birth and two deaths in a matter of days? Was the detail about the mourning dress there to draw attention to her postpartum circumstance or to disguise it altogether? Had Catherine come to Mable Rose to connect with the dead? Had she turned to Mable Rose and the Ouija board for comfort?

Amy exhaled. No wonder Camellia was bowing to the weight of it all. The house she and her sister inherited seemed full of restless spirits. Grandmother Ollie would call them haints. And Mable Rose had invited every single one of them inside her home. She had invited every one of them to sit at her table.

She remembered Sir Alfred Hitchcock's words.

I would ask you to join me, but as you can see, the seats are all taken.

Maybe he was talking about the table in the parlor at Piney Top. The parlor full of spirits surrounding the Ouija board.

"I don't know what to do with this," Camellia said finally, with a nod to the letter. "Is it something that needs to be turned over to someone? I don't want to lose this house because of some weird paper snag. And I don't know how to make the house good enough for Rose to come live here. The house is damp and spidery and…" Camellia looked at Amy with sorrowful eyes. "And it feels so haunted," she added. "The more I read about Mable Rose, the more I wonder if she really did just wander off like they said."

"Wander off? What do you mean?"

Camellia sighed again. "My family's story is that Mable Rose just up and left her house one day and no one ever saw her again. Depending on what part of the family you are talking to, it was either in late summer or early fall, but in both versions, they claim she disappeared without a trace.

"That's why the house sat empty for so long. Mable Rose's sister inherited the house, but she's been gone a long time, too. None of the family lived near and no one wanted to do anything about the old house in case she showed up again one day. I guess that possibility ended a long time ago, but it just never got dealt with. Someone paid the taxes. A family trust, I guess. I think they had a maintenance man squatting there for a while, but he's long gone, too."

Camellia pushed her hair behind her ears. "Our grandmother is the daughter of Mable Rose's sister. According to the family, Mable Rose never married and never had children."

"Is that why you were looking for old photos? Were you trying to find a family picture?"

Camellia looked startled. "How did you know about that?"

"This town has ears," Amy said. "And eyes. And tongues." She rubbed her temples. "You're right. It is overwhelming. How is it that your last name is deRossier?"

"It's my middle name," Camellia said. "I like it, so I've always used it as my surname, and no one ever seems to notice otherwise."

Amy nodded. "What can I do to help?"

"I want to be friends with you and the others," Camellia said. "I don't want to feel like an outsider, and I don't want to feel like I have to do everything myself all the time. For some reason, I thought if I let anyone help me, they would take it all away and now I see how dumb that is. I could use your help. And I think you and your friends are pretty cool old—" Camellia stopped and smiled.

"You were going to say old ladies."

"I was not."

Amy smiled. "If you say so."

Camellia rolled her eyes and grinned, her tears thinning, and Amy laughed so hard her cheeks ached.

What a day. She watched Camellia leave Tiddlywinks and slip onto the bike she had stowed against the building. Camellia invited her to stop by and have a look at the diaries for herself. She claimed she hadn't uncovered any love letters, but there were still lots of cupboards and tins and hiding places left to look.

Amy promised to bring the letters she found in the Ouija board. They belonged to Camellia. Not to herself. Of course, she would take pictures before she let them go. It wouldn't lessen the overwhelming nature of the project on Piney Top, but perhaps the more Camellia knew about Mable Rose, the more she would seem like a real person and not a haunted spirit in a strange family tale.

She would bring Rian again when she came by, and Rian could help Camellia decide what things needed to be fixed and what could slide. Rian was handy, and if she didn't know how to do something, she knew who to hire.

A pall of sadness had drifted in, and Amy opened the windows to let in the fresh air. It was crisp enough to drop the temperature inside the store by several degrees, but the breeze felt as good as it smelled.

She realized the shop day was nearly over, but she felt like hanging out at Tiddlywinks rather than going home to her apartment above. Victor would have to wait for his supper.

She was pleased when Zelda popped in again. "I'm closing up for the day," Zelda said. "What are you going to do this evening?"

"I'm going to hang out here for a little while," Amy answered. "I'm feeling a little unplugged and uncentered. Know what I mean?"

Zelda nodded. "I think we're like computers. If we're not working right, just unplug us, wait a bit, and then plug back in. I think that works for everything."

Amy agreed. "I'd offer you a glass of wine but I'm out. We drained that box last time we gathered here."

"Awful stuff," Zelda complained. "We need to get you a real wine cellar. Didn't you learn anything from the sommelier?"

Amy laughed. She had almost forgotten about the wine sommelier and their misadventures in the Arkansas wine country. Genna had dragged them on the Big European Tour of Arkansas for a publicity stunt she was heading up for a politician's election campaign. Amy, Rian, and Zelda went looking for a good time but found themselves steeped in a tricky state of affairs where they uncorked a murderous plot with poison in the wine.

"Tell me," Zelda said, her eyes searching Amy's. "What is it about all this Ouija and haint stuff that's got you so wrapped up and running tail and feather, to and fro? I don't understand why you think something that happened a hundred years ago has any bearing on today."

Amy raised a brow. "Haven't you been listening to Genna? Everything that happened a hundred years ago has bearing on us today."

"I don't mean women's rights," Zelda said. "I'm talking about the murder you're trying to solve. It's unsolvable. Even if you did manage to figure it out, there's no one to blame. Everybody's gone. What is so fascinating about this puzzle?"

She didn't answer at first, giving herself time to think. "That's it in a nutshell," she said finally. "Because it is a puzzle. I don't know how to walk away from a puzzle until I've found the very last piece. Aren't you that way about your accessories? Hunting down the perfect shoe to finish your look? It's not all that different."

It was Zelda's turn to ponder. "I guess you're right, Sparks. The right pair of shoes is the perfect finish."

"Besides," Amy added, "I opened my big mouth to one of the Langford brothers and now the other brother is dogging Camellia to sell at a low price. He's trying to push her out and take her land. I don't know how the necklace and the murder and the house at Piney Top are connected but I can't shake the feeling that they are. I don't know if this is the same Langford family that lost a property deed in a poker game a hundred years ago, but if I go digging for more information, I could make matters worse for Camellia. I have to figure out how to fix this. I have to put it right."

Zelda nodded. "Yeah, you do."

Amy smiled. "I could make us a cup of tea. The bakery is already closed for the day, but I have an electric kettle in the back. Want a cup?"

"Sure," Zelda said. "Got any of those yummy cookies to go with it?"

Amy smiled at her friend who was always after a treat. "It's a possibility. Let me look," she added, as she rose and headed to her little closet kitchen.

When she came back with two cups of tea and a plate of cookies balanced on one of the mugs, Banjo Man was seated at the table with Zelda.

"Well, hello," she said, putting the tea and plate on the table. "Nice to see you."

He nodded. "Likewise."

"You could have called," she said. "That's all I asked." She pushed the cup across to him. "Are you okay?"

He nodded again. His arm was in a cast and sling. For someone who used a cane to get around, that had to make mobility an issue.

"You wanted to ask me something? You said it was urgent." He moved the teacup closer but didn't drink. She could tell he was feeling low.

"At the time, I wanted to ask you why you broke into my house and stole that necklace I showed you. But then, I learned that it wasn't you after all. And you fell and I'm really sorry that happened."

"Thanks for the confidence boost."

"I wanted to ask you what these signs meant. The ones drawn on the pages. Specifically, the symbols drawn on these pages." Amy pulled out her phone and brought up the photos of the pages from the necklace. "This one for Cat, Catherine Duncan I'm guessing, looks like a donut. She was Winslow Duncan's widow."

Banjo Man glanced at the photo. "That means 'nothing to be gained here,'" he said flatly. "If it had an X in the middle, it would mean something else."

"Like what?" Amy asked, pulling in for a closer look. It looked suspiciously like an X has been rubbed away from the page, although she knew the pencil in the hinge had no eraser.

"That would change the meaning to a good place for a handout."

She turned to the page marked for Evangeline. "What about this cross? Or is that obvious?"

"It means if the hobo is willing to listen to a religious lecture, he will be fed."

"Hmm," Amy said. "That makes sense. And this one?" She showed him another picture. It was diamond shaped like a kite with a very short tail.

"That was a warning not to speak out," Banjo Man answered. "If you turn it the other way, it means you should be prepared to defend yourself. I'm not sure which way that was drawn."

"Whose page was that?" Zelda asked, peeking over Amy's shoulder.

"Maude," Amy answered. "M.A. Calhoun, the name behind the town newspaper."

The last shape appeared on several pages. Two vertical lines. Amy presented the picture.

"That means the sky is the limit," Banjo Man answered with a smile. "In modern terms—a cash cow."

Zelda and Amy exchanged glances. Mable Rose knew her target market, and Bella St. Claire was one of them.

"Is that all?" He shuffled as if he was about to leave. Amy put her hand on his sleeve.

"No, actually, I wanted to ask you why you were looking for a birth certificate from 1924."

Amy noticed the cup shook slightly in his hand as he set it on the table. Were those nerves? Or was it because he was recovering from a fall?

"I guess I owe you an explanation," he said finally with a deep sigh. "I did just up and leave that day without any word of farewell."

He was talking about the day at Tiddlywinks when she told him the story of the murder of Winslow Duncan and how Hobo Joe was blamed. He was shaken by the news then and he still looked uncomfortable about it now. She was ready to hear his side of the story.

"I guess I should start at the beginning," he said.

"That's a good place," Zelda piped in.

He looked at Zelda and smiled and she smiled back. Zelda could tame a wild tiger if she had to. For now, she was putting an old man at ease.

"I told you I got into the hobo stuff because of that postcard sent to my grandma. That's true. But only partly."

Amy remembered the scrapbook and the postcard cut from a box of cereal postmarked from Texas.

He closed his eyes and recited: "Fear knocked but faith answered. Your kindness filled my heart. Be ever watchful for the hand of God for he will make a promise. Please tell Miss M, I am beyond reach and blessedly grateful. Ever yours, Joe."

He opened his eyes. "I knew that postcard was from Hobo Joe. My grandmother's name was Della, and she was very familiar with Hobo Joe. He did a lot of chores at her house. And well, my favorite uncle was born in 1924. My grandmother was a war widow. I always figured Hobo Joe was my uncle's dad. My uncle was my hero. And so, I made Hobo Joe a hero, too."

Amy was silent.

"When you told me about the murder, I was devastated that Hobo Joe could have killed someone. And when I put the words to the postcard up against the crime you described, I couldn't help but picture that scene. Hobo Joe leaving town in a hurry. And then letting Granny know he'd arrived safe down the road.

"No one ever talked about any of it out in the open, but I heard things I wasn't supposed to hear. I didn't know who Miss M was, but she must have helped him escape. She and Granny both."

He took a deep breath and went on. "Duncan was not a well-liked man. I don't know that anyone was surprised he was killed like that. I didn't recall hearing that story when I was a kid, but when you shared it with me, it jogged my memory. I filled in the rest.

"Granny always said there were only three people in this world she would trust with her life. The dressmaker. The preacher's wife. And Hobo Joe. At least two of them were out in the snow that night. The night Duncan was shot and killed."

Amy leaned forward. Was Evangeline Hayes there, too? Mable Rose? And Hobo Joe, who helped Duncan free his car from the slush! Maybe the M in the postcard was Mable Rose, not Maude Calhoun. And maybe the ever-watchful hand of God was the wife of the good reverend and his penchant for preaching the gospel of gossip.

She didn't know whether she should share her thoughts or not. She remembered the article Genna had found in the local newspaper. A witness identified Hobo Joe as the man with

Duncan that night. They claimed Duncan gave him money for his help. Another witness said they saw him running from the scene but wouldn't swear testimony. The Rev. Hayes claimed he and his wife, Evangeline, were having supper and prayer with Hobo Joe at the time of the murder.

It was clear that Hobo Joe was the killer. Mable Rose was the witness. Evangeline and her husband came to the rescue. They knew what Joe had done and yet they lied to protect him. They lied and let him escape. They helped him escape! But why? If Rev. Hayes knew who committed the crime, wouldn't he be obligated to tell the police? What a conundrum of human nature.

"I'm sorry," Amy said at last. "I'm really, really sorry."

Banjo Man drank his tea in silence, but Amy wondered if he had more to say. He sat quietly and she waited for him to speak. "I'm tired and I want to go home," he said, setting his cup on the table. He grabbed his cane, rose slowly, and then hobbled out the door.

"See," Amy said to Zelda. "The past really does matter. What happened a hundred years ago is still with us today."

"Mystery solved," Zelda said and ate the last cookie.

Later, as Amy climbed the stairs to her apartment, she suddenly felt tired, wondering if the stairs had gotten steeper since the morning. Her legs felt as heavy as two fat hams. Her stomach grumbled and she realized how empty she felt. Was it hunger that was hollowing out her belly or was it hollow with the knowing?

She paused on the stair and took a deep breath.

She had been too eager to make a murder out of a molehill. The mystery was solved. There was no black widow society. There was no cold case. There was no reason to dig any more.

The necklace found in the graveyard was dropped by Camellia climbing a tree to eavesdrop. It wasn't a clue to a crime. It was simply a piece of jewelry that seemed to appear out of nowhere and meant nothing. The symbols on the pages might be hobo symbols and the numbers might be measurements. They could also be the sketching of a young girl learning a secret language to share with her friends about the boys they wanted to marry. There could be many stories behind the necklace, but Winslow's murder was not one of them.

CHAPTER TWENTY-EIGHT

"I just knew it!" Genna exclaimed as she entered Tiddlywinks like a wind-swept leaf. She was dressed head to foot in brown suede, a black Hermes scarf with a pattern of golden autumn leaves knotted at her neck.

"Wow! You look great!" Amy said. "Where are you headed all dressed up?"

"For an early dinner meeting in Little Rock with a new public relations client. Someone with m.o.n.e.y.," she spelled out with a toothy smile. "But my first stop today is to see my friends," Genna announced. "And I have the deets!"

"The deets?" Amy was confused.

"The details. The goods. The skinny on our not so honorable Rev. Hayes," Genna said. "Are Rian and Zelda here yet? Not a peep until they get here."

Before Amy could answer, Sammie Walsh from Crumpets and Cones next door entered, balancing a tray of goodies and a large pot of tea.

"Good morning," she said and set the tray on one of the tables. "Compliments of Genna, if I am right in me t'inking," she said. "And thank you. You are the one who ordered this?" She looked at Genna and smiled.

"I did," Genna said and nodded. "I've been jonesing for one of your crumpets with cream and a good cup of tea. We haven't had the likes of that since we left Ireland."

Sammie beamed. "Oh, be gone wit' ya." She wiped her hands on her flour-stained apron. "It's just a proper cup of tea and cream whipped stiff. The crumpets are still warm. That's always when they are best."

Sammie Walsh and her boyfriend, Beau, had moved to the Ozarks from Northern Ireland. She was part of The Cardboard Cottage shops, a very important part, since her bakery spiced up the air around the building and drew in customers following their nose. Amy tried to include her in their activities, but she found Sammie to be rather reclusive. She was not unfriendly. She was always warm and welcoming, but she seemed to prefer the quiet morning hours and the solace of her ovens. Sammie closed early in the day and Amy had no inkling what she did with her time away from the bakery.

"We don't have to wait for them to get started on this," Genna said as she piled a crumpet with raspberry jam and fresh whipped cream. "This is one of the things I miss most about Ireland." Genna poured tea for both of them. "I always thought the food in Ireland would be boring boiled potatoes, but we ate like royalty, didn't we? Delicious!"

She made a plate for herself, noticing that Sammie had included decorative china instead of paper plates and cups. What a nice touch.

Amy licked the cream from her lips. "What did you find out about Rev. Hayes?"

Genna wagged a finger. "Not a squeak until Rian and Zelda get here."

Amy looked at her watch. "It will be any minute now," she said. "They always open by ten or not at all."

She heard Zelda's shoes in the hall first. Rian was behind her.

Zelda clasped her hands as she noticed the tray on the table. "Breakfast!" she crowed. "Breakfast at Tiddlywinks? Sounds like a movie!"

When they finally settled, Genna tapped her cup with a spoon. "I've been doing more archive digging and I believe I have solved the murders."

"Murders?" Zelda asked.

"Murders," Genna echoed. "Winslow, Frank, Oscar, and Cecil. I believe there was a serial killer in Bluff Springs, and I think it was Bella St. Claire."

"Bella!" Rian exclaimed.

"Well," Genna began as Zelda reached for seconds, "I believe Rev. Hayes knew Bella was behind the murders and he said as much in his sermons. In fact, I think he said a little too much and that's what got him killed."

Genna now had their full attention, crumpets and cream or not. "I went through the newspapers and collected as many Monday sermons as I could find for around that time," Genna started. "It seems our good reverend was a master of gossip from the pulpit."

"We knew that already," Amy said and Genna put up her hand.

"What you don't know is who he was gossiping about. I think I have figured out who drugged them in their sleep to make it look like a heart attack. Everything points to Bella St. Claire. She's the one with the knowledge, but I haven't found her motive yet."

"Convince me," Rian said simply.

Genna pulled papers from her London Fog tote bag and rattled them with a shake of her hand. "Proof," she added. "It all seemed to start with Rev. Hayes's sermon about the incident where two young boys died after taking the wrong cure. There was no penicillin at that time, you know. That wouldn't come along for another twenty years or so. Remedies from that day were tinctures with a grain of this and a grain of that. Take two Bayer and pray it doesn't kill you. Everybody thought it was Oscar who mislabeled the drugs. But it may have been Bella."

"What?" Rian sputtered. "That can't be true."

Genna nodded. "We knew Bella was a wartime nurse who aspired to be a pharmacist. She trained with her husband to become the first certified female pharmacist in the state. But…"

Genna held up the paper, "but not before Oscar was out of the picture. And not before the rumors started that Oscar made mistakes. Hayes helped spread that rumor, but Bella was the one who started it!"

"That's all there in his sermon?" Rian asked. The frown on her brow said she was dubious.

Genna lowered her glasses to her nose and read. **"Even the kindliest among us who strive night and day to cure and comfort the ill, and aid others misled by the evils of addiction, still have moments of deep, abiding shame. No creature before God is free of such burden. No one knows this any better than the woman who stands in solidarity by his side and fails."**

"Doesn't that sound like Bella St. Claire confessed to Hayes that her husband was an addict and the reason those boys died?"

Rian refilled her cup. Genna looked pleased with herself.

"The week before Winslow was shot, the good reverend wrote about vice and charity and scandalous attitudes. Here, let me read a few lines:

"'Is it not a remarkable curiosity to the penitent souls of this community how one twenty-dollar Federal Reserve Bank Note is a meager sum when wagered to Lady Luck. But the same note donated to the great good of the church is viewed as an extravagance. Is this not perplexing? Where is our charity? Where is our conscience that guides the morals of men? Bad temper and vice are the poison that breed uncharitable and scandalous attitudes among our brethren. Pray you the Reaper does not come for what is his due.'"

Genna looked up. "That sounds like he was talking about Winslow Duncan. It sounds like he was extorting money. It almost sounds like he was calling the murder into being."

"Sounds like blackmail to me," Rian said.

"My gosh, he's all doom and gloom," Zelda said. "I don't think I'd be in his church pew very often."

Amy was listening to the words trying to picture Rev. Cecil Hayes standing at the pulpit, his collar buttoned to his throat.

She pictured him as a gout-looking guy with a ruddy complexion and a mop of brown hair. And then she pictured him as thin and stern and wispy, with his hair parted in the middle and slicked on either side. Did his words come from a barrel chest with a baritone voice? Or did he rattle and prattle like Jacob Marley's ghost until the congregation gnashed their teeth in despair?

She burst out laughing.

Three pairs of eyes turned curious.

"What in the world are you laughing at, Sparks?"

"I was trying to picture Rev. Hayes. We've never seen a photo of him, have we?"

Even Genna had to admit that was true.

"We saw pictures of Bella and Catherine and Maude. You even uncovered a photo of Winslow, but we've been living with these men in our heads, and we don't know what any of them looked like."

"You're right," Zelda said. "I guess we put our own mental spin on them. Winslow was dark and brutish but dashing. In my mind, Frank was big and tall and looked old long before his age. Oscar was tall and suave with a cleft chin. Sort of like Rhett Butler minus the dark and alluring charm."

She hadn't pictured Oscar that way at all. In her mind, he was thin and bent at the waist, serious-minded and a little jittery. Too many Coca-Colas.

"I don't believe it," Rian said to Genna. "If Bella made a mistake that took a life she would have so much remorse. But shame? That's more about having a husband who doesn't own up to *his* mistakes. If there was a serial killer, it wasn't Bella."

Genna frowned. "I see you need more convincing. Bella St. Claire was known for her herbal remedies."

"And she had them blessed before she used them," Rian added. "I read that somewhere about her."

"Now that's weird," Zelda said. "Hayes wasn't a priest for crying out loud."

"This dude sure had people wrapped around his finger," Amy said. "If you didn't pay the piper, he'd peep."

Zelda laughed. "If the pastor piper picked a peck of poison, how much poison did he peep!" She repeated it until she couldn't keep a straight face, and they laughed until Genna started coughing, spewing the dregs of her tea. She wiped her eyes on the Irish linen napkin Sammie included with their breakfast tray and then laid it back in her lap.

"The piper of poison," Genna said, finally recovering. "That's a good one, Zelda. I suspect Frank and Oscar and Cecil were poisoned with something that mimicked a heart attack. Hayes was the last to go. I think he knew something about the other deaths. I think that knowledge got him killed. Bella is the one who had access."

"Bella wasn't the only one who made remedies," Rian interjected. "Most country folk did. Many still do."

Genna nodded. "Point taken, but the thing about the reverend's sermons that I noted was they were all fire and brimstone and that tone that says, *'I know who you are, and I know what you did'* and then he completely changed his tune. Like he had been warned. Or threatened."

Amy sat forward. She had been waiting to unveil what she had learned in her visit with Camellia and Banjo Man. The Rev. Hayes and his wife Evangeline knew something about Winslow's murder and so did Mable Rose. What they knew was still hidden in the weeds. Maybe his sermons would spell it all out.

"You've got it all wrong, Genna," Zelda said boldly. "The hobo did it. He shot Winslow and took the money. Rev. Hayes and his wife helped get him out of town. Who knows why, but that's what happened."

"Thanks for stealing my thunder," Amy said crossly. "And you forgot to mention that Mable Rose was at the scene of the crime, too!"

Genna looked dumfounded.

"Banjo Man told us everything," Zelda continued. "His granny was friends with the dressmaker, the preacher's wife, and Hobo Joe. They were at the scene of the crime the night Duncan was shot. I told you before, the hobo did it."

Amy folded her arms. "No, you said the barber did it."

"Is that true?" Rian looked relieved that Bella St. Claire wasn't at the scene, too.

"True according to Banjo Man," Amy said. "And the reason he went looking for a birth certificate was because he thought his favorite uncle was Hobo Joe's son. He believed his grandmother Della and Joe were familiar, to use the language of that era."

Rian whistled under her breath and Genna sat back in her chair, obviously deflated by this turn of events.

"Winslow's murder wasn't related to the other deaths," Rian said, twirling a curl with her finger. "Which means the other three men were not murdered. Which means no serial killer." She looked at Genna. Genna looked disappointed.

"I'm sorry to bust your theory, but that's what I believe, too," Amy said. "Although I do think Hayes did a lot to provoke the community."

"Why did Hayes help the hobo escape?"

Amy shrugged. "I think maybe they were friends. I gather Hobo Joe had supper with the Hayes family often. Maybe the preacher was trying to make an honest man of him. Get him to settle down. Banjo Man told me about the hobo culture. These men weren't shiftless, they had wanderlust. Maybe Evangeline convinced her husband that helping Hobo Joe escape was best for everyone. Hayes would lose faith if the man he befriended was captured for murder. Shoot, Hayes may have known about Della's situation, which would compound the situation. I'm sure Evangeline knew about Della and Hobo Joe. She and Della were friends."

Amy exhaled. "This is all my fault. I found a necklace and had a dream that was probably not even a snippet, and I made a mystery out of a molehill. It was nothing more than a cool old necklace. It wasn't really a cold case because everybody knew who killed Winslow and no one seemed to care.

"Not even Catherine," Amy added. "She was too grief stricken to care. I think she was the one who gave birth a few days before her husband's funeral, and the baby didn't live."

The room grew quiet, each to their own thoughts, the content of which Amy could only imagine. Of the four, only Genna had children, and they were now grown.

"No wonder she was so determined to be mayor," Zelda said. "Catherine made something good of her life, something really good out of something very sad."

"But what about this sermon right after Oscar died?" Genna asked when their silence had lasted a while. "The newspaper called his death an overdose, but Hayes called it redemption. He wrote that some lives were destined to flail while others gained glory. He said there was only one Judge in the lives of man, but that all men served on the jury. He quoted that passage. You know, the one about, *'Ask, and you will receive. Knock and the door will be opened to you.'* What was he implying and about whom?"

"For all we know, he could have been talking about anybody in town," Zelda said. "We only know the people you've introduced to us, Genna. And if there really was a serial killer in Bluff Springs, he or she was never found out."

"It's pretty obvious Hayes had his nose to the ground," Amy said. "He knew things others didn't, and he didn't seem to mind sharing it with the jury, as he so aptly called them. Anyone sitting in his congregation with a load of guilt might assume he was talking about them."

"Which may have been the truth of the matter," Rian said quietly. "Guilt and paranoia."

"That's a possibility," Amy added. "Camellia told me that Mable Rose felt that everybody who came to see her for spirit work took a little piece of her with them and left a piece of themselves behind. It was in her diary. She felt she was losing herself in a place between two worlds. They were different— Mable Rose and Cecil Hayes—but I can see both of them feeling the strain of other people's secrets weighing them down."

"That and Datura," Rian said simply.

"Datura who?" Zelda asked.

"Jimsonweed. *Datura stramonium.* You've seen Georgia O'Keefe's painting. Most people think it's a morning glory, but it's really a datura trumpet flower."

"What does this have to do with Hayes?" Genna asked.

"Nothing. Just another take on how people approach spiritual life," Rian answered. "Amy and I found a stand of Jimsonweed at

Camellia's on Piney Top. I can't say it's been reseeding itself for a hundred years, but that would not surprise me.

"Jimsonweed is known as a visionary hallucinogen. Shamans used it to intensify their visions. It was a way to remove the ego and open the veil to mystical experiences."

"Like with Spiritualism and the Ouija board," Amy said.

Rian nodded. "But if it's overused, it can cause delirium and confusion, even paranoia."

"Mable Rose was losing herself and she knew it," Amy said. "Maybe Hayes felt the same way."

Genna pounced. "And what about its use in traditional medicine? Like homemade remedies that a pharmacist might use?"

Rian frowned. "Yes, Genna, Bella St. Claire would know about that, too. It was a gamble, a few grains too many was deadly, but in the right measure it could relieve pain and fever, ease childbirth, and even treat insomnia."

Amy inhaled. "Insomnia. Permanent sleep."

She thought of her snippet and Alfred Hitchcock's words came back to her once again.

I have it on good authority that unfavorable habits lead to sleepless nights. I also have it on good authority there is a most useful remedy for insomnia.

He had placed a single bullet on the table.

Guaranteed to put you to sleep. Forever.

Amy blew into her cup. Would her snippets ever make sense?

CHAPTER TWENTY-NINE

It was cold and windy when they arrived at the house on Piney Top. Amy zipped her hoodie as far as it would zip and pulled the hood over her head. Rian had parked the Fiat at the back of the graveyard, and they walked through the back gate and up the road to the house.

Camellia's bicycle was leaning against the side of the porch, but she didn't answer when they knocked.

"Maybe she walked downtown to hear music in the park," Amy suggested.

"You said she asked us to come to look at repairs," Rian said, opening the screen door to knock on the solid door behind. When she reached for the doorknob, it twisted in her hand and Rian looked at Amy with the question in her eyes. "A city girl leaves the door unlocked?"

"It was unlocked last time I was here to…" She decided not to add *here to snoop*. And she was almost caught in the act. "Maybe there is no key. Or the door only locks from the inside. It's an old door and nobody locked their doors back then. I guess that should be one of the repairs on the list."

Rian opened the door a few inches. "Hello? Anybody home? Camellia? It's Rian and Amy."

With the door open a few inches, Amy could see over Rian's shoulder. A lamp lit a side table near the door, casting a small yellow circle of light. At the base of the table sat a suitcase, an old-fashioned one with tan jute sides and a brown Bakelite handle.

"She's going somewhere," Rian said and backed out of the door jamb. "Unless she's planning on selling that vintage suitcase to the antique shop."

"Shouldn't we check to see if everything's okay?"

"You mean go inside?" Rian looked surprised. "That's how you get blown to smithereens."

"I doubt if she has a gun."

"Okay then hacked with a pair of dressmaker's shears."

"You're just being cantankerous." She reached around Rian and pushed the door open. "We need to at least make sure she's not hurt."

"I'll wait here," Rian said and planted her feet on the porch.

Amy stepped into the parlor. "Camellia? It's Amy. Are you here? Are you hurt?" She glanced back at Rian and shrugged. "I don't hear any cries for help. Do you think I should check all the rooms?"

"No," Rian said sternly. "I do not."

She backed out of the door jamb and shut the door. "Well? What now?"

Rian pulled a flashlight from her pocket. "We can at least take a look in the basement. You can tell a lot about an old building by its bones below the surface. That's really where I wanted to start anyway. You can see how well a house stands up to time from the bottom up."

Amy shook her head. "And that's not trespassing?"

Rian grinned. "Not so much."

They left the porch, walking around the side of the house, where Amy gave the trumpet flowers wide berth as she passed, the crunch of fallen leaves beneath her feet. Just beyond the kitchen steps was the basement door, and Rian pulled the metal plate from the staple loop of the lock as she had done before.

"What are you looking for?" Amy whispered as Rian pulled the door open on its rusty hinges.

"Rotten floor joists. Water leaks. Evidence. Why are you whispering?"

"Evidence of what?" Amy repeated.

Rian didn't answer. Even though it was daylight, the basement was dark. The light coming through the door only illuminated a small arc and when Rian pulled the light chain hanging just inside the door, the chain crumbled in her fingers.

Amy followed Rian in. It was a typical old Ozark homestead basement built into the side of the mountain like an earth berm. The floor was rocky dirt and the beams above them were barely head high. If Genna was here, she would have to stoop. At the back of the basement, which would be the front of the house, the floor joists from above met the ground. The porch would sit beyond that, but it didn't look accessible from here.

Amy looked at the circle cast by Rian's light. Spiders and spiderwebs. She stepped closer to Rian.

"People kept food in the basement where it's always dark and cool," Rian said, moving the flashlight beam quickly around the basement. "There's probably a shelf of home-canned goods down here."

"You mean like pickles and pears?" She felt Rian leaving her side. "Wait! Don't leave me alone here in the dark."

Rian chuckled. "Scaredy cat. There's nothing down here but dirt and dead spiders. Hey, look at this." The beam illuminated a wooden shelf built into the wall. The wood was rotted through down the middle, but at one time it had been a sturdy cache of preserved goods. There were a few jars still upright, but most had fallen into a pile of broken glass and rusty lids heaped on the floor where the shelf had given way. Rian moved her flashlight beam to the heap.

"You mean we're down here looking for old jars of rotten food?" Amy asked incredulously.

"Not exactly."

"Then what exactly?"

"Wait? Do you hear that?"

In the quiet, Amy heard the drip drip of water coming from somewhere above.

"That's not good," Rian said. "There's a leak somewhere." She bounced the flashlight over the beams. They looked dry. She swept the room with the light and the basement looked maybe ten- or fifteen-feet square. As Rian passed the light over the walls, Amy saw the remnants of rural life lived in 1920. Farmyard implements hung from heavy nails on one of the wood walls. A rusted spade. A rake. A wooden bucket hanging by a rusty handle.

The wind whistled through the cracks in the plank wood siding.

"It's getting colder," Amy said. "Let's hurry up with whatever we're doing and get out of here."

"Look at this," Rian said as her beam focused on an area against the wall.

"What is that?"

"I think it's a scullery, of sorts," Rian answered. "For herbs. And other things."

Amy studied the area in Rian's beam. It did look like a place set aside, similar to those from Victorian times, where pots were scrubbed and stored. Kind of like Zelda's pantry-sized shop. Against the wall sat a porcelain sink with a faucet and a drainboard counter. A butcher block extended the surface area and a kerosene lamp stood in the center, the red paint now mottled rusty brown.

"Why is that down here?"

"So, she wouldn't contaminate her kitchen," Rian said.

The wall above the table was studded with nails, and strings drooped like broken spiderwebs. The flax threads were empty of long dead plants, the crumbled bits fallen away from where they were hung to dry. Also suspended and long forgotten were scissors and snips. A metal funnel dangled from a metal chain. One of the nails was vacant and Amy wondered what tool had been kept there once.

On the other end of the sink was a cabinet with a key lock. Grandmother Ollie had one similar in her kitchen, except hers had screen doors. A pie safe, she called it, an airy place to store pies and cakes safe from the flies. This one was metal, and it was spotted with rust everywhere the flashlight beam touched.

The wind whistled, blowing dry leaves through the basement door, rustling as they settled to the dirt. Rian nudged the metal cabinet with her shoe. Nothing moved. The lock held and the door stayed closed.

The flashlight beam scanned the ceiling in a grid pattern, light illuminating an area no bigger than a dinner plate. The beam lit a shadow in the corner of a joist and she saw that hanging from a nail was a key. Swiping cobwebs out of the way, Rian grabbed the key and inserted it into the lock, but the door still did not budge. She wiggled the key in the lock and then kicked the door gently with her toe, until finally, the cabinet creaked open.

"Pheew," Amy said as the stale stench billowed from the cabinet. "That really stinks."

"I bet that's why it's down here," Rian said, stepping back from the cabinet. "Don't breathe. I think those are Mable Rose's *Datura stramonium* concoctions."

"You mean poison?"

"For lack of a better word."

They moved back a few steps, the light beam trained on the inside of the cabinet. There were a dozen or so brown medicine bottles with rusted lids and rotten corks lined up on the shelf. Two of the bottles were cracked and a thin line of dark goo hung in a stiff permanent drip from the edge of the shelf. The bottles were labeled, but from where she stood, she could not make out the writing. She wasn't venturing any closer.

"I was wondering how she avoided contaminating her kitchen," Rian said. "She did everything down here. That stuff may be all dried up by now or strong enough to kill the army."

"The army? Whose army?"

"That's how the plant got its name. Jamestown. As in Virginia. The James-town-weed of colonial times. It rendered soldiers helpless so they could be overcome by their enemies."

"Is there no botany tidbit you don't know?"

"To be fair, I went looking for that tidbit," Rian admitted. "I knew about *Datura*, but I didn't know as much as I do now. 'Blind as a bat, dry as a bone, red as a beet, mad as a hatter, and hot as a hare.'Those are the symptoms of Jimsonweed poisoning."

"I don't remember hearing anyone described like that."

"No, but Camellia told you that Mable Rose's diary entries got weirder as time went on," Rian explained. "That's what made me think of it. That and the plant we saw on the side of the house. It's possible she was using it to enhance her visions. I read it was pretty common in spiritual and shamanic practices."

"What did she do with it?"

"I guess she drank it. Maybe she shared it with other Spiritualists and Ouija enthusiasts so they would have visions, too. Who knows."

"You think it tasted as bad as it smells?"

Rian chuckled. "Toxic things taste bad. Honey might make it more palatable, but that wasn't the point."

"What do you think we should do with it?"

"We? We do nothing with it. But I want to make sure Camellia doesn't dump it. It can't go in the sewer, and it shouldn't be dumped in the woods. No need to take a chance on it killing an animal."

A gust of wind screamed through the slats and Amy watched with wide eyes as the door of the basement swung closed. She lunged forward to catch it, but she was too late. The door banged shut and she heard the tinny sound of the hasp lock flipping into place over the staple. She shoved at the door with her shoulder, but it held fast, with only a thin thread of light shining around the edges of the door.

"No!" she screamed and pushed at the door again. "We're stuck! We're trapped!"

Rian shoved the door with her shoulder and the wood creaked and cracked, but the hasp did not give way. She shoved her shoulder against it and groaned.

Amy felt her panic rise. "How do we get out of here?"

"Don't you have your phone?"

"I left it in your car. Don't you have yours?"

"I left it at home."

Amy suddenly felt fiercely angry at Rian. "Who in their right mind has a mobile phone they leave at home?"

"Uh, people in their right mind who don't think being tethered to a phone 24/7 is such a good thing," Rian spat back. "It's an old door; we'll break it down if we need to."

Rian shoved the door again, but it did not open.

With her nose buried in her jacket, Rian kicked the door of the smelly cabinet closed with the toe of her shoe. She shoved the flashlight into Amy's hands and then, pulling the spade from its nail on the wall, she jammed the spade into the tiny thread of an opening in the door. The spade edge was too thick, and the effort was futile. She banged the wood with the shovel where the lock would be on the outside. That, too, didn't help.

Amy felt her stomach drop. They were stuck. It was getting colder and darker. And they were trapped.

Rian clenched the handle and with one big heave, shoved the spade over her head and into the ceiling. Amy felt dirt and debris falling on her shoulders as Rian rammed the floor above, again and again.

"Hey!" Rian yelled. "We're down here!" She bumped the floor again and then waited in silence.

There was no answer from above. They could hear no footsteps. They could hear no sound at all, other than the drip, drip of water somewhere in the dark.

"I don't see another way to get in or out," Rian said.

Amy bounced the beam around the room. "Maybe there's a trap door somewhere."

"Oh, you mean like a secret passageway? This isn't a castle, Amy. It's an old Ozark homestead."

"Don't get all snide and snarky with me. I'm not the one who dragged us down here."

Rian banged the shovel against the ceiling again and dirt rained down with a soft hiss.

"Warn me next time," Amy barked, brushing the debris from her hair and shoulders. She stepped aside and Rian rammed the ceiling again. Still there was no response.

Amy made her way to the opposite wall with the flashlight beam leading the way. Dropping to the soft dirt floor, she sat against the wall with her legs splayed in front of her. She refused to panic. Refused to feel defeated. At least she wasn't here alone.

She had been trapped alone before. Trapped and alone and frightened. She felt an ache swell in her chest and her eyes burned with tears.

Rian dropped down beside her.

"Camellia has to come home at some point," Amy declared. "She'll find us."

Rian didn't answer.

"Maybe we could take the hinges off the door."

"The hinges are on the outside."

"Maybe we could dig through to the front porch."

"Be my guest," Rian said, pushing the spade handle toward Amy. "It's just a few feet of Arkansas rock."

They were silent, with only the sound of their breathing and the steady drip, drip.

"Does this remind you of anything?" Amy said when the silence had grown too still. "Us being stuck in a basement in the dark?"

Rian exhaled. "You know it does."

"Well, we got out of that without harm. We'll get out of this, too. Someone will find us. Zelda will notice we're missing, and someone will see your car, and someone will come looking and we'll yell, and they'll hear us and—" She paused. She was rambling, as if the sound of her own voice would soothe her nerves. She was rambling as if her voice in the dark was better than nothing but dark. Rambling because she once had been trapped deep in the woods where no one would hear her anyway. And then again, locked in a closet with a storm raging outside, boat rolling in the waves like some horrible carnival ride. And, locked in a storm cellar with no way out.

"We got out of that without harm," she said again, fighting back hot tears. "We'll get out of this, too."

"It better not take two days," Rian said abruptly. "I'm already hungry."

There was a two-beat pause then Amy burst into laughter. "Are you saying what I think you're saying?"

Rian laughed. "That you would be my picnic? I'd rather eat hundred-year-old plums from that pile over there. And you can't say we got out of that without harm. The Jaguar was completely destroyed. The guy who bought it was so sad I thought he would weep."

"That was such a horrible tornado," Amy said quietly, as the memory closed in around her. "If you hadn't pulled into that farm for shelter, we wouldn't be here today."

"I know that," Rian said. "Things have a way of happening the way they do."

Amy nodded, knowing there was always a reason things happened as they did. Cause and effect. Yin and Yang. Ebb and flow. Choice and consequence. Synchronicity and chance.

She fell silent as she remembered what seemed impossible to forget. Two days trapped underground. Trapped in a storm cellar somewhere between Bluff Springs and Missouri.

Rian was delivering a vintage car to Kansas City. She and Zelda and Genna went along for the ride. She had not known them very long, but she knew they were friends she wanted to keep.

The tornado came up behind them on a hilly narrow back road, black clouds on the periphery in every direction but one. Rian was eyeing the storm in her rearview mirror when she abruptly pulled off the road into an old homestead.

Luckily, the gate to the farm was open. Luckily, there was a storm shelter right outside the abandoned house. Luckily, they escaped down into the shelter with a picnic basket and a bottle of wine just in time. And then they were not so lucky. A tree fell from the storm and blocked the shelter door, trapping them in the bunker. It took two days to be found. The mangled Jaguar was like an SOS fire to the helicopters circling the area in a county-wide search and rescue for survivors of the tornado. It was a bright blue SOS in the middle of an empty farm.

Others were not as fortunate. So many people suffered that day. The tornado slammed into the town of Joplin with a mile wide swath of destruction. It had taken years for the city to recover. Some of its residents never did.

This was not a memory the four of them talked about, but it was a memory that cemented their friendship. It wasn't an adventure they could rehash with laughter, and yet it was never too far from her mind because it was the reason four unlikely friends became four inseparable friends. Amy knew they would do anything for each other. Like sisters. A sisterhood of determination and perseverance. The realization gave her hope.

She flicked the flashlight beam over the floor joists above, over the ruined jars, over the sink, the cabinet with its lethal contents, and then turned the flashlight off. Better to save the battery. She realized she was getting used to the dark. The panic had eased. Her heart rate slowed, and she knew there was nothing to do but wait. If they could survive the storm cellar, they could survive this if it didn't get too cold.

She felt Rian shuffle her legs in the dirt beside her.

"How would a dose of that stuff affect you anyway?" Amy ventured.

"Fever, thirst, rapid heart rate—I guess you would hallucinate for a couple of days. Or a couple of weeks. Depending on your metabolism."

"Why would anyone do that to themselves?"

"It's that old love-hate relationship with altered states I was talking about," Rian answered. She sounded calm and resigned to sit in the dark and wait. Perhaps she had come to the same place in her thoughts. They would find a way out. "Mable Rose had to know what she was doing because every part of that plant is toxic."

"Which part is the most toxic?"

"I'm not sure," Rian answered. "But I do know that every seed pod has about a hundred seeds of pure atropine. That's more than lethal."

They were silent again, listening for the sound of footsteps above and the chance to make themselves known.

"I am beginning to think Mable Rose was more mysterious than anyone knew," Rian said after a while. "No matter where we turn in this strange little case you dug up, all roads seem to lead back to her."

"Well, the necklace was hers," Amy admitted, "but she was only a dressmaker who moonlighted as a spiritual medium. And maybe she took some strange drugs," she added.

"She was more than that," Rian replied. "She lived alone and obviously had enough money to be self-sufficient. That was a big deal in the 1920s. She knew people intimately because she made their clothes. She heard their secrets if they came to her for spiritual guidance from the beyond."

"Are you saying she blackmailed them?"

"I'm saying she had a lot of power for a woman in the 1920s."

"The same kind of power Rev. Hayes had," Amy agreed. "He knew secrets, too."

"Do you remember what was in those letters you found in the Ouija box?"

Amy reached for her phone, remembering it was still in Rian's Fiat. She had taken pictures of the letters, but that didn't do them any good now. Why had she left her phone behind? That really was stupid. Snooping with no phone in her pocket. Never again.

Rian shifted beside her.

"I remember the gist," Amy began. "She was in love, and they were getting married. They were going to leave town, and she was very excited. And then something happened, and she was heartbroken."

"Was she going to get married and leave town or leave town and get married? Those are two very different scenarios."

"Interesting. I don't know that she said. The letters weren't dated, so I don't know in what order they were written. Something important was going to happen and she confided in someone she trusted for help."

"Someone like Rev. Hayes?"

"A pastor and a Spiritualist? That's a leap."

Rian laughed. "Well, I'm in love with a cop."

"So, you're in love with Ben," Amy echoed, smiling at the admission. "I've never heard you admit that. Although we all knew it."

"I think I just realized it. Just now. While sitting in the dark thinking about keeping secrets and why people do that. And how other people get caught up in the web."

"Like Hobo Joe," Amy added. "I think he was the one who carried the letters to and from Mable Rose. And then her man went silent. I believe Hobo Joe came back with the letters she sent, and they were unopened and unanswered."

"It sounds to me like she was in love with a married man," Rian declared. "She thought he would leave his wife and run off with her and they would live happily ever after. Just like in the fairy tales."

Amy heard the disdain in Rian's tone. "Or maybe they did run away. The family claimed she disappeared. They say she walked out the door and never came back. Maybe she disappeared with her man."

"Well, she didn't take her suitcase," Rian declared. "It's still upstairs."

Amy laughed and turned on the flashlight, swooping the beam around the room.

"What is that?" She trained the flashlight beam on the ground where the dirt met the floor above. Something winked in the dirt.

"Broken glass," Rian said dismissively.

"I don't think so." Amy rose from the ground and walked toward the dirt berm as far as she could without stooping. She kicked at the object with her toe. "It's a chisel." She turned the flashlight to the wall above the sink. "I bet it belongs on that vacant nail over there. I wonder what it's doing over here?"

She moved the flashlight back to the beams above her. "Rian!" She flashed the beam at her friend, who raised her hands to block the light from her eyes. "There's something up here etched into the wood. Probably made with that chisel! Maybe it's a hobo symbol!"

She leaned in as far as she could and studied the mark.

"T.e…

"…d.d —

"Teddy. It says Teddy!"

Amy scrambled in for a closer look and her shoe kicked something in the dirt. She glanced down at the object near the toe of her sneaker, now illuminated by the flashlight. She bent down and brushed the dirt away. Was it a bone? She reached to brush away more dirt and then froze. It was not just any bone. It was a skull.

CHAPTER THIRTY

Rian scrambled from the ground as Amy trained the flashlight on the skull at their feet. Only part of the bone was showing above the dirt. "Is it human? How would you tell?"

"By size and shape, I guess," Rian said.

"Do you think it's… do you think it's Teddy?"

"Who is Teddy?"

"The infant who didn't survive."

Rian looked up. "Why would he be buried down here?"

Amy realized they were whispering as if they might disturb the grave they had found. Her heart was fluttering but her hands felt cold. Her feet were rooted to the ground, but her head was spinning. Her ears prickled from an unseen heat and a whispering in her ear sounded oddly familiar.

I knew you would be along shortly.

Rian interrupted her thoughts. "It could be an animal skull."

"The *boogeydog*!" Amy exclaimed. "She complained of the *boogeydog* barking all night long. Maybe the dog was in the basement. Maybe she didn't know it was down here!"

A feeling of relief and sorrow washed over her at the same time. And then logic landed. An animal that etched the wood with a chisel before dying? Only in a far-fetched dream.

Then whose bones were buried here?

Rain reached down and brushed the dirt away from the bone, clearing more of its fragile structure. "That's not a dog. It's clearly human. An adult human."

Amy stood rooted as she stared at the skull. It was as if her feet would not move. Could not move.

I knew you would be along shortly.

Did Camellia know this was in the basement? Could that have been what drove her to Tiddlywinks in tears and overwhelm? Camellia just wanted to make a home for herself and her sister. She faced so many obstacles in this inheritance encumbered by an uphill battle. There was an aggressive neighbor. Lots of expensive repairs needing money she didn't have. There was uncertainty about where the aunt had gone. And now, bones in the basement. Her sadness felt overwhelming.

She could feel the weight of it on her shoulders.

Mable Rose and her Ouija boards. Was she trying to find the one that would speak to her? Is that why she had so many? If one board didn't reach the spirit world, another one would.

Who was so dear to her that she spent her life trying to reach them? Who was she trying to find on the other side of the veil?

Someone she loved. Someone she lost.

Teddy.

Her heart thumped. Teddy Duncan? As in Winslow T. Duncan?

Mrs. Teddy Duncan. All those little curlicues drawn in the pages of the necklace were not the scribblings of a young Catherine. Those were the markings and wishful dreams of the dressmaker! Mable Rose had dreamed of being Mrs. Teddy Duncan. Teddy and Rose. Secret nicknames that would go unnoticed if someone saw the love letters. Mable Rose was the one who hoped and waited. She was the one sending the letters that would be returned unanswered. She was the one whose hopes and dreams were dashed beyond repair.

Amy glanced at her feet. Whose bones were buried here?

Somehow, she knew the answer.

"If we call the police, Camellia's house is going to become a crime scene," Amy said quietly. "I don't know that she will be able to overcome that. Emotionally or financially. And if we don't call the police, we're breaking the law."

"Since when did we let that deter us?" Rian countered.

Footsteps sounded overhead and they realized Camellia had returned. They glanced at each other and began banging on the floor above.

CHAPTER THIRTY-ONE

Camellia opened the basement door and stared at them with a horrified look. "What are you doing down here?" Her tone was shrill.

Rian grabbed Amy's elbow and ran toward the door. Camellia stepped back as if they were aiming for her. "No!" she yelled, stepping back from the door.

"Wait, it's okay," Amy said, reaching out. "It's just us. We got trapped in here when the wind blew the door shut."

Camellia put her hands over her ears and shook her head. "All I could hear was that banging on the floor. It was coming up from below my feet like some creature from a bad dream! I don't think I've ever been more frightened in my life!"

Amy exhaled and took a deep breath of cold air. She glanced at Rian, who seemed to be in the same place. Grateful to be out of the dark. Grateful to be away from the moldy stench in the cabinet and the bones buried in the dirt.

"What were you doing, anyway? What were you doing in the basement?"

"We were looking over your repairs." Rian said. "Sort of."

Camellia cocked her head. "Sort of?"

Rian closed the door and secured the hasp.

Amy inhaled deeply. "Do you think we could go inside and maybe have a cup of tea? Something nice and hot?" She rubbed her hands on her jeans. The wind had died down, but it had left the air cold with infinitely more dead leaves to crush underfoot as Camellia led them back up the slope.

The house was dark on this late afternoon in November. The curtains were pulled against the windows and a near dusk filtered through the material. The suitcase was still on the floor in the circle of light and Camellia's sling bag was thrown to the surface of the table.

She motioned to the chairs, now placed in a sitting area rather than set along the wall. She turned on the lamps and the room grew cozy.

"I'll make tea. And then you can tell me what you were doing in my basement."

Amy caught the possessive. It was her house now. And they had been trespassing; there was no way around that. Even if their efforts were well-intended, she and Rian had been snooping on private property.

Amy could see that Camellia had been making herself at home. The fall asters on the mantle had been replaced with fresh stems. A group of flameless candles flickered in the fireplace. She would need to replace them with wood before long or she'd never get her house warm. The table that had been in the center was moved to one side to make a dining table, with a single chair pulled to the edge. How lonely that looked. The floor length tablecloth was gone, and she noticed the ornate pedestal legs. The wood gleamed and she smelled the lemon linseed scent still lingering.

This was not a large room, but the absence of the table in the center made it appear bigger. The rug was worn but swept clean of decades of dust. The round dressmaker stool was pushed between two sitting chairs. A squat white glass lamp cast warm light on a stack of cloth-bound books. Were those the diaries Camellia had been reading? They looked old.

Amy heard the whistle on the kettle and minutes later Camellia carried a porcelain teapot to the table and then went back for cups. "It's herbal," she said. "No need for sugar or cream. But it needs to steep a minute."

This touch of old-fashioned hospitality struck her as sweet and unexpected. Living in this old house had brought out old-school manners. Maybe Camellia's life seemed to be melding into one from another era. She seemed taken with the clothing left behind. Today she was wearing an old-timey looking cotton slip over leggings and a turtleneck sweater. A thin belt cinched her young waist. Her dusty Doc Martens were back on her feet.

They sat in silence until Camellia poured the tea.

"You must make a decision. You have to decide what you want to do," Amy said.

"About what?" Camellia asked. "About whether I call the police on you for trespassing? That's not really my Zen."

Amy felt like hiding behind the steam in her cup.

"Not about that," Rian said, after taking a cautious sip.

Camellia looked confused. "About what then? Decide about what?"

"I think you already know," Amy said.

"Know about all that crap in the basement that I don't want to clean up? That foul smelling cabinet with who knows what died inside?"

"You really don't know?"

Camellia glared at Amy. "I don't know why you were in my basement," she snapped. "Unless you were pranking me back for going through your closet!"

Amy exhaled and steam rose from her cup. "There are bones in your basement," she declared.

Camellia jerked and sloshed her tea. "Bones! Whose bones?"

"That's where your decision comes in," Rian said calmly. "It's probably Mable Rose."

"Mable Rose!" Camellia screeched. "You mean she's been in the basement all this time!" She looked at Amy with pain in her eyes. "Oh, this is too much. Too much."

She set her cup on the table, nearly missing the edge and the tea sloshed on the wood. As she reached to swipe the drops away from the surface, her hand caught the cup, and it went flying. The crash was loud, and the jarring sound startled them all. Camellia burst into tears.

"She was in love with him, and he dumped her," she sobbed. "He promised to marry her when she got pregnant. But he didn't. He let her suffer alone. It was so sad!"

She sobbed loudly and then wiped her eyes with the sleeve of her sweater. "It was heart breaking," Camellia said, quietly, her tears thinning now. "He was so cruel to her, and he had no reason to be. All she wanted was to love him. All he wanted was a mistress. She refused him that. She would have nothing to do with him after he married. He was angry about that, and violent, and she feared he might hurt his wife as revenge."

Amy studied Camellia's profile in the growing dark. She could be looking at a young version of Mable Rose. A modern version of the dressmaker born nearly a hundred years later. She studied the strong jaw and the straight nose. The curve of her cheek and chin. The flash in her dark eyes. A flash of what, she wondered. Madness like Mable Rose? Or determination? Both could be in her DNA.

Amy set her cup on the table. "Winslow," she said quietly. "Mable Rose was in love with Winslow Duncan."

Camellia nodded. "They danced all night at a Valentine's ball. She fell in love, but he married someone else because, well, because he did. The woman had family money, and her father was insistent. But Catherine was never in love with him. She was obligated to marry, and no one knew why. Mable Rose never stopped loving him, even after he married, but she would not betray her friend. She would have nothing to do with him. But she could not stop loving him. It was an impossible situation."

Amy nodded and spoke quietly. "Teddy was his child. Mable Rose must have hid her pregnancy the whole time. She was already pregnant when Catherine and Winslow married." Amy looked at Camellia, whose eyes were still full of tears. "She was anticipating a new life with a child and husband. That didn't happen because he married Catherine. I thought they were forced to marry because Catherine was pregnant, but that wasn't it at all.

It was about money and status and tradition. The marriage put an end to Mable Rose's romance. It's in her letters."

Camellia looked confused and Amy grew quiet. She knew the letters hidden in the box belonged to Camellia simply because they belonged to Mable Rose. But she purchased the Ouija boards, and that meant she bought whatever was hidden in them, too. It was a fine line she wouldn't argue, but she felt a certain possessiveness over them. A feeling of ownership she couldn't quite grasp. It was as if by letting them go, she was letting go of more than old paper and sad dreams that had soured with age. It was as if by letting them go she was giving up on her own dreams.

"I think Catherine knew. They were friends, she and Mable Rose." Amy pictured the photo in the museum. Mable Rose was looking at someone outside the frame, her gaze intense and her smile tender. Was she smiling at Winslow? Was he smiling back?

"I think Mabel Rose was the one who met him at his car that night. She wanted to tell him what happened with their child. She braved the cold to share her sorrow. She hoped for compassion. For closure. For anything that eased her grief."

Camellia looked wide-eyed. "How did you know?"

"A hunch," Amy said, remembering the photo of Winslow. A man who was broodingly handsome. A man who looked like he would be fun to be with. Fun until he wasn't fun, and then he would be cruel and unforgiving. She pictured Mable Rose writing in her diary about love, then grief, and then guilt that would disconnect her from reality.

"She fell in the snow and that hobo saw her and helped her up and brought her to a friend's house in town." Camellia's eyes were shiny with tears in the lamplight. "The friend's name was Della. She wrote that Della was good at keeping secrets."

Amy nodded. Della had a secret of her own. She thought of Banjo Man's postcard. The kindness of strangers, he wrote. Mable Rose was the Miss M mentioned in the postcard. Not Maude. Mable Rose was a friend to Hobo Joe. She and Della knew he would be made guilty of the crime because he was an easy target. He was seen at the car at the wrong time. If he was captured, he might say more than he should, and then three lives would be ruined instead of one. No, more lives ruined than that.

Hobo Joe wasn't helping Duncan out of a rut. He was helping Mable Rose up from the snowy slush. Mable Rose in her fur coat. The one Winslow gave her. The one that came all the way from St. Louis with a purchase receipt Catherine kept along with her fur collar. It would be hard to tell the two of them apart in the dark from a distance. Two fur coats in the cold. One on Winslow. One on Mable. No wonder the witness was confused. Was Duncan also watching them struggle in the snow? Or was he already dead?

Amy thought she knew the answer.

Rian rose to pick up the cup shards from the floor and then carried them to the kitchen. Amy followed with the teapot and the empty cups.

"Do we call the police?" she whispered.

"It's her call to make," Rian said. "I'm not going to make that decision for her. And it certainly doesn't have to be made tonight. This is not an emergency. Those bones have been down there a long, long time."

When they returned to the parlor, Camellia was holding one of the books from the makeshift reading table. She opened the diary to a page marked with a piece of ribbon. A paper fluttered to the floor and Amy picked it up.

"I don't know when the dog started barking because she stopped dating her diary entries, but it had to have been some time later," Camellia began. "The *boogeydog*, she called him. She thought it was a haint she had called up from the Ouija board and she couldn't drive it away. And then she realized the barking was coming from the basement."

Camellia stopped and looked at her feet. "That's the last entry in her diary. There are no more."

"She went to the basement to rescue the dog!" Amy exclaimed. "She opened the door, and the dog ran out and she was locked in. Just like Rian and I were locked in!"

"A door with no lock," Rian added. "There is no padlock on that basement door, and yet we could not budge it from the inside."

"Someone wanted us to find those bones," Amy said. "Someone or something."

"You are the one," Rian said looking at Camellia. "The Ouija board was talking to you."

Camellia shivered noticeably.

Amy remembered the board spelling out WAIT before Camellia had arrived at Tiddlywinks. How it moved effortlessly when Camellia's fingers were on the planchette. It was as if Mable Rose was reaching out from the other side to solve the mystery. And not just one mystery. A whole necklace full of mystery. Was Mable Rose the haint in the Silent City? The restless spirit who wanted to make things right for this next generation?

"You are the one," Amy repeated. She thought again about her snippet. The bullet was for Winslow. The lace handkerchief was Catherine's. The thimble was not the Monopoly piece she thought it was. It was a dressmaker symbol. Did the apothecary jar belong to Mable Rose? Or was Bella St. Claire involved, too?

Amy glanced at the paper that had floated to the floor. Opening it, she stared at the scrawl. The signature for J. Earl Langford was penned across the bottom. The promise note from the poker game. A smear of something dark spotted across the page.

"It's just a piece of paper," Camellia whimpered. "It doesn't prove anything!"

"Where did you find this?" Amy asked.

Camellia sighed with defeat. "It was tucked in the pages of a diary."

"You knew!" Amy said. "You knew she killed him! You knew all along!"

"I didn't want to believe it! I couldn't. He was so cruel," she wailed. "Didn't he deserve it? Didn't he deserve to die?"

Amy sighed. That was the $64,000 question, wasn't it? She didn't have the winning answer.

"Did she mention anybody else in her diary like Oscar St. Claire, or Frank Calhoun? Or even Cecil Hayes?"

Camellia looked startled. "Why do you ask?"

"They were there that night, too. At the poker game. I don't know about Hayes, but I always wondered if the other players saw what happened. Or thought they saw what happened and never let on."

Camellia took a long time to answer. "She only mentioned the wives," she said finally. "They asked for a tonic for insomnia."

Amy gasped. Four queens. Catherine. Bella. Maude. Evangeline.

Four wives and the dressmaker.

The hair stood up on the back of her neck.

Four queens. Zelda. Rian. Genna. Herself. And Camellia. Four queens and an ace.

Was that coincidence? Had Alfred Hitchcock known it would take all of them to solve the mystery? Not just Amy. Not just Camellia. All of them.

Insomnia. The word in her Hitchcock snippet sounded in her head.

Wives who wanted their husbands gone. And then… they were gone.

The black widow society of 1924.

Amy stared at the note in her hands.

Zelda was right. The puzzle was unsolvable. They could never prove anything. Even if she could put this last piece of the puzzle in place, there was no one left to blame. No evidence of a crime. No reason to change how history was written. A man had been shot and killed. A hobo had escaped into the night. A woman had slowly gone mad in her own wretched torment. Three wives had sent their husbands to their final sleep.

But Zelda was also wrong. She had said something that happened a hundred years ago had no bearing on today. That wasn't true. Camellia deRossier was proof. Banjo Man was proof. Living, breathing proof.

Camellia turned to a page in the diary marked with a piece of black ribbon and handed the book to Amy. Rian moved to look over her shoulder.

March 20, 1924

The moon will rise soon, full and bright in a clear winter sky. The Worm Moon, the harbinger of spring when the robins come and feast until they are so heavy one cannot imagine how they take flight.

I have not written in so long; my pen feels unfamiliar to my hand. I wait every day for a knock on the door, though it does not come. The newspaper blamed Joe for Winslow's death. They claim it was a robbery gone wrong. I know this is not the truth.

My heart aches for Della. Hobo Joe is gone. The rails have taken him somewhere safe; I trust. The town seems satisfied with their conclusion. If I do not tell my story here, I may never tell it, not to a soul living or dead.

I was familiar with the poker schedule, aware that if I was to see Winslow, this would be my ways and means. I went out that night, many months past, now. I waited in his auto in the cold, wearing the beautiful fur he gave me. The coat was the only solace he offered when he and Catherine wed. The fur came all the way from St. Louis. He told me, "If you will not let me keep you warm, this must suffice. It is a poor surrogate, indeed." What arrogance he wore like a shroud. I see that now. I wish I had seen it then.

There was no other choice for me. Catherine was my beloved friend. Winslow was now her husband. I took myself from the picture, although Catherine sought my council often to share her news. I wanted to share mine. A baby on the way. The baby's father? Catherine would ask me without judgement because that is who Catherine was. How would I answer that?

I hid my pregnancy for as long as possible, which was long enough. The year came in cold and bitter, and when my back pained me terribly, I knew this was a sign the baby was coming early. I called for Della's help, and she knew without words what I was asking when I rang her home.

I named him Teddy. He lived five days. Or perhaps it was six. I have difficulty recalling how the time passed. I suffered to let go, but Della's gentle hands took him from me. She made a promise I knew she would keep. She never revealed to me where he was buried, but I knew she would lay him to rest in a place of peace.

I rose from my bed and went out in the cold to meet Winslow when I was able to stand. I wanted to tell him the sad news. I wanted compassion I knew I would not receive. I wanted love he would not give. I wanted forgiveness as any woman who has failed her child wants. I wanted to forgive him, and I wondered if I could. Love is no small matter. The heart does not stop beating because you wish it to stop. Forgiveness does not unfold simply because you speak its name.

Hobo Joe and Rev. Hayes were walking in the road when I climbed into the seat of his automobile and hugged the coat against me. I do not know if they saw me. We did not speak. They were headed toward the church, and I remember wishing I could find the courage to join them. I would throw myself on the altar and into strong arms to weep until my grief ebbed. I stayed where I was and waited. When I saw him stumbling from the game hall with Langford following him, I drew against the seat and made myself small.

The gun glinted in the lamplight. I heard the rustle of the two men scuffling and I feared shots would ring out. I heard Langford curse him before stumbling away and then Winslow opened the door and slid inside, surprised to find me waiting.

He made a move to kiss me as if he thought that was why I had come. I pushed him away. His eyes went wild, that dark unforgiving place I've seen at least once. He growled for me to get out. When I didn't move, he reached across to open my door, nearly shoving me from the seat.

I could smell his breath. Cigars and drink and malcontent. How had I fallen for this? Why had I given so much for so little?

When he raised his hand to strike me, to backhand me with his ring, I know I flinched. I knew the feel of that steel and sterling. I don't remember grabbing the gun from him. I don't remember the look of horror and surprise that must have fallen upon his eyes as the bullet pierced his flesh. I don't remember tumbling into the snow.

I remember Joe, dear Hobo Joe, picking me up from the ground where I lay crumpled and shivering. I remember him partly carrying, partly dragging me to Della's on German Alley. I remember him telling me that Winslow was dead.

Had I killed him? Had I put an end to that cruel but wondrous heart? Why could I not remember?

I heard Della talking in hushed tones to Rev. Hayes. I knew they must know what I had done, and I waited for the constable to find me. He never came. And they sent Hobo Joe away. Della gave me tea to sleep, and soon their words faded from my ears. I could not open my eyes. I could not lift my head. I dreamed of nothing, and nothing dreamed of me.

Catherine asked me to make her mourning dress. I could not bear to refuse her. Her measurements had changed, and I feared the worst. A widow with child. Teddy's child. How would I ever smile into her eyes again? I sewed with numb fingers and cold tears. I did not feel the prick of the needle even once, though I know there were many.

My heart soared when I learned my fear was unfounded. My relief was immense. Catherine was not with child then, or ever, and she looked regal and resigned to her fate, blissfully unaware of what I had done. Still, as much as I loved her, I could not share my secret. I could not tell her about Teddy, as I named him. I could not tell her about Winslow, who she would soon be lowering to the ground. I could not tell her, although somehow, I believe she knew.

The ground was a cold and frozen ground the day Winslow was laid to rest. My heart is frozen cold and hard as I write these words. I fear my days will be as numb and dream-filled as I slowly disappear.

Amy closed the book and looked up to see fresh tears in Camellia's eyes. Her own vision was blurry. She could hear Rian sniff behind her. No one seemed to have words.

"You can't stay here by yourself tonight," Amy said quietly after a long silence. "I don't have an extra bed at my apartment, but I do have a couch and a cat who might snuggle with you. Although maybe not. He does like to hold a grudge."

Camellia looked up and smiled faintly. "I would like to snuggle with your cat if he will have me. Let me grab clothes."

"Don't bother," Amy said. "I'm sure I can find what you need."

They left the house, the porch light shining in the now dark sky. There was no wind, but the air was nippy enough to frost the leftover pumpkins, wherever they might be.

The three of them went through the back gate of the graveyard and Amy felt Camellia shiver beside her as they made their way to the Fiat. It would be a very tight fit for the passengers, but she sure wasn't going to wait in the Silent City alone.

CHAPTER THIRTY-TWO

It was too cold to be on Genna's deck in the woods, even with the fat-bellied chiminea roaring. They moved inside, carrying their mugs of hot spiced cider with them.

"I am loath to say goodbye to fall," Genna said, dumping the dominoes on the table. "Thanksgiving is around the corner and winter is right behind."

"I like winter," Rian said. "I like how quiet it gets when the snow blankets everything and people stop rushing around."

"I like not having to worry about driving in the snow," Amy added. "All I have to do is come down the stairs to open Tiddlywinks. I've never gotten the hang of driving on icy roads."

"I like having a whole new wardrobe to choose from," Zelda added. "Every season is a fashion adventure."

Amy laughed at her friend's penchant for clothes. "How is your 1920s clothing line coming along?"

"We hit a snag," Zelda admitted.

"Oh?" Genna murmured. "What kind of snag?"

"Vito," Zelda said with a frown. "He simply can't keep up with the demand and he's not willing to outsource any part of the process. He says if they can't afford the price tag and the waitlist, they aren't the right client."

"That doesn't sound like Vito. He's such a nice guy."

"He is a nice guy," Zelda agreed. "But he's a terror to work with. We're like two cats in a closet. We argue. We spat. He wins."

"Ah, I see," Amy said. "That's the snag. He wins."

"Every time," Zelda said with an exhale. "I've decided that I'm done with this." She waved her arm dismissively. "And anyway, fashion cycles are fickle. Roaring Twenties inspired designs are already showing up on racks everywhere. Glamor meets practical for the modern woman. I don't know what I was thinking."

"You were ahead of the curve," Amy said.

"I am the curve," Zelda declared with a smile "What is there to eat, Genna? I've got the munchies," she said changing the subject.

As if on cue, Genna went to the kitchen and Amy scattered the dominoes in the middle of the table. She could hear her banging around and soon smelled popcorn. Genna made popcorn the old-fashioned way on the stove and then sprinkled M&Ms on top. Hot apple cider and popcorn. It couldn't get more hygge than that. When Genna returned, she set the bowl in front of Zelda, whose eyes lit up.

"Has she decided what to do?" Rian asked, stuffing her mouth and then dusting her fingers on her jeans.

"You're asking about Camellia?"

Rian nodded.

Rian had dropped them off after their discovery at Piney Top. Amy made toast and scrambled eggs for herself and Camellia and Victor, too. He loved scrambled eggs with ricotta cheese. She was hoping to soften him on Camellia's behalf. Ease his grumpy attitude a little. They had stayed up way past Victor's bedtime talking about Mable Rose and what came next.

Amy had already shared the gist of that conversation with her friends and the diary entry from Mable Rose describing the night that Winslow T. Duncan died. They had shared their experience of being locked in the basement and their discovery of the skull. The memory of being locked in the dark had drawn a solemn quiet. She could sense they were reliving the silent terror of two days in a storm shelter with only themselves for company and comfort.

"She's going to stay near her sister for a little while," Amy explained. "She wants them to decide what to do together."

"You think she will have the skull tested for DNA?" Genna asked. "To see if it really is Mable Rose?"

"That's expensive," Rian answered.

"She doesn't have that kind of money," Amy agreed. "The police might run the DNA at their expense, but only if they decide the basement is a crime scene. There is nothing to indicate that it is. Not really."

"Besides, we don't know how much of the remains are there," Rian said. "Bones disintegrate, and a hundred years is a long time. There may be nothing left other than what Amy saw. A skull and a couple of brass buttons. If it goes to Little Rock for testing that could take a while, maybe even a year."

"And what happens in the meantime?" Genna asked.

"She won't be able to sell the house with a crime scene in the basement if that's how it goes. Not even to her neighbor, who wants to tear the house down anyway. She won't be prevented from living there, though," Amy said. She and Camellia had searched the Internet looking for first-level answers.

"If the authorities get involved, they can choose to investigate the scene of a missing person. Mable Rose was a missing person, but Camellia didn't think anyone in the family filed an official report. We couldn't find where they even had missing reports back then. Legally, Mable Rose could be declared deceased after seven years. That's how it works today, anyway. That had to happen somewhere along the way, or the property would never have passed on to her sister.

"We couldn't find a death certificate online, either, but there's a way to request one. Especially since Camellia is a relative. She considered talking to the lawyer who handled the estate, but she's not ready to get them involved. Lawyers take money."

Amy splayed her fingers on the table and looked at her friends. "Other than Camellia and her sister, Rose, we're the only ones who know about the bones."

"I didn't even tell Ben," Rian added. "If they go to Little Rock, chances are she won't get them back."

"Why in the world would she want them back?" Zelda asked.

"To bury Mable Rose proper," Amy said. "In the graveyard. In the Silent City."

Zelda shivered. "What was Mable Rose doing down in the basement, anyway?"

"I think she went to the basement to rescue the *boogeydog*," Amy answered. "Who knows what state of mind she was in by then, but when she realized where the barking was coming from, she had to do something. I'm sure she was relieved it was a real dog and not a haint."

"We believe she opened the door to let the dog out, but the door slammed shut behind her," Rian added. "Just like it did with us."

"She didn't even try to shovel her way through Arkansas rock," Amy added, with a sour glance at Rian. "She gave up. She was ready to give up. She had lost everything she loved."

The room grew quiet again, even their munching ceased.

"So, Mable Rose shot him with his own gun because he was a cruel and insensitive cad," Genna said slowly. "I guess she took the poker money, too. Does that poker real estate IOU have value?"

"No," Amy said plainly. "It's nothing more than a piece of evidence with no chain of custody."

"And what about the other husbands?" Zelda asked. "Did she kill them, too?"

Amy shook her head. "It doesn't fit. There was no motive. Her diary tells how she shot Winslow out of grief and white rage and then spent the rest of her life suffering for it. Just because her diary claimed the wives asked for a sleeping tonic, doesn't mean she killed them. Or their wives, either. Maybe the husbands died as reported. We will never know the answer. It's a cold case. Cold cases are rarely solved. I think we made a big jump in conjecture," Amy added.

"We?" Rian countered. "I don't believe I was ever on the black widow train."

"Me either," Zelda said. "It was a puzzle with too many missing pieces. Even you can't make it fit, Sparks. I told you it was unsolvable."

"Oh, come on," Genna said. "You were the conductor of the black widow train."

"I was not."

"You also said the barber did it," Genna added. "So, there's that."

"Spoilsport," Zelda snapped.

"I gather I got carried away interpreting his sermons," Genna admitted, apparently acquiescing defeat without so many words. "I think Cecil Hayes thought they killed their husbands and used that guilt for his own gain. In the end, it did him in.

"His last sermon," Genna added, "it was about how the weak and mild would not inherit the Earth. I thought he was misquoting. He turned meek and mild into weak and mild and *would* into *would not*. I think he was talking about women as the weaker sex."

"Weak and mild," Amy said. "Evangeline must have hated who he had become. He was an angry man who judged everyone before he judged himself. She must have felt helpless to stop him. He may have swept her off her young, innocent feet with his smooth talking, but he did not deliver on the happily ever after. She couldn't divorce him. None of them could. Or none of them would."

"Were the husbands really that awful?" Zelda asked. "Weren't they just men being men?"

"As if that's an excuse," Genna said.

Amy shrugged. "I didn't find anything terribly bad about any of them. It was a man's world, and women were trying to do their best to thrive. I'd like to think these women did amazing things after their husbands passed, proving they could do a better job than their husbands did. But I am ashamed that I jumped so quickly to believe that women had to be killers to do so. I think their husbands' deaths were natural, albeit timely, and widowhood simply gave them the opportunity to step in and be stellar women. Bright women. Competent women. Confident. Compassionate. Eager to make the world a better place."

"Boy," Rian said and whistled under her breath. "Aren't you on Genna's soapbox today?"

Amy grinned. She didn't think Genna would mind.

"And what about Rev. Cecil Hayes?" Zelda asked. "Do you think his wife did him in?"

"About that," Genna said, "I found his death notice. He had bad asthma and was trying a new-fangled treatment injection program down in Little Rock. Ephedrine. It gave him a heart attack."

"Ephedrine?" Amy asked, her eyes wide. "You've got to be kidding."

Genna grinned. "Déjà vu."

"Déjà vu vu," Zelda echoed.

Amy nodded. "It appears that Della and Rev. Hayes helped Hobo Joe escape because no one would believe he was innocent. And Della wasn't about to throw her friend under the bus."

"There were no buses, yet," Rian added. "They didn't show up for another few years and certainly not in Bluff Springs."

"Well, whatever they threw people under back in 1924," Amy said curtly. "Della didn't throw Mable Rose under it, even though she knew about Winslow.

"You know what I think?" Amy said after a long pause. "I think we should have Thanksgiving at Tiddlywinks. We could make it a Friendsgiving celebration. We can eat and play games and be thankful for the people in our lives."

Zelda clasped her hands. "What a great idea! I'll make my famous orange floof. Rian can bring the brownies."

"No," Amy said quickly. "Rian cannot bring the brownies!"

Rian rolled her eyes. "It would be so much more fun if I did."

CHAPTER THIRTY-THREE

Amy looked out at Tiddlywinks Players Club. The tables were full of people and food. Or people and games. Everyone looked like they were having a great time.

She had brought out the candles she bought for the Ouija night, deciding the candles fit this event with the same prayerful intent. The candlelight took center stage on each table, and Camellia had braided a wreath of fresh flowers and greenery to go around them. The smell was intoxicating—candles and greenery and Thanksgiving food.

Sam Ford and Ben Albright were talking shop in the corner. A private investigator and a cop. A great combination. Sam had popped into her life when they were sleuthing the murder of a wine merchant, and their friendship was growing. She glanced again at Ben, wondering if Rian had told him how she felt. Probably not yet. He knew, of course. They all knew.

Sammie and Beau had come, too, much to her surprise since Thanksgiving wasn't an Irish holiday. They came bearing a tray overflowing with pastries like pilgrims from the North. Amy noticed Beau was entertaining a table with an expressive story that had them all laughing. No doubt his brogue and good looks were part of the appeal. Sammie looked at him with nothing less than awe.

Camellia and her sister Rose were two of those at his table laughing at his story, and Amy saw how much they resembled each other. They had not spoken yet about the house on Piney Top, and Amy knew it would take time for everything to settle out the way it needed to settle. Between the two of them, Rose and Camellia would make the decision that was right for them.

Banjo Man arrived with a plus one date, and Amy recognized the lady from the porch, although she didn't seem to recognize Amy. It didn't matter. She was happy to have all of them share her table at Tiddlywinks. She was happy to know them. Happy to know they were doing well. *Happy Happy Happy.*

She smiled at Genna and Rian and Zelda in turn. Three best friends of a deeply bonded tribe. A sisterhood of troublemakers. A clutch of old chicks ready for the next adventure. A posse of women who loved to snoop. She had so much to be grateful for.

Genna clanked her glass with a spoon and all eyes turned toward her. "It is a day to give thanks," Genna began. "I know Amy is the master of this feast, but I want to give thanks to the three women who allow me to call them best friends." Genna looked at Amy and Rian and Zelda in turn. "I also want to give thanks to all the women who have paved the way for us to be here celebrating this great day. There are so many to thank, which we learned as we looked back at the history of the 1920s. I'd like to thank…"

Someone groaned. Amy thought it sounded like Rian.

"The list is long," Genna continued. "Because many, many women have paved the way for their sisters in every generation and in every field. Every act of courage and leadership. Every expression of intellect and genius. Every gesture of kindness and compassion. Every effort of faith that supports the rise of women to their rightful place in society is worthy of our gratitude." Genna paused and smiled.

"Every woman paves the way for the next generation in line. We cannot forget this as our lives get easier. We cannot forget how much our sisters invested in us, never even knowing who we are. They sacrificed because they knew it was the right thing to do. We live history every day. We make history every day. And today we're making history for tomorrow."

"Here, here!" Amy said, raising her glass.

"Here, here!" the room echoed.

Here, here. She couldn't have said it better, even if Genna had let her try. Her heart swelled. She felt humbled thinking of all the women who had toiled for justice and equality and human rights. Not just for themselves but for her. And not just for her, for everyone. History really did matter.

CHAPTER THIRTY-FOUR

Camellia rushed in through the door of Tiddlywinks and Victor was so surprised by the loud jangle that he jumped from the back of his favorite wingback in the window and arched his back.

"Easy, buddy," Amy cooed. "It's your friend Camellia. Remember?"

"He really holds a grudge," Camellia said and laughed. "I don't think he will ever forgive me for pushing him off the shelf in your closet. It made the mess worse, anyway."

Amy smiled and glanced at the bag in Camellia's hands. "What have you got there? More old games?"

"What I have is much better than an old game," Camellia said and with an exaggerated flair, pulling a tin from the bag.

"The money tin!" Amy exclaimed. "You found it?"

Camellia placed the tin on the table and lifted the lid. She reached in and pulled out a wad of cash. "The money tin!" She laughed. "You said there would be one! It looks like play money to me, but it's not! It's real!"

Amy eyed the bills. There were tens and twenties showing. She had to admit, it did look a little like play money, something that might be used in a 1920s movie.

"There's more than two thousand dollars here," Camellia said. "And it's worth a whole lot more than that!"

Amy could feel her confusion creasing her brow. "What do you mean worth more?"

"These bills were printed in 1920 and earlier. That makes them collectible. Some of them are worth thousands. Can you believe that? A ten-dollar bill worth two thousand bucks!"

Amy took a closer look. The grin on her face widened. "It's the poker money," she said. "Mable Rose had the poker money and hid it all those years. Where did you find it?"

"It was under the floor. I was trying to fix a creaky, rotten board where water had been dripping, and the can was hidden beneath it."

Amy pulled a piece of paper from the tin. "What's this?"

Camellia beamed, her bright smile as genuine as her look of satisfaction. "That's the icing on the cake," she said. "Read it! You've got to read it now!"

Amy opened the letter and read.

October 14, 1926

Evangeline will bring this letter under the pretense that I am having trouble breathing again. Asthma they tell me. As bad as it has ever been. I have asked her to procure for me one of your remedies, which you will find odd, given our disparities in belief. She does not know the content of this letter and must not know, now or ever. Send her home with something that will satisfy her curiosity.

I write to say that I saw him strike you. I saw you tumble from his vehicle. I write to claim that a rage welled in me I have no courage to own and even less to deny. His hand was on the grip of the gun as if this would be his coward's way out. That a bullet delivered as you lay helpless would save himself from whatever inconvenience he suffered by your hand. I dare say your suffering was far deeper. There was but one shot. He died swiftly as I prayed for his salvation, knowing he would be no more saved than I.

There is not much breath left in this life for me, and I have but one regret. I allowed you to believe you pulled the trigger. That was my coward's way out. May God have mercy on my soul. May you have mercy on yours.

Cecil G. Hayes

The hand that penned the letter had trembled over the strokes, but its meaning was clear enough. The Rev. Cecil Hayes had aimed the gun at Winslow T. Duncan's black heart. The Rev. Hayes had fired the fatal shot.

CHAPTER THIRTY-FIVE

Amy held the bouquet of violets to her side as she stood silently in the grass, a gentle breeze blowing. The sun was bright, and the new spring forsythia bloomed bright against a deep blue sky free of clouds. Spring had arrived with sun and color and a welcomed reprieve from the cold. Camellia touched the headstone, and Amy noticed the tenderness behind the gesture. It had taken them months to get this far and maybe a thousand phone calls.

"Ashes to ashes, dust to dust," Camellia said, her voice trembling. She clutched her sister's hand. "Here lies Mable Rose deRossier. First Class Dressmaker."

"Welcome to the Silent City," Amy whispered. "May you rest in peace."

She left Camellia and Rose to the quiet of their thoughts and walked the path through the graveyard, stopping when she reached her destination. She bent down and placed the violets against the headstone. Catherine Duncan. Silent City resident since 1967.

"It was you all along," Amy said. "You were the one. Not Mable Rose. You were the restless haint who could not rest until the dressmaker was found. Until the mystery of her disappearance was solved. Until all the pieces could be laid to rest. I believe you knew about Teddy and Rose. I think you knew the choice she made because she was your friend. She was your friend to the end. And you were hers."

The wind seemed to carry her words.

"May you rest in peace, Catherine."

The wind blew gently past her once more.

I knew you would be along shortly.

THE END

Acknowledgements

Friends who endure the ceaseless nattering of a writer in the throes of a new plot are special people indeed. They smile while listening to bits of fact and fantasy as characters and coda come into being. You know who you are, and I am grateful for your genuine interest in what goes on in my head.

While researching the 1920s for *Ouija & Haints in the Silent City*, I learned so much about the history of that era far beyond what we think we know about the Roaring Twenties. Comparing 1924 to 2024 was a captivating exercise. I learned about inventions, culture, fashion, and the history behind women's right to vote. And, true to my theme, the games people played.

People may have felt differently about reaching their loved ones on the other side after the heavy losses of war. Whether faith or fantasy, people found solace in the invention of the mystical talking board. I am neither a fan nor foe, just a writer exploring humanity. While this is not a historical novel, I hope I have woven a thread of history true enough to give the reader a glimpse of a decade more than 100 years ago. Perhaps you will have as many "I didn't know that!" moments.

From zero words to 80,000 is a process of many little grey cells, as Hercule Poirot would call them in Agatha Christie's first book, published in 1920. Not all of that grey cell creativity makes it to the page. A lot is left behind in the trash bin. What lands in the reader's hands is the best I can do for now.

A big Arkansas thanks to Red for sharing his passion and knowledge about hobo lore. Deep gratitude to fellow authors Susan Clayton and Sarah Barbour, artist legend Mary Springer, and Zeta Muffin Michelle Hannon for reader guidance and earnest enthusiasm. A big welcome to editor Jessica Gang at Silver Lining. Special thanks to Elise Roenigk, history preservationist and proprietor of the most haunted hotel in America, for her eagle eye and generous, nononsense approach to life. And finally, a bow in awe to the resilient women of all eras who endeavor to uplift and unite women's voices in our pursuit of equality, change, and progress.

About the Author

Jane Elzey is a mischief-maker, storyteller, and bender of the facts. A retired career journalist, she now writes cozy mysteries without much regard for the truth. Born and raised in Florida, she now lives in the Ozark Mountains of Arkansas with her fur family, a neighborhood of deer, and an occasional and very fat groundhog.

An insatiable world traveler, Jane turns bucket list travels into story settings, sharing destinations with armchair readers on the hunt for whodunit. She loves to play board games and is always up for a Scotch served neat, a trip downriver in a kayak, friends, great food, and a good laugh.

In the Cardboard Cottage Mystery series, Jane Elzey writes about four best friends who play to win... while the husbands die trying. The husband always dies. *Ouija & Haints in the Silent City* is book five in the series. Bucket list adventure and book six, *I Spy a Dead Guy,* is slated for a 2026 release. Be on the lookout for a new Jane Elzey cozy series launching soon: *A Snooty Foodie Mystery with a Pinch of Magic.*

If you are looking for the perfect gift for a friend who has everything (including a bad ex) consider gifting them membership in the Killer Club for her/his own literary revenge.

Hunt details at JaneElzey.com where you can join the VIP Club for gossip and arrange an author signing or book club event. Please follow Author Jane Elzey on Amazon to hear about upcoming releases.

Books in the Cardboard Cottage Mystery series by Jane Elzey
Scorpius Carta Press
Available in in E-book, Paperback, and Hardcover

Dying for Dominoes (2020)
Dice on a Deadly Sea (2021)
Poison Parcheesi and Wine (2023)
Killer Croquet on the Emerald Isle (2024)
Ouija and Haints in the Silent City (2025)
I Spy a Dead Guy (2026)

Join Jane Elzey's VIP Club for author gossip, special offers, autographed copies, and fun merch at JaneElzey.com. There's always room in the Killer Club for one more. #TheHusbandAlwaysDies

To schedule author signing and book club events, contact Jane Elzey at CardboardCottageMystery.com